Drayling

By

Terry J. Newman

First published in Great Britain by Pen Press

All paper used in the printing of this book has been made from
wood grown in managed, sustainable forests.

ISBN13: 978-1-907499-91-3

Printed and bound in the UK
Pen Press is an imprint of Indepenpress Publishing Limited
25 Eastern Place
Brighton
BN2 1GJ

A catalogue record of this book is available from
the British Library

Cover design by Jacqueline Abromeit

Acknowledgements

Many thanks to Debs, Laura, Bernard, Richard and Roger for their invaluable input during the gestation of this book.

1

"It is, of course, well known that the world was in constant turmoil throughout the 22nd and 23rd Centuries. From the time that Europe finally abandoned the pretence that its many countries possessed similar ideals, right through to the collapse of the Sino-Australasian pact, there's been war and bloodshed raging somewhere on our planet.

"Now, I certainly don't propose to dwell upon the details of this sad period in the history of mankind.

"We all know of the China/Indostan troubles, the civil war in the Franco-German Republic and the Trans-Saharan conflict, to name but three. From these, and from all the other examples of human lunacy, sprang the same old problems of disease, homelessness, starvation, corruption and so on.

"That's why, ladies and gentlemen, we're so privileged to live in the Britain of Dunstan Heathfield."

Uri paused and took a sip of water. He was enjoying himself immensely. He was Drayling's Local Historian and had been given the honour of making the celebration speech at the opening dinner of the annual People's Festival. Now 38 years old, he'd lived in the small South Country district of Drayling all his life. He was an only child. His parents were both now deceased, but had lived long enough to see him become a well-known and respected member of the local community.

Before resuming his speech, he turned, and with outstretched hand – palm uppermost, he referred his audience to the statue of the great man in the centre of the end wall behind him.

"It was a hundred and twenty-nine years ago, in 2320, that Dunstan formed the Government of National Unity, and then went on to show the world how, by non-violent, yet determined, political means, the global peace that we all now enjoy could be won."

He paused again for effect.

"And what a colossal achievement it was!

"This was international diplomacy at its brilliant best, and has since deservedly become known as 'Dunstan Heathfield's Revolution'.

"It was Dunstan himself who renamed our country 'The British Friendly Federation',…and I'm proud, ladies and gentlemen – as I'm sure you are – to be one of its citizens.

"I therefore ask you to raise your glasses for the loyal toast – to…'The BFF'."

Uri held his wine aloft, and the people stood and echoed "the BFF" as one. They then rewarded him with a generous and sustained round of applause.

Smiling broadly, he returned to his place at the top table alongside his wife, Della, and proceeded to enjoy the remainder of what was a relaxed and well-organised social occasion.

Uri Graves was a big man in all but physical stature. His fellow citizens would consult him routinely on issues large and small, and he'd give of his time gladly. A beak-like nose dominated a friendly, narrow face, and his mop of dark hair showed advanced signs of greying at the temples. Despite being only five feet six inches tall (the BFF had long since reverted to using traditional British measures), he'd developed a slight stoop – the result, almost certainly, of many, many hours spent happily at his desk. Uri was a learned man.

Della, on the other hand, was taller, at about five feet nine. Slim and attractive, she had long dark hair and a ready smile. Having been childhood sweethearts, they'd finally married some seven years ago, when Uri was thirty-one and she twenty-eight, to the delight of all who knew them.

It had taken time for her to fall pregnant – partly because Uri was opposed to the modern, guaranteed, methods of conception available. He was a man of strong principles, and a passionate traditionalist. He believed firmly that "the old natural methods are almost always the best in the long run".

Having been a member of the local Council – a 'Worthy' – for two years now, he was justifiably proud of his position in the local community.

The following morning, Uri slept in a little later than usual, and Della took care not to wake him. When he finally appeared, she was sitting in the kitchen.

She looked up as he entered, and smiled. "Uri Graves, if that grin gets any wider, the bottom of your face'll fall off!"

Uri chuckled. "The fact is, my darling, that life couldn't be any better. If I can't smile the way things are today, then when can I? Just think! I'm Drayling's Local Historian, and the loveliest wife in the world is about to give birth to our son! Tell me, isn't that excuse enough to be thoroughly pleased with myself?"

Della had to admit that it was, and raised her face to allow him to kiss her.

She watched as he selected a bowl of steaming soup from the multimeal, and then, as he sat down opposite her, observed, "You know, it's absolutely right that we go out of our way to celebrate the achievements of Dunstan Heathfield. The life we enjoy here in Drayling could hardly be happier, and it's important that we realise it. We're very, very lucky…and if Dunstan Heathfield's responsible for that, then it's certainly fitting that we acknowledge it."

Uri nodded and swallowed another mouthful.

"Mmm…yes…I couldn't agree more…and…on top of that…to know that similar peace and contentment exists all around the world is even further reason to celebrate. His achievements really were quite, quite incredible."

A couple of hours later – not long before noon – as they were relaxing and enjoying a warm drink, the front entrance sensor buzzed.

Della looked up at the day-screen. "We have a visitor, darling. It's young Hayden Burcher – Clement's boy." She de-activated the entry-lock, and the door opened.

Uri rose to greet their visitor. "Good morning, Hayden. What can I do for you this sunny day?"

"Um…Good morning, Sir Uri," replied Hayden, respectfully using the formal title traditionally accorded to a Local Worthy, "I hope you don't mind, but having listened to your speech yesterday, I just had to speak to you."

"Well, of course, lad, of course…come in and sit down," replied Uri, secretly flattered. "Here…"

He pointed to a hospitality chair.

"Thank you, Sir," said the boy, and sat down. As was the custom, he made a selection from the drinksmade console in the armrest.

Uri studied him as he made himself comfortable. A tall, intelligent boy of around fourteen, Uri knew from conversations with his father that he was interested in history.

"What would you like to know?"

"Well, Sir, I'm curious about what you said in your speech. You see, ever since I can remember, people have talked about Dunstan Heathfield's Revolution, and what a good thing it was and everything, and obviously I was told the basics at education facility, but I'd like to know more about the background to it – the reasons and so on – and my father suggested I should talk to you. He said that, as well as being the Local Historian, you've been friends for many years, and you wouldn't mind – Sir."

He grinned sheepishly.

Uri laughed out loud.

"Your father knows me well, Hayden! He knows that I love to talk about the past – and the lessons to be learned from it. Where would you like me to start?"

Hayden swallowed, and said, "Well, Sir, I suppose what I really want to know is – what was so great about Dunstan Heathfield? I mean, why do we think he was so special?"

Uri settled down into his chair opposite the lad, took a deep breath and began to speak enthusiastically about his favourite subject.

"For around three hundred years, prior to the introduction of the Government of National Unity in 2320, the whole world was in constant turmoil.

"Consider the major world events since the mid-21st century. In 2041, the European Union was abandoned to prevent war, and the Northern European Alliance – the NEA – was formed. Then the United Nations Organisation, as it then was, facilitated the recolonisation of most African countries south of the Sahara, ostensibly to deal with the climatic, economic and social tribulations which – it was said – "a political levelling of wealth" would alleviate, but, in reality, it was to prevent war."

The boy was enthralled...and, encouraged by his clear display of interest, Uri ploughed on with relish.

"In 2194, the Iberian Alliance and the Eastern Baltic Republics all joined the NEA, thereby leaving the Franco-German Republic as the only member of the Central European Union. It seemed there was just one crisis after another!

"For around a hundred years after that, constant wars in Asia and the Far East created major refugee problems, and the China/Indostan Cold War culminated in the unfortunate events which led to the Sino-Australasian pact..."

At this point, Della – who was listening – could take no more.

"Uri – stop! For goodness' sake! You're swamping poor Hayden with detail! Does he really need to know all that stuff?"

"Uh?" responded Uri, briefly perplexed. Then, almost immediately realising that she was right, said, "Oh, I'm sorry, Hayden. I'm afraid I do sometimes get a little carried away when I'm talking about my favourite subject!"

Hayden, embarrassed, gave a quick half smile and replied, "No, Sir…please…don't stop. I'm interested." He then turned to Della and added, almost apologetically, "Really…I am."

Uri needed no further encouragement.

"The detail of this sorry period in the history of the world is no longer important, but suffice it to say that, for the whole of that time, there was war and bloodshed raging somewhere on our planet.

"Goodness me, Hayden, even our own country got involved from time to time!

"It was Dunstan Heathfield who stepped up onto the world stage determined to do something about it."

"Yes, but *how* did he do it?" persisted the lad.

Uri smiled. "Well, he made many speeches in many countries. He gained the trust of political leaders and peoples. He was awarded the highest honours in several countries around the world, and soon people realised that here was a man who really could change things for the better. Of course, he made many speeches here in Britain also, both in parliament and across the country, and his popularity soared.

"Dunstan Heathfield knew what was needed, and had the energy and determination to make it happen.

"He made us realise that minor changes to the British way of life were necessary to facilitate the monumental achievement of world peace and harmony – and a similar message was received and accepted all around the world.

"By his 'comprehensive prioritisation programme' he showed us that "to be able to change the most vital pieces of the jig-saw, *every* piece of jig-saw must change to a greater or lesser extent. After all, the most important feature of every jig-saw is, and must always remain, the overall picture." In fact, this became his most famous quotation.

"…And, as a result of this, international travel stopped completely in 2318 and, subsequent to that, inter-district travel also.

"As peace and harmony returned, the wisdom of his words became abundantly clear. He'd shown that travel – and indeed many other forms of communication – needed to become things of the past. Soon, *all* non-administrative communication between districts had ceased completely.

"He'd shown that, by making these simple changes to our way of life, peace really could be established and maintained."

He paused and leaned forward, as though to emphasise his words.

"By peaceful diplomacy, he achieved what years of violence had failed to achieve, and, as a result, he was revered by the British people, and headed the single-party 'Government of National Unity' for 35 years. He proudly announced our new state name, 'The British Friendly Federation', in 2334.

"That, Hayden, is why Dunstan Heathfield is so special."

The boy said nothing, but sat, absorbing every word.

"He'd shown the world how to solve its problems of starvation, deprivation and envy by political prioritisation and moral leadership. Who would have thought that international trade would become a thing of the past, or that religious intrigue and strife would be consigned to history – that we would realise that such things were, in reality, actually barriers to world peace?

"In the BFF, all major decisions are now taken by common consent, with the wider needs of our species in mind, and here, in our little corner of this great land, every person is objectively graded according to intellect and motivation so that he or she is able to make an appropriate contribution to the community. That applies to every one of us, whether we be a Worthy Councillor or whoever we are. Each individual has all that he or she needs. Everything is well-ordered and nothing is left to chance."

Uri paused again, and looked at the boy.

"I think you'll agree, young Hayden, that such an achievement really does make Dunstan Heathfield a great man indeed."

Hayden had to agree that it certainly did and, after a few moments, he rose from his chair.

"Thank you for taking the time to explain, Sir. I can see it all much more clearly now. Er…Goodbye, Sir."

He took his leave, and Uri grinned at Della. He loved his subject passionately, and it was always pleasing when someone else showed an interest too. He hadn't enjoyed himself so much for ages.

2

Uri's son, Marius, was born in the spring of 2450, and daughter Urania arrived three years later.

Both were happy, healthy children, and both intelligent, but it soon became apparent to Uri that Marius possessed a particularly strong desire to learn.

The year 2455 saw the centenary of the death of Dunstan Heathfield and it was Uri's responsibility, as Local Historian, to arrange and coordinate a series of events in Drayling to pay suitable tribute to the great man. Even at the tender age of five, Marius was keenly interested in all that was going on, and bombarded his parents with a barrage of searching questions.

His boundless curiosity was, of course, a source of great satisfaction to them both, although Della was driven, on more than one occasion, to remark that it would be nice if he could ease off – just for a little while – if only to give her time to draw breath.

Uri could see much of himself in Marius, and made up his mind to suggest that they sit down once a week to discuss the happenings of the week, and any other subject that either wished to raise. He assured Della that he wouldn't pressurise the boy, and agreed that, if he didn't want to talk, they wouldn't.

But they needn't have worried. As Uri had suspected, Marius thought it was an excellent idea, and a routine quickly became established. Marius had inherited his father's love of heritage and tradition, and throughout his childhood they spent many, many hours together, exploring every kind of subject – ancient beliefs, monarchs, rituals, wildlife, wars, – the list was almost literally endless.

At one particular session, Marius asked Uri to explain the purpose of the 'identiscreen' – the flat, black device, about the size of a man's hand, that all adults carried.

"Ah, the identiscreen is a very impressive and important tool," replied Uri. "But to understand it properly, we need to trace its development from as long ago as the Middle Ages."

Marius grinned. That meant he could settle back and enjoy another of his father's long, but invariably fascinating, history lessons.

Uri was soon in full flow.

"Way back in those ancient times, information was brought to the people by 'town criers'. These were men with exceptionally loud voices, who simply stood in the streets and shouted the news. Then, for over three hundred years, newspapers – printed sheets of paper – were produced each day, and people would pay a small amount of money to read about the latest events, and all sorts of other things besides.

"In addition, in the 20th Century, radio and television gave almost every home in the country access to an increasingly diverse range of information and entertainment.

"The computer, and all its derivatives, proliferated throughout the 21st Century, and you'll recall that we've already discussed the consequences of the poorly-controlled early days of what was then known as 'the internet'.

"In the year 2066, our government, perhaps belatedly, realised that the march of technology needed to be controlled rather more closely for the good of all, and the identiscreen was conceived. It quickly became apparent that this simple device could fulfil many functions. Nowadays, for example, it's replaced the identity card, and, for that reason, it's mandatory for every citizen over the age of fourteen to carry one."

Uri was now well into his stride, doing what he did best, and Marius sat in happy silence, absorbing every word.

"The IDS, as it's now generally referred to, has replaced most written publications – any book in the National Archive is accessible on its screen – and it provides daily news information automatically to us all.

"It also incorporates such mundane personal tools as diary, clock, calculator, voice and written communicator, personal development record, time manager, personal alarm, personal grading and achievement information, location monitor and so on.

"In fact, it's now got to the point that we all treat it as a personal friend without whom we'd be lost. Of course, when you're fourteen, you'll receive one also."

"How does it work?" enquired Marius.

"Well, it's powered by something called 'proximetry'," explained Uri. "Every human being – in fact, every living creature – is surrounded by something called 'innate ambium'. It was discovered in the 21st Century by a scientist called Anna Pavel. It's a sort of invisible cloud around you, which is the essence of life itself. Everyone's is different. Each IDS incorporates a sensor which can detect its owner's innate ambium and draw from it all the power it needs. For that reason, it's a legal requirement that no one is ever more than 50 yards from their IDS."

As Marius' knowledge grew, his desire to learn more grew also. He wanted to know the story behind everything – how and why things were as they were, and how such seemingly impossible changes to the human condition had been brought about by purely peaceful means.

He realised that he was in a uniquely advantageous position. He had direct access to, and an established weekly audience with, Drayling's Local Historian – his father – who was equally passionate about the momentous events that had led to the creation of the BFF. However, he had an insatiable curiosity, and certainly did not wish to restrict his learning opportunities to the formal sessions with Uri.

One day, he told his father that he wanted to find out how starvation had been eradicated from the world. Uri suggested that he borrow his IDS to look it up.

"As you're my son, and still under fourteen, it's all right for you to borrow it," he explained, "provided I stay within 50 yards of you, of course."

He took it and settled into a chair. Soon, after locating the section headed 'Nutrition of the People', he began to read.

Following the endorsement by the Witan of the lack of need for travel and non-administrative communication within the BFF, the nutrition of each district's citizens became the responsibility of its Worthy Council. It is the responsibility of the Worthy Council to ensure that the district is self-sufficient. In addition to this, however, the Witan keeps geography, geology and climate under review and provides supplemental provision as appropriate. As a result, malnutrition does not exist in the BFF.

Marius was already engrossed, and read on.

A similar approach has been successful in the rest of the world. The world has been divided into zones appropriate to the efficient management of world resources, and, as is now always the case, all decisions are taken with the wider needs of our species in mind. (See also 'Abolition of International Trade'.)

Marius followed the link to the suggested section.

In addition to the abolition of travel and non-administrative communication, universal agreement was reached to discontinue international trade also. This has removed all sense of deprivation and envy between peoples, with the result that international strife has been eradicated. (See also 'Phasing Out of Currency'.)

Marius was dipping in and out of the relevant sections now. He was beginning to see what Uri had meant when he referred to Dunstan Heathfield's famous quotation that 'each piece of jigsaw affected every other piece in the picture.' Under 'Phasing Out of Currency' he read:

In the year 2340, the many improvements in the quality of life in the BFF led the Witan to conclude that currency was no longer necessary. This development coincided with the introduction of the 'Just Utilisation of People Act', whereby each person is objectively graded according to intellect and motivation so that he or she is able to make an appropriate contribution to the community.

Throughout their childhood, Marius and Urania submitted themselves for formal schooling at the Drayling education facility on four mornings each week, as was required by law. Since the inception of the Compulsory Literacy Act (2339), each district had its own facility, run by the Worthy Council along strictly prescribed lines. Three subjects were covered: History, Literacy and Citizenship. These were provided by the relevant Worthies – the Local Historian, Local Culturist and Local Assessor respectively. Under the law, all other education was provided subsequently, as appropriate, in accordance with Personal Gradings, which were first assessed at the age of sixteen.

As Local Historian, it was therefore one of Uri's responsibilities to give basic history lessons to the children. His remit – which he didn't especially enjoy due to its rather simplistic and repetitive nature – was to summarise the story of the creation of the BFF and the consequent phasing out of all religious beliefs. The lessons were required to be formally structured and 'of an informative nature'. Young citizens were not encouraged to ask questions or seek further detail whilst attending the facility.

It was this latter aspect which Uri found so frustrating, as it was totally alien to his natural inclinations. However, he consoled himself that he was providing a service to the community, and that "most young people want to get out of the classroom as quickly as possible anyway."

Neither Marius nor Urania were disadvantaged by the cursory nature of this formal part of their education, as they were fortunate enough to have parents with the foresight and capability to give them access to a much wider range of information and human experience. Marius had his weekly sessions with Uri, and Urania (to whom Uri had, of course, made the same facility available if she'd wanted it) had opted for regular chats with Della. Whilst certainly not stupid, Urania didn't possess the burning passion for knowledge that was already driving Marius.

On the day before his fourteenth birthday, at their weekly formal session, Marius informed Uri that he proposed to make History his career, and that, after completing his 'Local Service', he planned to follow a similar path to that taken by his father. This came as no surprise to Uri, who could see already that his son had the potential to eventually succeed him as Local Historian, if circumstances allowed. The thought made him feel exceedingly proud.

"As you know, father," continued Marius, "I've spent some time recently with your identiscreen researching various aspects of the development of our country. There are a couple of things I'd like to ask you to clarify."

As always, Uri was delighted to be asked, and replied, "Of course. What are they?"

"Well, I'd like to know exactly how the political pyramid works...and how did its evolution bring about the ending of all religious beliefs?"

Once again, he knew he was setting Uri off on one of his comprehensive discourses – which was precisely his intention. Nobody knew more about their subject than Uri.

"The political hierarchy in the BFF is basically simple. The Government of National Unity, or 'Witan', is headed by the Archwitan, or Premier, and, as you know, that is currently Spencer Curtis. There are five or six other members, or 'Witanates', working directly with him. Each has sworn to work with the others to uphold the principles and values established by Dunstan Heathfield."

"What happens below that?" asked Marius.

"Well, immediately beneath the Witan, are the six Regional Administrations, who are charged with implementing the Witan's decisions. The R.A. for this area is called 'South Country Regional Administration', and it consists of four Honourable Officers – Regional Assessor, Regional Culturist, Regional Historian and Regional Provider. As a matter of courtesy, whenever referring to more than one of the Honourable Officers, it's usual to refer to them in alphabetical order. These are the people who are in direct contact with the Worthy Councils of the various districts. Drayling is officially designated an 'Area Entity', and therefore has its own Worthy Council, which deals with all local issues, and receives any instructions arising from Witan decisions via the Regional Administration. There are normally six members of a Worthy Council. These are the Archworthy, who is the head of the Council, plus the Local Historian, Local Assessor, Local Culturist, Local Provider and Local Genworthy. Each member has very clear responsibilities. Traditionally, Worthies are addressed as 'Sir', but I'm afraid there's no polite alphabetical order for us!"

"What exactly are your responsibilities, father?" asked Marius.

"The easy answer to that is anything related to our history," replied Uri. "My statement of duty reads 'To teach historical fact to all as needed, and to personify its importance in the local community'. That means – teach history to the children at the education facility, look after all local historical records accessible on identiscreens, keep local

15

mapping up-to-date, coordinate local events which have an historical significance and provide one-to-one tuition to individual citizens as required by the Local Assessor. In practice, it's the latter that takes the bulk of my time."

"And this system is the same as the one set up when Dunstan Heathfield first formed the Government of National Unity in 2320?" interrupted Marius. "Would you say it's worked well?"

"I've said many times that I believe we're fortunate indeed to live in the BFF. Since Dunstan Heathfield's Revolution, mankind has lived in harmony. The world is no longer ravaged by war, and starvation and deprivation have been banished. We, and the rest of the world, are at peace, and we have all that we need. Yes, I'd say it's worked very well."

"We were told at education facility that all religions were officially abolished in the year 2335. The records obviously confirm it, but I can't find any detailed reasons. Can you explain the thinking behind it?"

"One of Dunstan Heathfield's famous speeches is reproduced in full in the archives. You can access it via identiscreen. In it, he explains in detail how the unprecedented advances achieved by what we now call his 'Revolution' prompted a 'grave and momentous agreement' with all of the main religions that there was no longer any need for them to exist – there being no point in 'travelling to the same destination along separate, parallel railway lines which were built for days which are now long gone'. He said he'd been 'deeply moved by their unanimity and vision', and that 'all main lines have now merged at a common junction of civilisation, and a single line will now carry us all forward in peace and unity'."

"Yes, I know it says that," said Marius, "but what was the real reason? I mean, can you explain exactly what it all means?"

Uri was a little surprised. "Well, it means what it says. Since the Heathfield Revolution, we've all lived in harmony.

Every decision is now taken with the best interests of mankind in mind, and each individual has all that he or she needs. Everything is well ordered. Strife, envy, greed, starvation and deprivation have all been eradicated.

"It must have become apparent that a defining moment in the development of the world had been reached, which was beyond anything that anyone had hitherto dreamed of. As everyone now desired to move in precisely the same direction, it was recognised that a greater good could be achieved by total unity."

"Come on father," persisted Marius. "Is that the extent of it? What do you really think?"

Uri wasn't used to being challenged in such a way, but he knew that his son was, by nature, as logical and intelligent as he was, and they both loved to debate. He realised that the point was well made and, after some thought, continued, "Well, I don't think we should dismiss it. I think the development is essentially a practical one. Remember Dunstan's jigsaw analogy, and the changes that had to be made to our way of life to achieve the huge overall advances that we all now enjoy. This is just another piece of that jigsaw."

He paused, and then added, "but having said that, I suppose some might also say that much of the strife in the world over the centuries has been religion-related in one way or another. Maybe the various leaders were moved to acknowledge the fact, and to realise that a brand new world perhaps requires a brand new approach. I don't know – but maybe."

It seemed to Marius that the more he delved into history, the more interesting it became.

The following day, the Archworthy of Drayling presented him with his own IDS.

3

One spring morning a couple of years later, Uri and Marius were eating breakfast together in the kitchen. Neither had spoken for some time – each being completely comfortable in the other's company.

Eventually, Marius broke the silence.

"Father, I'm thinking of conducting an archaeological excavation of the Northern Agricultural Area."

Uri looked up from his food. "Oh, really – what do you have in mind?"

"Well, as you know, they're going to build our new Worthy Hall up there. Construction starts in a few months time. I thought I'd see what I could find out about the site they're going to put it on. In fact, apart from details of crop planning and allocations of responsibility for the various food production uses to which it's been put in recent years, the records are pretty sketchy – but what little information there is seems to suggest that the site, or at least part of it, may have been used for recreational purposes at one time."

He paused and looked at his father.

"If there is anything up there to be learned, then I think it makes sense to take the opportunity whilst it exists."

It did, indeed, make perfect sense, and Uri was immediately determined to encourage and support his son's efforts. Of course, as Local Historian, he'd need to be involved on a formal level also.

"You'll have to seek permission," he observed, "but I can't imagine that anyone's going to object. On the contrary, you'll need help, and I'm sure the Local Assessor would be delighted to select some suitable people to participate. It's the kind of project that'll arouse interest, as well as being of educational value."

Marius was pleased by his father's positive response – although, in truth, not surprised. It wasn't unusual for them to think along similar lines.

The excavation got under way a few weeks later. In addition to four selected nominees, the Local Assessor also sent along his son, Hayden. Despite an age difference of fourteen years, Marius already knew him well, because he'd often accompanied his father on his visits to their home in the past.

Having assembled the team on the spot where the new Worthy Hall was to be built, Marius addressed them confidently.

"We're fortunate that it's a clear day, and not too cold. It rained a little during the night, so the soil should be workable. In fact, I'd say the conditions are probably more or less ideal. The Local Historian has arranged for a multitron scan of the area, and this has already been carried out."

Although all those present knew that he was Uri's son, it seemed to Marius more appropriate, in the circumstances, to use his father's formal title.

He wanted the project to be as authentically traditional as possible, and hadn't been keen to accept Uri's insistence on the multitron scan, but he'd had to concede that the area was far too large for purely random excavation. He knew also that primitive geophysical surveys had been used as long ago as the 20th Century, so, despite the virtual infallibility of modern multitronics, he consoled himself that this was not too great a departure from his original plan.

"The scan has produced a 'geomitron map', and if you look at it on your IDS, you'll see that it highlights two clear areas of anomaly and a line running diagonally across the site.

"I propose that we start by opening two trenches, one across each anomaly, using the old-fashioned manual digging tools. By avoiding the use of metrographic and aditronic technology, which would give us detailed prior knowledge of what we're going to unearth, we'll hopefully experience the full thrill of the discovery, in the same way that archaeologists did in the past.

"Hayden, if you'll take Caleb and Gil over to the anomaly next to the Eastern boundary and start Trench One, I'll go with Dan and Ali to the Northern one and establish Trench Number Two."

None of them was used to using manual tools. The march of technology over the years had meant that there was almost invariably a labour-saving device available for every kind of physical task, and, whilst exercise was encouraged and practised, it tended to be under scientifically controlled conditions, rather than through simple, hard toil.

Very soon, they began to experience discomfort, and abrasions began to appear. Hayden quickly became concerned and approached Marius to suggest that they should cease digging for a time and reassess their priorities. He pointed out that, whilst the four nominees were unlikely to complain openly, it was apparent that they were being asked to carry out tasks for which they weren't really prepared, and hadn't been trained. He questioned whether it was reasonable to push them.

Marius realised immediately that he was right, and called the team together to ask them how they felt.

On discovering that they were all already suffering from blistered or bloody hands, he called a halt for the day, and apologised profusely for his oversight. He'd not foreseen the problem.

There was very little conversation as they made their way directly to the medical facility for treatment.

Marius was furious with himself. How could he have been so stupid? As he sat alone in his room that evening, staring into space, Uri knocked on the door.

"Can I come in?" he asked.

Marius grunted, but raised no objection.

Uri sat on the bed beside him. "It's not the end of the world, you know. Everyone makes mistakes. In fact, the man who never made a mistake never made anything."

"I was stupid," retorted Marius. "I was so blinded by my ideas that I failed to see the obvious. As a result, in addition to humiliating myself, I've probably lost the goodwill of the team as well."

Uri smiled inwardly. This display of self-recrimination showed clearly just how much his son cared, both for the project itself, and for the men who were helping him.

He replied quietly, and in an even tone.

"I think a number of positives have come out of today's events. Firstly, you realised you'd made a mistake, and were quick to admit it. Provided you learn from it, you'll have gained from it.

"Secondly, your aim was to experience traditional archaeological methods. Well, whilst uncomfortable, you've certainly already discovered that the process consisted, at least in part, of plain hard slog."

He stood up and turned to face Marius.

"And thirdly, Hayden called to say that the others all realised how annoyed you were with yourself.

"The message is that, if you give them a day to recover, they'll see you at the site at nine o'clock on Friday morning."

Marius looked up at his father.

"They're right behind you," smiled Uri, and put his hand on his shoulder. "…But I tentatively recommend that you use an aditronic probe when you resume digging."

Without waiting for an answer, he left Marius to his thoughts and went to bed.

The excavation duly resumed at nine o'clock on Friday morning. All were wearing gloves. Marius had taken Uri's advice, and within a short time they were all clustered together next to Trench One examining aditronic images on their identiscreens.

"Whatever it is in Trench Two is enormous," observed Hayden.

"And metallic," said Marius. "Trench One is less clear, but the four circular features must be wheels, mustn't they? A cart of some sort, maybe?"

He made a decision.

"I propose we concentrate initially on Trench Two, and see if we can identify our metal giant."

They all readily agreed, and strolled together the three hundred yards or so to the Northern trench. As they walked, Marius said, "We have the use of a metrographic earthworker today, which will shift the bulk of the heavy soil without interfering with any archaeology. It requires one person to operate it, and I understand you know how to use it, Gil, so could you take charge of that please?

"I'm going to use a hand-trowel when we get close to the object. If anyone else would like to do the same, I've brought enough with me. But please remember, it's not a race – take it slowly, and try to enjoy it. Also, we don't want to damage anything that might be flimsy or brittle. Whatever is under there has been there for a long time. A few more hours won't make any difference – and let's avoid wasting any more of the medical facility's time."

They all expressed interest in having a go, and Hayden pleased Gil by asking him to explain how the earthworker 'read' the soil to avoid damaging anything of importance.

It wasn't long before a large quantity of earth had been removed, and they set to work with their trowels. Soon, metal began to appear. They scraped on eagerly – keen to ascertain exactly what the object was.

Uri had been monitoring proceedings from a distance. He knew that Marius wished to maintain the authenticity of a 'traditional dig', but was unable to curb his curiosity any longer. He strolled over to the trench, and, as casually as he could, said, "Many congratulations on your achievement, gentlemen. You're all clearly tired from your efforts, and, have now experienced the thrill of the discovery. May I suggest that an aditronic picture at this point would almost certainly identify precisely what you've found?"

They all looked up at Uri, and then turned, as one, to Marius.

He was certainly tired.

For a tense moment, he didn't reply. Then, accepting that he'd been cornered, he shrugged and nodded.

He stood up, and, as he did so, realised for the first time that his back ached excruciatingly.

"It's what they used to call a heavy roller," announced Uri a little while later. "Since this excavation was first mooted, I've been doing some research of my own into the uses to which the site may have been put. I think this find proves conclusively that it was indeed used for sports and leisure activities. It would probably have been known as a 'recreation ground' or 'park', and it's likely that the main activities would have been the games of football and cricket – typically football in winter and cricket in summer. As you know, football is still played informally by young children, whereas cricket died out around the end of the 21st Century. Interestingly, it seems to have died out more or less of its own accord – some 250 years before Dunstan Heathfield's Competition Discouragement Measures finally brought an end to every kind of organised sport throughout the world. This roller would almost certainly have been used to prepare the cricket playing area."

"But it's huge," said Marius.

"Yes. It would've been operated manually – simply manhandled by several men at once – similar to the methods used to build Stonehenge and the Pyramids. It would simply have been pushed and pulled – back and forth – across a selected piece of ground, using its sheer weight to flatten the earth. The game of cricket needed the playing area to be as smooth and level as possible."

Trench One was not quite so straightforward. Whilst the excavation itself was fairly easy – they all enjoyed it – the day came to a premature end without a definite identification of what they'd uncovered. However, they were all extremely tired, so they went their separate ways with Marius promising to contact them again as soon as he had something further to report.

It took nearly three days of puzzling over the evidence with his father before Marius reassembled the team in the foyer of the Worthy Hall.

"At first, we thought we were looking at some kind of cart – perhaps used for transporting posts for the football goals, which archive records confirm would have been quite heavy. But, after looking into the game of cricket in a little more detail, we've come to the conclusion that what we probably have here are the remains of what was known as a 'sight screen'. This would have been a large mobile contraption, similar to a section of fence, standing something like 15 feet high by about 12 feet wide, on metal wheels. The body of the structure would probably have been made of wood."

"What was it for?" asked Hayden.

"It would've been positioned behind the person bowling the ball. The records say that the screen would've been white in colour to enable the batter to see the ball more easily. It seems to me that the game of cricket mainly involved the manoeuvring of heavy machinery!

"Anyway, that left us with the line on the geomitron map which runs diagonally across the site from South-East to North-West...and my father can tell us more about that."

He deferred to Uri.

"Yes...thank you, Marius. As you know, official permission was necessary for our excavation – and that was no problem. However, as a matter of routine, it was recorded in the weekly report to South Country Regional Administration. To my surprise, the Regional Historian showed great interest in what we were doing, and has been monitoring our progress on his identiscreen. He's asked me to congratulate you all on your efforts. He was able to tell me that the diagonal line is one of many cable conduits which were laid across the whole country in the early 21st Century as part of the great internet fiasco. He asks that we leave it undisturbed at this time, as any investigation into that would ideally need to be conducted on a national scale.

"As Local Historian, I'd like to add my own congratulations to you also. It's been a most instructive experience, and I hope you all feel that you've got something positive from it."

Marius made a particular point of thanking everyone for their help and forbearance, and then, after chatting for a while longer, they said their goodbyes and went home.

4

The archaeological excavation had aroused much interest amongst the people of Drayling.

In response, whilst Marius and his team had been digging, Uri had made arrangements for spectators to view the proceedings from a safe distance, and had also produced a daily progress report – accessible to all via IDS. In fact, the interest level was such that the Archworthy had informed Uri that, quite apart from the obvious historical significance, both the Local Culturist and the Local Assessor had reported perceived benefits in their areas of responsibility also. A special meeting of the Worthy Council was therefore convened, at which Uri was asked to arrange a series of appropriate public lectures as soon as practical.

Later that evening, when he told Della what he'd been asked to do, her reaction took him by surprise.

"That's a superb idea," she enthused, "…and Urania and I can help you do the necessary research!"

The look on Uri's face – and his open mouth – showed clearly that this was not the response he was expecting, and he didn't reply immediately.

Before he could say anything, Della continued, "Remember how we helped to scour the records when you were puzzling over the cricket sight screen? Well, the whole thing intrigued us so much that, since then, the two of us have been delving deeper into cricket – both the game itself, and its place in the community. It's fascinating, you know – I can't really understand why it died out. For years it was part of the fabric of communities. People of all ages would get involved, in all sorts of different ways, and it was a thoroughly civilised and sensible way to spend a summer's afternoon.

"We really enjoyed looking into it...and I think Urania summed it up perfectly when she commented that a cricket match was a sort of communal picnic – complete with organised game!"

It was obvious that Uri was still off-balance, and she laughed at his discomfort.

"Oh, Uri, I know I don't normally get quite so directly involved in your official duties, but I think, in this instance, both of us could be a real help to you."

She gazed straight into his eyes – a ploy that she knew from experience immeasurably improved her chances of getting her own way – and Uri finally rediscovered his voice.

"My love, I...I'm sorry if I seem a little...er...confused. Of course, I know perfectly well that you always give me your full support in everything I do, and I certainly wouldn't want to imply otherwise.

"Your obvious enthusiasm for the subject is a pleasure to see."

He paused and swallowed.

"Actually, I had in mind two illustrated talks – one to be entitled 'Archaeology Over The Years', and the second to be called 'The Drayling Of 300 Years Ago'...but I'll now unhesitatingly add a third, and call it 'Cricket'."

The following day, Uri advertised that the public lectures would take place in the Worthy Hall on the next three Wednesday evenings. During the days running up to the first of them, the whole family spent many hours trawling diligently through the various records available – and, from the results, Uri composed his presentations.

One evening, about a month later, when the four of them were relaxing together in their easy chairs, Della remarked, "You know, Uri, your lectures were extremely well-received.

A number of my friends have said how much they enjoyed them – particularly the last one."

Uri grinned. "Yes, I've had a few compliments too."

"I think everyone liked them," Marius chipped in. "In fact, I've been thinking…if there's so much interest in cricket, why don't we organise a game, and experience it all for ourselves? I'm sure, with a little bit of ingenuity, we could make the bats and wickets and things."

The family's reaction was immediate and positive. They all thought it was a wonderful idea – and so Uri undertook to have a word with the Local Culturist without delay. He could see that the proposal probably impacted on both of their areas of responsibility, and the formal approval of the Worthy Council would obviously be necessary before they could go ahead.

Urania, who was particularly excited by the idea, took Marius to one side to make a point of her own. "Obviously, there's a whole load of things to think about, but one thing needs to be made clear right from the start – women are included."

Marius thought quickly. He could see that this was a potentially sensitive issue, and he agreed straightaway that, when they sat down to discuss the various points to be dealt with, the question of the inclusion of both men and women would be the first to be considered.

The idea of a cricket game found favour with the Worthy Council. The Archworthy reported that the timing of the request couldn't have been better, because "only recently" he'd been instructed by Regional Administration to arrange "appropriate events" in the forthcoming months to commemorate the 400th anniversary of the introduction of identiscreens in 2066. They agreed unanimously that a "Drayling Cricket Match" would be an "entirely suitable addition" to those celebrations – although Uri was careful to point out that Heathfield's Competition Discouragement Measures were "still an integral part of his jigsaw," and that they should therefore make it very clear to all that the important features were the "participation and enjoyment," and that the result of the game was of no consequence whatsoever.

As the original idea of the game had come from Marius, they also agreed that he should organise it, with Uri's guidance, of course.

When the Graves family sat down to dinner that evening, the sole topic of discussion was the forthcoming cricket match.

"I suppose the first thing we need to do is find out how many men want to play," said Uri.

"No," replied Urania in a steady voice, "the first thing we need to do is find out how many men or women want to play."

"Yes, absolutely," added Della quickly. "There's no reason at all why this should be restricted to men."

Uri and Marius looked at each other enquiringly – and then, realising that it made no difference whether they thought it was a good idea or not, they nodded simultaneously.

"Agreed," said Marius. "There's obviously a lot of things to think about. Perhaps we could each take responsibility for a different aspect of the preparations for the game. Let's make a list of everything we think needs to be done."

About two hours later, Marius said, "Right, that's it, then. This is what we've agreed. Father will be responsible for preparing the playing area and ensuring that everyone involved knows the rules. Mother and Urania will make all the arrangements, put together two teams and organise a mid-game meal – and I'll address the problem of providing all the equipment we'll need. We don't think there'll be any lack of people willing to help, so we can each get others involved as and when we need them."

With that, he said, "Goodnight," and went to bed.

Uri picked up his IDS and recorded the plan in his diary.

Many miles away, at Witan Central Office, Turner Zeal had not been assistant to Archwitan Spencer Curtis for very long. Still only eighteen, he'd been recognised as a prodigy by his Local Assessor as a young child, and, at the age of fourteen had been "officially identified for potential elevation." His official duties weren't at all onerous at present. Tall, fair-haired and blue-eyed, he'd accompanied his boss on a couple of special appearances in North BFF, and was required to carry out simple administrative tasks as the need arose. Generally, however, his brief was to "identify aspects worthy of further personal investigation with a view to gaining as much beneficial knowledge and experience as possible for future governmental responsibility."

He'd carried out all his duties efficiently to date, and displayed an eagerness to learn. For his part, Zeal realised that fate had dealt him a unique opportunity to achieve power and influence, and that, for the moment at least, cultivating the trust and respect of Spencer Curtis was an essential precursor to that.

It was now two o'clock in the afternoon, and the rest of the day was his own. He took a cool drink from the drinksmade, picked up his identiscreen and re-accessed South Country/Drayling. A few weeks ago, one of the Witanates had suggested to him that he "take a look at an archaeological excavation being carried out in that part of the country."

It had been intriguing.

The excavation had come very close to an embarrassing and potentially difficult exposure of a BFF Power-Route, but the Regional Historian had managed to spin a story about "21st Century internet conduits," and a major incident had been averted.

The instigator of the undertaking was surprisingly young – a sixteen-year-old youth named Marius Graves, who was the son of the Local Historian. He'd applied for permission on the grounds that "we should learn what there is to learn from the site before the new Worthy Hall is built on it, and the opportunity is lost."

Zeal had wondered about the youth.

It hadn't been difficult to investigate his IDS activity over the previous two years, and, in addition, the searches on his father's screen in the few months leading up to his fourteenth birthday weren't in any way consistent with the older man's previous access patterns, so it wasn't unreasonable to assume that they too had been made by the son.

The subject-matter and persistent nature of the searches seemed to Zeal to be altogether more questioning than the norm. He noted the depth of inquiry into the reasons behind previous Witan decisions, and the extent of his investigation into why things were as they were.

"This fellow's no fool," mused Zeal, "...and now he applies for permission to play cricket."

He skimmed through the latest notes, which recorded detailed plans for the organisation of a game, which the local Worthy Council had decided would form part of the forthcoming identiscreen anniversary celebrations.

He then turned his attention to a gentleman in North Country who claimed to have discovered a new way of making bread.

The next two weeks were a blur of activity for the Graves family, as they set about their respective tasks to bring Marius' cricket project to fruition. The idea was something new and exciting, and it wasn't difficult to find friends who were keen to help. Soon, Drayling was abuzz with anticipation.

When the day of the game finally arrived the weather was mercifully dry and by early afternoon it seemed that the entire population of the area entity had assembled at the recreational facility, eagerly awaiting the big event.

The teams that Della and Urania had put together were to be captained by Marius and Hayden, and each consisted of six men and five women. Ages ranged from around sixty to as young as thirteen – the latter being Urania herself.

The game took a while to get going, but when it did, it quickly became apparent that no one really knew what they were doing. Although every one of the players had attended Uri's cricket classes only a few days previously, they weren't finding it quite as easy as they'd expected to turn the theory into practice.

Whilst there was much laughter and running about, it seemed to Uri that some kind of concerted action was necessary. Being one of the 'umpires', and therefore already standing in the middle of the playing area, he assumed his natural demeanour of tutor. Although only able to draw on what he'd learned from reading IDS records, he began to direct operations.

This of course meant that, for a while at least, the proceedings became little more than a lesson in how to play the game. However, the need was already plainly apparent to the players, so there was no argument, and soon, as they gradually gained more confidence, a general appreciation of what it was all about began to emerge. This slowly developed into a contest and, by the end of the afternoon, both players and watchers had had their first taste of the game of cricket.

In the late afternoon of the following day, the Graves family sat down to have dinner together.

"I think you've created a monster, Marius," remarked Uri. "Your game of cricket's been the only topic of conversation in Drayling all day. Despite its popularity in years gone by, no one these days has ever seen anything quite like it. I haven't heard a single negative comment. In fact, they're all asking when we're going to do it again."

Marius grinned. "Yes, it was great fun. The only down-side for me was that my team didn't hit enough runs!"

"That doesn't really bother you, does it?" queried Urania.

"No, of course not," chuckled Marius. "What was important was that everyone enjoyed themselves – but that won't stop Hayden reminding me that his team were the winners!"

"And would you do it again?" asked Della, as she spooned soup into Uri's bowl.

"I'd certainly like to. What do you think, father?"

Uri paused for a moment, and then, with his characteristic thoughtful expression, replied, "I think the Worthy Council will undoubtedly have more to say on the subject. Both the Local Assessor and the Local Culturist have reported that they've noticed benefits in their respective areas of responsibility already, and I would definitely say the same.

"That being the case, we'd be failing in our duty if we didn't capitalise on it in some way. We've already exchanged IDS messages, and there's a formal meeting at the end of the week, so I suggest you wait to see what that brings."

5

Growing concern in the Witan about the threat of inbreeding in the BFF, brought about by the travel restrictions imposed as part of Dunstan Heathfield's Revolution, finally forced Spencer Curtis to act.

He ordered the Regional Administrations to put every Archworthy in the country on notice that changes needed to be made to resolve the problem. All existing area entities would be enhanced by amalgamation with two immediately neighbouring districts to create fewer, larger entities – to be known as 'Local Geographical Units'. These LGUs would continue to operate on precisely the same basis as the existing system, so that all essential features of Dunstan Heathfield's famous jigsaw would be preserved.

He summoned Turner Zeal to his office.

"Zeal, I have a job for you. You're already aware of the communication to Archworthies notifying them of the action being taken to deal with the inbreeding problem. I want you to work with the Quality Controller to draw up the necessary detailed instructions for Regional Administrations to pass on to the Worthy Councils. The QC will liaise with the other Witanates as appropriate. The new political structure is to be in place, and fully operational, within six months, and LGUs will operate precisely as the area entities do now.

"The Regional Assessors will need to identify an Archworthy for each LGU from the three current incumbents. The Assessment System is totally objective, so the decision will be straightforward. I've encoded your instructions into your IDS, and incorporated all necessary authorisations."

Zeal acknowledged that he understood the Archwitan's instructions, and the two men parted. He did not know, at that stage, that Spencer Curtis was a very sick man, and that he would never see him alive again.

Della, Urania and Marius were sitting chatting at home when Uri returned from his regular Worthy Council meeting. He spoke as soon as he walked in.

"I have some really surprising news," he said. "Sir Bedford Coote, our Archworthy, is stepping down.

"Although he's only 82, and still, therefore, three years short of the normal retirement age, he's decided to go now."

"Really?" said Della, "that doesn't sound like Bedford. Why's he going so early?"

"He says he's been considering it for some time," replied Uri, "and has concluded that he'd like to relax and simply enjoy life with his family as a free citizen.

"On top of that, he also said that, whilst he was in touch with Regional Administration, he agreed with them that we can arrange a game of cricket against a team from Stowly Heath! In fact, he said they were so impressed by the success of our recent game, that they suggested we might also like to include the people of Burshaw as well!"

All three jaws dropped.

No one said a word. They just stared at Uri as though he'd gone completely mad.

"I promise you I'm not making this up," he said, throwing up his hands. "I'm just as amazed as you are. I've just had half an hour longer to get used to it, that's all."

They were all stunned, but Marius was nevertheless quick to react.

"Father, what you say is puzzling, to say the least. Forgive me for being sceptical, but, if I understand you correctly, you're saying that a relatively spontaneous approach to the RA by our Archworthy has resulted in his premature retirement and received a response which has potential repercussions far beyond Drayling. On the face of it, they appear to be prepared to relax the Jigsaw Laws – key features of Dunstan Heathfield's Revolution – just so that we can play cricket. If that's the case, then I don't think it adds up. What's going on, father?"

Urania spoke before Uri could reply. "Oh, Marius, don't be so cynical! Why shouldn't a man who's worked so hard for us all his life retire and enjoy a rest?

"The RA obviously knows that Sir Bedford's been a loyal servant, and simply wants to agree to one of his final suggestions as a parting gesture!"

Uri smiled. He would love to believe Urania's version of events, but he knew – and clearly Marius could see also – that these apparently trivial minutes of a Worthy Council meeting simply could not be the innocuous local matters that the Archworthy had clearly tried to present them as.

Neither Uri nor Marius slept much that night. At first light, Uri went straight to the Archworthy's house. Bedford Coote had seen him coming on his day-screen, and was at the door before the sensor confirmed his approach.

"Hello, Uri," he said without smiling. "Come in. Clement's already here, and the others are on their way."

Uri wasn't surprised. He followed the Archworthy into his reception room, nodded at the Local Assessor, found a chair and selected himself a drink. Within ten minutes, the other three members of the Council had arrived also.

Uri and Clement looked at each other enquiringly. They were generally regarded as the senior members of the Council after the Archworthy and, this time, the latter took the initiative.

"This isn't a Council meeting, Bedford. We're a group of close friends who've known each other for a long time. Nothing's being recorded. We're all here because we know that something out of the ordinary's happening, and also out of concern for you. What's going on?"

Coote looked at the faces of his colleagues of many years, and said, "At next week's regular meeting, I expect to have the full story for you, and I ask you as friends to treat everything I say now as confidential until then. I know you're here as…" His IDS buzzed loudly. "Oh…excuse me a moment."

He looked at his screen and his face changed colour visibly.

"Are you all right, Bedford?" asked Uri, immediately concerned for the old man. "Is it bad news? Would you like us to leave?"

"No…no…don't go," said Coote, almost absent-mindedly, "there's more to say now…and I don't know if it changes anything."

He settled back into his chair and took a sip of the drink that the Local Culturist had handed to him. He took a few moments to compose himself.

"I've been advised by South Country Regional Administration that all area entities – of which Drayling is one, of course – are to be amalgamated with two neighbouring entities to form one larger entity, to be called a 'Local Geographical Unit'. The new 'LGU' will operate in exactly the same way as the previous entities. It'll have a single Archworthy, who'll be selected from the three existing incumbents. I've told RA that, in view of my age, I'd prefer not to be considered."

The Local Genworthy, Donovan Chard, interrupted.

"Does the same apply to all other Worthies?"

"I think it must," replied Coote, "although I've not yet had it confirmed. I've already asked that question."

"Well, that explains why a game of cricket against Stowly Heath and Burshaw is permissible," observed Uri. "Presumably they're the other two members of our new Local Geographical Unit. Why is this happening? Why are RA seeking to change something that's worked so well for so long?"

"They say the Witan's been concerned for a long time about the insidious effects of inbreeding, and that, after years of monitoring, it's got to the point at which action simply has to be taken. They say that, by increasing the size of district units in this way, they can retain all the essential features of Dunstan Heathfield's Revolution, but at the same time strengthen the gene pool. They also propose to introduce one new, healthy male into each LGU from elsewhere. Apparently, detailed research has shown that such a move will also have a significant strengthening effect on the overall gene pool within a few generations. I have to say that it sounds a little trivial to me on the face of it, but I'm sure they know what they're talking about."

"Right," began Clement Burcher, "What are we…"

"Hold on, Clement," interrupted Coote. "There's something else I have to tell you. The IDS message I just received told me that Spencer Curtis has died."

No one spoke for several moments, but, having already been subjected to a steady stream of numbing information in a very short space of time, the news didn't have quite the same deleterious effect on those present as it would undoubtedly otherwise have had.

Clement Burcher continued. "Well, obviously the death of the Archwitan is very sad, and no doubt we'll be sending a suitable message via the RA from the people of Drayling, but it's not likely to change anything. If it's acceptable for one male to be introduced to strengthen the gene pool, why can't a larger number be introduced to strengthen it still further? I agree with Uri. Why is it necessary to change the Area Entity system as well?"

Whilst the Local Assessor had been talking, Sir Bedford Coote had decided that enough informal discussion had already taken place. In his official voice, he said, "Gentlemen, we'll need to debate these matters formally in council. I'll call an extraordinary sitting shortly due to the death of our Head of State. I'll give you all relevant information received on all the issues at that time."

He rose, and the others, knowing the discussion was over, went home.

At the formal Council session they examined the Regional Administration's instructions in great detail. Even so, at the end of it, Uri's mind was in complete turmoil. For years now he'd extolled the virtues of Dunstan Heathfield's famous vision – that every part of the jigsaw was key to the composition of the overall picture – and now, the Area Entity system – clearly fundamental to the whole – was to be abolished. Of course, he understood that the new LGUs were planned to operate along the same lines as the AEs, but he'd always laid great emphasis on the absolute integrity of the old arrangement – the very indispensability of every detail – to countless people over many years. How could he now simply forget all of that?

What on earth was he to think? He was a Worthy for goodness' sake! What are others going to think? People looked up to him. They would expect him to explain it all.

He shut himself in his private office for the rest of the day, and that night – once again – he hardly slept at all.

As was often the case, it was Della who eventually came to the rescue – over breakfast the following morning. She knew instinctively how troubled he was, and motioned to Urania and Marius to keep quiet.

For a long time all was silent. Uri, indifferent to his surroundings, was deep within himself, tormented and clearly still wrestling with his predicament.

"Uri," began Della in a matter-of-fact voice seemingly insensitive to his discomfort, "what's a government for?"

"Uh?" grunted Uri, rudely dragged from his private thoughts. "Well, it…"

He paused and frowned. Then a slow dawning began to ease his pained expression. He stared into space for a few moments more.

As his realisation grew, he allowed his gaze to fall on Della's face, and he broke into a smile.

"Wife, it's long been a source of wonder to me just how well you understand me," he said.

Of course! It really was as straightforward as that! It wasn't his job to make such decisions. That's what a government's for! For goodness' sake, what was he thinking? His way was perfectly clear. The decision had been made, and was therefore the right one. It only seemed strange to him because he wasn't in full possession of all the relevant information from which such important decisions have to be made. He felt a little ashamed of himself. It was a very simple point, but an important one, nonetheless. What's the point of having a government, if every decision it makes has to be dissected and approved by every citizen?

Suddenly, he was completely comfortable. He stood up and walked over to his wife. As he kissed her, he said, "Thank you my darling," and left the room, pausing for a second to reflect, "sad about Spencer Curtis though."

Marius and Uri's regular weekly chat had long since become an institution to which they both looked forward, and which they both valued. Of course, it was now more a meeting of thinking minds than an educational exercise. It had become a forum in which any subject could be raised and explored in confidence. Both had absolute trust in the other.

The latest meeting was no exception, and they had much to discuss.

"A lot's been happening in recent days, father," said Marius. "It's been difficult to keep up with all the events."

Uri nodded and smiled thoughtfully. "Yes, that's certainly true. We do indeed have much to occupy our minds."

It was a measure of their closeness and mutual understanding that Uri already knew instinctively that Marius had been curbing his natural curiosities ever since the announcements – undoubtedly with difficulty – to allow his father to deal with matters in his own way, and without interference.

"Are you happy with the way things have gone, father? I mean, as a Worthy, it obviously affects you more than most."

"Well, yes, that's true, although I don't think there's too much to worry about. On a personal level, I've been retained as Local Historian to the new LGU, and the world isn't coming to an end. There's just a range of different issues to deal with, that's all. I shall reassure the people of Drayling that there's no reason for alarm, and that their way of life is not in imminent danger of collapse!"

"Things are certainly different," conceded Marius. "First, the old area entity system's scrapped, then Drayling's incorporated into a larger entity along with Burshaw and Stowly Heath. Sir Bedford Coote resigns, or is pushed, and the Stowly Heath Archworthy becomes ours also. On top of all that, Spencer Curtis dies of an illness we didn't know he had, and we now have a new, and completely unknown, Archwitan who calls himself…what is it?…'Tujo'?

"When you put it like that, I agree it does all sound rather radical," acknowledged Uri. "But if you take a moment to examine the issues separately, I think you'll find that it does all start to make some kind of sense. For example, it's perfectly feasible that the restriction of travel would, in time, lead to a weakening of the gene pool due to inbreeding. Indeed, the Witan has confirmed that this is what their tests have shown. For that reason, the relatively minor adjustment to the new LGU system does seem entirely appropriate. Also, the area entity system itself isn't being scrapped, because the new, larger areas will operate in precisely the same way.

"I suspect that, on reflection, Bedford Coote will embrace retirement gracefully, and will enjoy the freedom that the increased leisure time will give him. I'm told that Sir Grindon Blane, our new Archworthy, is forthright but fair, and that he's respected by the people of Stowly Heath. At 56, he's certainly a lot younger than Sir Bedford! Also, I'm pleased to say that Clement Burcher's going to continue to be

41

our Local Assessor, so that'll help to provide further continuity for the people of Drayling.

"The death of Spencer Curtis was, of course, very sad news. He kept his illness secret right to the end.

"Apparently, he'd known that his condition was terminal for some time. As you say, the new Archwitan is unknown to us. In fact, we did contact Regional Administration to ask for his full name, but it met with a rather terse response. They said that we'd already been told his name – Tujo – and that if any further information was considered appropriate, they would pass it to us."

He gave a little shrug. "However, overall, I don't think there's anything to worry about."

Marius wasn't at all surprised at the approach his father was taking. Whilst Uri was a brilliant historian and academic, he was, first and foremost, a Worthy. His sense of duty to the Council, and to the people of Drayling, would always take precedence, and he admired him for it. Nevertheless, Marius, as a logical thinker and avid student of BFF history, remained fully aware of the magnitude of the events that were unfolding, and was more than a little concerned.

It wasn't until later that he realised just how significant this latest discussion with Uri had been. For the first time in his life, he'd chosen not to share his disquiet with his father. In deference to Uri's position, he'd consciously decided to keep the full extent of his unease to himself.

However, he was also realistic enough to know that, whatever his personal views, the changes were going to happen anyway. So, for the moment at least, he decided to turn his attention to the question of cricket. He contacted Hayden Burcher by IDS and arranged to meet him at four o'clock that afternoon.

At about two o'clock, however, Uri brought Marius news from the new Archworthy.

"Sir Grindon has had discussions with Bedford Coote, and has expressed great interest in the archaeological discoveries that you made, and also in the obvious success of the cricket match. He says he's keen to use the proposed games with Stowly Heath and Burshaw to help cement the new kinship which arises from the amalgamation of our communities. He suggests a "Grand Cricket Day," involving all three teams, in about four weeks' time. What do you think?"

It certainly seemed like an excellent idea to Marius, and so plans went ahead accordingly. The Worthy Council made much of the significance of the forthcoming event in daily IDS messages and, together with many willing helpers (plus some designates identified by Clement Burcher, who'd already taken the opportunity to exercise his authority in the two districts new to him), everything was made ready. In the lead-up to the day, Uri conducted informal classes to teach prospective players – and a surprising number of others – the rules of the game. Marius asked Hayden if he would be the captain of the Drayling team, and he readily agreed.

When the big day arrived, the weather was kind. Three matches were to be played – sixteen overs for each team – and, as the Drayling players had already had some previous experience of playing the game, it was considered fairest that the first encounter be between Stowly Heath and Burshaw.

It resulted in a runaway win for Stowly Heath – which Urania loudly observed wasn't altogether surprising, as the average age of the Burshaw players "appeared to be approximately twice that of their opponents!"

After a light lunch, the second game was played between Stowly Heath and Drayling. It was a keenly fought, close game, which Stowly Heath eventually won by just two runs.

During the break that followed, everyone agreed that the day had been hugely successful. The captain of Burshaw, Norton Greatley, stood up and congratulated everyone involved with the initial idea and the arrangements. He said that, whilst his team were enjoying themselves immensely, some of "our more venerable members" were already rather tired, and perhaps Drayling wouldn't be too offended if he asked some of the younger members of the Stowly Heath team to make a guest appearance for his team in the final game. Nobody raised any objection, and the final match was played in a carnival atmosphere, with Drayling winning by some margin – the exact figure being uncertain, however, as proceedings descended into friendly anarchy when Greatley put the ball into his pocket and announced that he was going to "run about thirty" on the last ball.

6

One afternoon about ten days later, Della was relaxing in an easy chair, reading her identiscreen, when Uri returned from his Council meeting. He kissed her and asked where Marius and Urania were.

"Not far away," replied Della. "Why?"

Uri grinned. "Just you wait and see," he replied.

This, of course, had the intended effect of awakening her curiosity, and she called them immediately by IDS.

Within minutes the family were all together.

"I have some rather wonderful news," began Uri, in a voice that suggested – to Urania, at least – that he was about to make a speech. "I've just come from a full Council meeting, and one of the items discussed was the recent Cricket Day."

He paused in his characteristic way.

"The Archworthy, Sir Grindon Blane, was absolutely delighted with it. So much so, in fact, that he referred to it as 'a triumph', and insisted that it be officially designated as 'a notable achievement for our new LGU' in the records.

"After further discussion, in which I was asked to take no part due to a rather obvious conflict of interest, it was decided that you, my son...," he turned to face Marius, "...should be publicly honoured by the people of Burshaw, Drayling and Stowly Heath."

Marius opened his mouth to speak.

Uri held up his hand and continued, "Before you say anything, please let me finish."

He paused, and then, in a slightly more measured voice, said, "Marius Graves, I'm instructed by the Worthy Council of Burshaw, Drayling and Stowly Heath to ask you to formally accept the title of 'Thinker'. This accolade is rarely bestowed upon a non-Worthy, but in this case is considered to be well-deserved. You are being given this distinction in recognition of the major contribution you've made to your local community – specifically your archaeological excavation and subsequent reintroduction of the game of cricket. The rest of us..." he gestured towards Della and Urania "...have also been thanked officially for our contributions."

"Father..."

Once again, Uri raised his hand to silence his son.

"The Local Assessor has also asked me to inform you that your achievements have been officially recognised as being the equivalent of your Local Service – which is therefore now deemed to have been completed. He said that he considers the people of our LGU to have been well served."

Marius could take no more.

"Father, please stop," he spluttered, "what on earth are you talking about?"

"I promise you I'm not joking," insisted Uri, "...and I can't tell you how proud I am of you. Many, many congratulations, my boy."

He turned to Della. "And I'm sure your mother and sister are as proud as I am."

"Oh, darling," squealed Della, and hugged her son. Urania just gaped and grinned.

"W...what's a Thinker?" stumbled Marius, still reeling.

"It's a courtesy title, but very, very prestigious. I'm not sure how many times it's been awarded, but it's very few. And, as I said, it's almost never been awarded to anyone of lower rank than Worthy. It really is a momentous honour."

He paused.

"Oh, and Sir Grindon has asked that you meet him at the Drayling Worthy Hall tomorrow morning at eleven."

With that, he grinned at all three of them, collected his wife with an arm around her waist and marched her off to a drinksmade. This was truly a day he would never, ever forget. He was so proud he could burst.

The following morning, Marius was up by five o'clock, despite having had very little sleep. Adrenalin was still flowing freely through his veins, and he didn't feel tired at all.

After fetching himself a warm drink, he picked up his IDS and settled into an easy chair to see what he could find out about the title of 'Thinker'.

It didn't take him long to discover that the accolade had only been awarded seven times since its introduction in 2339 – the year that literacy was made compulsory – and that no one of lesser rank than Worthy, or younger than forty-seven, had ever received it before. It had last been awarded forty-six years ago, and its recipients were entitled to add '(Th.)' after their name. He learned that the honour could be bestowed by the authorities for particularly outstanding service to the community, and that, in every case, the express approval of the Witan itself was required.

Marius gasped audibly. His father had said that it was a prestigious award, but it was only now that he was beginning to grasp the true magnitude of what was happening to him. The Witan's approved this? The central government of the BFF?...But I'm only sixteen years old...And I'm not a Worthy...What's happening to me...?

He suddenly felt very ill. His stomach was churning now, and he was breathing heavily. He sat back in the chair and tried to relax. He was sweating and shivering at the same time. He closed his eyes.

The next thing he knew was his mother shaking him gently.

"Marius, wake up. It's ten-thirty. You have to be at the Worthy Hall at eleven."

Marius opened his eyes and looked up into her smiling face. It took a moment for her to come into focus.

"Gosh, mother – then I wasn't dreaming?"

Della smiled down at him. "No, my darling, you weren't dreaming. Now, quickly, go and get yourself ready. You don't want to be late."

Marius arrived at the Worthy Hall with about a minute to spare. As he approached the main entrance, he could see Sir Grindon Blane and the rest of the Worthy Council waiting for him outside. The Archworthy held out his arms as though to greet an old friend.

"Marius, my dear fellow. It's indeed a privilege on this bright, sunny morning to announce officially, on behalf of the people of Burshaw, Drayling and Stowly Heath, your elevation to the rank of 'Thinker'." He raised his fist into the air, and bellowed, "Let it be so affirmed!"

With that, a strange, and very loud, noise filled the air. Marius was startled, and took a step backwards. The Archworthy smiled. "Don't worry. That's the sound of the ancient bells to herald the investiture of a new 'Thinker'. It's an exact simulation of the traditional salute – and it hasn't been heard for over forty years. Since 2420 in fact, when the last 'Thinker' was proclaimed. It's sounding in your honour, Marius Graves. At this moment, every IDS in our corner of the BFF is ringing out at maximum volume to celebrate your new eminence.

"In addition to that, I'm also delighted to tell you that I've been asked by South Country Regional Administration, on behalf of the Witan itself, to accord to you the 'Distinction of Guardianship' of one of the great inventions in the history of our country – the 'Cipherslider Mark One' – of which you will have learned at education facility. It's particularly appropriate, as this fine antique computer dates from the very year in which the rank of Thinker was inaugurated. I've asked the Local Historian – your father, of course – to explain to you the significance of this additional honour, and that he will do later. Meanwhile, I am proud to record officially that, as of this day, the 2nd September, 2466, our LGU has become the home of both a new Thinker and one of the BFF's greatest treasures. It is indeed a momentous day for us all."

Having completed the formalities, he turned and looked enquiringly at Uri, who'd been stoically refusing to succumb to tears, but who was forced to shake his head gently to indicate that he wasn't in a position to speak at this point.

Before anyone else could say anything, Marius said, "Sir, I'm really not sure what to say, but I must say something. To say "Thank you" doesn't seem sufficient, yet I'm not sure what else there is.

"Obviously, this is all very new and a little frightening for me. I'm immensely proud, of course, not only for myself, but for my father..." he glanced at Uri, "...my family,...and all those who helped with our archaeological dig and the cricket. It was really all done because it was, well...fun. I'm really not sure that all this is deserved. I don't feel..."

"Enough!" interjected Blane. "Your modesty does you credit, young man, but please accept that the decision has been made, and that it's ours – not yours." Then, beaming hugely, he put his hand on Marius' shoulder and ushered him into the building. "Come, the Local Assessor has someone he'd like you to meet."

As soon as they'd passed through the general entrance IDS checks, Blane said, "They're waiting for you in the Heathfield Room." And then, without further eye contact, he disappeared into the main Council chamber. Marius, left to walk the short distance to the Heathfield Room alone, assumed – rightly, as it turned out – that his IDS had been authorised to permit his entry.

As he approached the door, it opened and he overheard the automatic announcement inside. Sir Clement Burcher came to meet him.

"Ah, Marius, do come in. I'd like to introduce you to Stin Goodman." He turned and gestured towards a young man standing in the centre of the room behind him. "Mister Goodman, this is Marius Graves, our new Thinker."

Marius walked over and shook hands. He had no idea at all to whom he was being introduced, but assumed that it must be something to do with his new status of Thinker, or perhaps the 'Distinction of Guardianship' that the Archworthy had referred to earlier.

Burcher clarified the matter straight away.

"As you're already aware, a new male is being added to each LGU in the BFF. Mister Goodman here has the privilege to be ours. From today, he'll be a permanent member of our community and, as Local Assessor, I've determined that you, Marius, are the man to ensure that his introduction is as smooth and efficient as it can be. I'll leave you to get to know each other."

He then turned and, without further comment, left the room.

Marius looked at the stranger. Slightly taller than himself, probably a little older – but not much. Longish dark hair, and – impossible not to notice – green eyes.

It was the newcomer who spoke first.

"I'm guessing that they didn't warn you," he ventured. "You seem a little surprised."

"Oh, I'm sorry," replied Marius hurriedly, "I didn't mean to be rude. But you're right – they didn't warn me."

He smiled nervously, and they looked at each other. After an uncomfortable pause, they laughed simultaneously and Marius said, "Well...I'm very pleased to meet you, Mister Goodman. Er...welcome to Drayling and to our new, larger, Local Geographical Unit."

"Thank you," replied the newcomer, "...and please call me Stin. Apart from Sir Clement, you're the first native I've spoken to. Er...congratulations on being made a Thinker, by the way. You must be very proud."

Marius – who was just now beginning to feel a little more at ease after his rather unusual morning – answered, "Yes…thanks…and don't worry, we're actually quite friendly. Sorry if I appeared a bit slow. Here…" He gestured towards the hospitality chairs. "Why don't we sit down and have a drink?"

They walked over to the chairs, selected drinks and made themselves comfortable.

It wasn't long before they were chatting freely. Stin told Marius that he'd come from a district in Mid-BFF called Feardleigh-in-the-Vale, and that, from what he'd seen so far, Drayling was not unlike it. Both his parents were dead, and, because he had no other close family ties, he'd taken the opportunity to apply for the area-transfer when it arose.

"At the age of eighteen, I thought a change might be good for me," he reasoned.

"Where are you going to live?" asked Marius.

"They've given me the living accommodation here in the Council building. Apparently, it won't be needed by the new Archworthy because he lives in Stowly Heath."

"You're honoured," commented Marius, "…but it makes sense. Look, I expect you'd like to get settled in. Why don't we meet again tomorrow? I'll give you a grand tour of the district."

They parted, having agreed to meet the following morning at ten o'clock, and Marius walked home reflecting on a full, and undoubtedly life-changing, day.

That evening, he and Uri would have much to discuss.

"As you know, the Archworthy has asked me to explain to you the significance of the Distinction of Guardianship," began Uri, once they were comfortably settled into their chairs. "What do you know of it already?"

Marius had to admit that he knew very little, but what he did know was that his father would relish telling him the full story, so he was very happy to just sit back and listen.

Uri began.

"One of the effects of Dunstan Heathfield's revolution, after inter-district travel had necessarily become a thing of the past, was that the people of the BFF were no longer able to travel to the big museums to view the great treasures owned by our nation. As a result, a new system was introduced whereby the many valuable articles were distributed all around the country – shared out amongst the various area entities. For each artefact, a local citizen – usually an eminent one – is made nominally responsible for its safety. In practice, of course, the item is kept in a safe place such as the Worthy Hall – usually on show – but the award of the Distinction of Guardianship is, nonetheless, a very prestigious one. In fact, in your particular case, it is perhaps even more so, because it just so happens that the previous guardian of the Cipherslider Mark One was none other than Archwitan Spencer Curtis himself. Conventional practice is that an artefact moves to a new district on the death of its guardian.

"You, Marius, have been given two national honours in one day, and I suspect that's unprecedented in the history of the BFF. Words really can't express how proud you've made me, son."

Marius quickly thanked his father for his words, but told him that he was becoming a little embarrassed by 'all the trumpeting' that the honours had created, and pleaded with him to 'return to normality'.

"Yes," accepted Uri, "I can understand that. It's all rather unusual, to say the least. Very well, enough said. How did you get on with our new male? Sir Clement told me he'd asked you to look after him."

Marius, relieved at the change of subject, replied, "Yes. He seems all right. I quite liked him actually. We're meeting again tomorrow morning. I'm going to show him around."

"That's good. Where does he come from?" asked Uri.

"Mid-BFF somewhere. A place called Feardleigh-in-the-Vale, I think he said. He doesn't have any family, so the move doesn't present any problems for him in that respect. I think he'll fit in well, once he gets used to us."

Uri nodded.

"There's one thing I thought a little strange, though," continued Marius, "he says he was told that, by agreeing to move permanently to another district, he was doing 'special service' for his country, and that, in return, he'd be given 'preferential treatment' by the Local Assessor. He was told that the 'rewards would be tangible'…whatever that means."

Uri looked a little surprised. "That's very interesting. I wasn't aware of that. I'll ask Clement what he has in mind."

He thought for a moment, and then said, "He's been given the living accommodation at the Worthy Hall, hasn't he? That's certainly very comfortable."

"Yes, but it does make sense," observed Marius. "It's empty, and it isn't going to be used by the Archworthy any more."

"That's true," agreed Uri. "Did he have anything else to say?"

"He said he's interested in history, and he seemed fascinated by our archaeological dig, so I'll certainly take him up there tomorrow."

"It sounds like you'll get on well," smiled Uri. "I think Clement knew exactly what he was doing when he decided to ask you to look after him."

Marius grinned. They chatted on about lighter matters for a little while longer, and then retired to their beds.

This time, Marius slept deeply and well.

7

The following day started dry, but dreary. Marius met Stin outside the Worthy Hall as arranged, and greeted him with a cheery, "Hello! Did you sleep well?"

"Yes, very well thanks," replied Stin, "...and I'm really looking forward to looking around my new home district! Where do we start?"

"Well, I've decided to stick to showing you Drayling to start with, because that's obviously the part of the new LGU that I'm familiar with." He looked up at the sky and pulled a face. "...And, frankly, I'm not sure that the weather's going to hold out for very long.

"There'll be a lot of functional similarities in Stowly Heath and Burshaw anyway, so there doesn't seem much point in duplicating things unnecessarily at this stage. Perhaps, in a few days' time, I could enlist the help of someone who knows those districts better than I do, and ask them to show us both around!"

"Sounds reasonable to me," grinned Stin.

"Right...well...let's get started, then," said Marius, beginning to walk. He gave an indicative sweep of his arm. "You already know the Worthy Hall...and those buildings attached to it are the Council offices.

"That large white building at the end is the Local Service Centre – the LSC – which is Sir Clement Burcher's domain. I can't tell you much about it though, because I've never actually been inside it.

"Frankly, it doesn't look like I ever will now, either, because I've been told that I'm not going to have to do my Local Service. The Archworthy said that it's 'deemed to have been served'.

"Quite why that is, I'm really not sure. To be honest, I don't follow the logic. I'm sure there must be things to be learned there that I'm never going to learn now."

As he said it, he made a mental note to seek his father's views on the subject.

"What about you, Stin, have you done your Local Service?"

"Yes I have," replied Stin. "About two years ago, although, to be honest, I don't remember much of the detail. I suppose I really ought to revisit the record on my IDS."

Marius acknowledged with a nod and, as they walked on, continued, "That annexe at the back of the LSC is the Clarification Facility – where people go if they're having problems with their gradings or work or whatever."

Soon they were strolling along at a comfortable pace and, as they got to know each other better, so their conversation began to flow more freely. Marius was finding it very easy to talk to the newcomer.

"This next building is the education facility and, unlike the LSC, I've been here many, many times! In fact, it's where my father spends much of his time, too."

"It must be quite a boon having the Local Historian for a father if you happen to be interested in history," observed Stin, "although, having said that, I suppose the fact that he's in that position may well have been a major factor in you developing your interest in the first place."

"Yes, that might well be true," agreed Marius, "but I have to say he really is an excellent source of information!"

Soon they reached the Public Gardens and recreational facility, and Marius took great pride in pointing out the cricket area that his father had prepared.

A number of other people were also out enjoying the fresh air, and the two young men were hailed with several

"Good mornings" as they walked along – prompting Stin to remark that it was extremely heartening to find everyone so friendly.

They strolled, chatting lightly about many things, past the storage, processing and distribution buildings for food and non-food, and on through one of the residential areas with its central grassed space and surrounding trees. After that, they headed out, between the medical facility and the machine maintenance buildings, towards the animal shelters, general pastures, waterfowl wetland and reservoir, before veering northwards.

Ten minutes later, they were in the Northern Agricultural Area.

"This is where our new Worthy Hall was going to be built," explained Marius, "but, of course, it's been cancelled now, because the Council's going to be based in Stowly Heath. As you can see, it's all food production land now, but our archaeological investigations proved that, at one time, at least part of it was used as a recreational facility."

"What made you come up with the idea of an archaeological excavation in the first place?" asked Stin.

"It seemed like a good way to try to get closer to some of our history," replied Marius. "To actually experience some of it first hand – to feel how it used to be – and, hopefully, at the same time learn something of value. I scoured my IDS for anything that might be helpful, and although I could only find fragments of anything relevant, it did seem likely that part of the Northern Agricultural Area might at some time have been used for recreational purposes. As there were plans to build the new Worthy Hall here, it seemed a sensible place to start, whilst the opportunity still existed."

"Well, you certainly did learn something of value," said Stin. "I have to confess that I read all the IDS records of your excavations last night. As I said yesterday, I too have an interest in history – which I suppose is why Sir Clement put us together – and I must say I really enjoyed reading them.

Your results were fascinating. Do you have plans to dig anywhere else?"

Marius was flattered that Stin had taken the trouble to read the records of the dig, and wished briefly that he could answer the question in the affirmative. However, he had to reply that he'd no particular plans at present, but agreed that it was something that he ought perhaps to think about.

As he was speaking, he noticed black clouds gathering in the sky, and added, "Come on, we're going to get wet if we stay here. Let's go back to my house and have a drink. We can sit and talk in comfort there."

Stin accepted readily, and they walked the short distance to Marius' home.

As the rain pattered on the window, Marius settled back into his chair and sipped his drink.

"What got you interested in the past in the first place?" he asked.

"One of the jobs I was given shortly after my Local Service involved regularly sitting around without much to do, so I used to spend the time exploring the national records on my IDS. There's so much knowledge available, if one is prepared to make the effort to find it. I delved into all sorts of subjects, and became particularly interested in the Roman Empire of about two thousand years ago – especially the conquest of Britain."

Marius nodded.

"Yes, it was certainly a fascinating period in our history. Did the Local Assessor reflect your interest in your personal grading and subsequent assignments?"

"Well, no – at least not specifically that one. As I said, I had a lot of time to myself, so I got quite deeply into other areas as well – particularly language and computers."

Marius was intrigued.

"Language? In what sense?"

"Well, I don't mean speaking in a foreign tongue or anything like that," replied Stin, "I mean our own language

57

particularly. I like to understand where words have come from, how they're made up, that sort of thing. I find them fascinating…and I enjoy playing around with them too – for fun."

"What do you mean – playing around with them?" queried Marius.

Stin chuckled. "Well, for example, did you know that the Roman Emperor Constantine – who, incidentally, had a British mother – had a name that can be mixed up to form the phrase 'Note Stin Can'?

"It's of absolutely no use to anybody else, but it amuses me."

Marius laughed. "And what about computers?"

"Well, of course, there has to be a serious side as well. Computers have played such a huge part in the development of our society in the last four hundred years, that I felt it's a subject I ought to take the opportunity to study properly." He paused, as if in reflection, and then added, "You see, I don't actually see the three subjects as entirely separate anyway. In sort of the same way as Dunstan Heathfield said that all the different pieces of a jigsaw affect each other, so History, Language and Computers all affect each other. All words and numbers have evolved from usage by our ancestors over time in one way or another, and computers use both to analyse and communicate. Actually, most of the assignments I've been given since my Local Service have been computer-related in one way or another."

Marius nodded his understanding.

"That's an interesting way of looking at it," he said, pausing thoughtfully. "So did you come across the Cipherslider Mark One in the course of your studies?"

"Oh, most certainly," replied Stin without hesitation. "The Cipherslider Mark One was a watershed. It was the first computer to incorporate cognitive capability to any degree. In addition to all the usual stuff, it was the first machine with the ability to comment on, evaluate or think around a subject and give a point of view. It could explore an issue and suggest courses of action, or areas warranting further investigation, which weren't necessarily immediately obvious. It could also highlight coincidences or similarities to other concepts of which it was aware.

"But it was the Mark Two, introduced a few years later, that actually became widely known as the 'First Thinking Machine' – after it was linked into the IDS network. That gave it access to an almost limitless record of BFF life – and infinite licence to observe and comment.

"The Ciphersliders are generally recognised to be the greatest single step forward in the history of computer technology."

"Gosh," said Marius, "I didn't realise it was as important as that."

"Oh, it's of huge significance in our heritage," said Stin. "You should be really proud to have such a close association with it."

As they continued to talk, it became more and more clear to Marius that Stin was a highly intelligent individual, and that he shared his own thirst for knowledge. He concluded that he was grateful to the Local Assessor for assigning him to mentor this new arrival to their LGU.

8

A week later, The Cipherslider Mark One arrived, and was put on show in the Drayling Worthy Hall between the replica of the British Friendly Federation Declaration of 2334 and the statue of Dunstan Heathfield. In the intervening days, the two young men had spent a lot of time together and, as a consequence, had developed a mutual respect and become friends. Amongst other things, they'd visited Stowly Heath and Burshaw, met and talked to a wide variety of local people and enjoyed an evening meal with Marius' family. Afterwards, Della had observed that he seemed a very pleasant young man, Uri had declared that he thought he would make "an excellent addition to our community" and Urania had chuckled and congratulated Marius on bringing a new and extremely tasty dish to their dinner table.

"…And did you see those eyes?" she said to Della a little while later when they were alone.

Her mother faked a weary look.

"Young lady, you're thirteen years old and much too young…but, yes, I did," she replied.

"And you're much too old, not-quite-so-young lady," admonished Urania, and they looked at each other and dissolved simultaneously into laughter.

Meanwhile, Uri and Marius were lounging in their hospitality chairs musing over the momentous occurrences of recent days.

"We're living in interesting and exciting times, Marius," observed Uri.

Marius nodded in agreement.

"That's certainly true, father...and, by the way, I have something to ask you. You remember that you were going to ask the Local Assessor about the preferential treatment that Stin was promised? Well, if you haven't spoken to him yet, do you think you could also ask him why he's decided that I don't have to do my Local Service? I can't help thinking that there are things I could learn, and that, by not doing it, I'll miss them. If that's the case, it seems, well, an unnecessary omission."

"Actually, I've already spoken to him," said Uri. "...Or at least I tried to. He wasn't very forthcoming, I'm afraid. He seemed...well...rather distant. I think he must have a lot on his mind at present. Anyway, what he did say was that he's going to invite you, by IDS tomorrow morning, to meet him at the Stowly Heath Worthy Hall. He wants to talk to you, although I don't know what about.

"But I'm sure you'll get the opportunity to ask if there's anything you'd like to clarify."

Sure enough, shortly before ten o'clock the following morning, Marius was invited to meet the Local Assessor at Stowly Heath at eleven o'clock. Whilst the message was couched in very polite language, it was given 'Required' status, which meant that attendance was mandatory. This compounded Marius' curiosity. What could be so important as to warrant such an approach? He had no idea, but he knew he wouldn't have to wait long to find out.

He arrived at the Stowly Heath Worthy Hall about an hour later, to be greeted by Stin at the foot of the entrance steps.

"Hello. I saw you coming," said Stin. "I guess you've been summoned here too."

They walked into the building together and were ushered straight into the Local Assessor's private office. Four others were seated there already. Three were strangers – two male, one female – and the fourth was Hayden Burcher.

Before anyone could say anything, a door at the other end of the room opened and Sir Clement Burcher strode in. He began speaking as soon as he appeared, and continued as he walked to, and then sat at, his desk.

"Lady and gentlemen, thank you for coming, and for your promptness. I know you're all wondering why you're here, so I'll come straight to the point. You've all been chosen to become Local Worthies."

There was a moment's silence, and then audible gasps around the room, as the six stared at him in surprise. Marius happened to notice Hayden's reaction, and it was apparent that, despite being Sir Clement's son, he'd not been given prior warning of this bombshell either.

The Local Assessor continued, "This assignment is an objective recognition of your capabilities, and is the contribution that your LGU requires of you. Your training will take place over the next eighteen months or so, after which you'll be allocated duties in accordance with the designation you'll by then have been given. This will continue for an indeterminate period until an appropriate position on the Worthy Council becomes vacant. Your training will commence at nine o'clock tomorrow morning at the Drayling Council Chamber. I suggest you all now go next door, and get to know each other. You're important people now, and have reason to be proud that you're being asked to serve your LGU in this way."

He rose and marched from the room.

The six young people, unsurprisingly in varying degrees of shock, rose in silence and made their way through to the reception area in the main foyer. No one said anything as each went to a hospitality chair, selected a drink and wrestled with private thoughts.

As they looked around at each other in bewilderment, Stin spoke first. "Well, Marius, I think this probably explains why you don't have to do your Local Service, and why I was told I'd be getting special treatment."

One of the others added in a low monotone, "I was told that my Local Service was to be delayed for a time whilst they reviewed the content."

It was some time before the mood changed, but eventually there was a flurry of conversation as each recounted the story they'd been given. Hayden confirmed that the news had, indeed, come as a shock to him, and that he certainly intended to tackle his father on the subject as soon as he got home.

Despite having had no inkling of their forthcoming status, they were all delighted to have been selected and, after about an hour – by which time they'd introduced themselves – the group had unified. The three previously unknown to Marius were Glebba Day, the only female amongst them, aged 17, from Stowly Heath; Zeke Darwin, 16, also from Stowly Heath; and Gordy Wester, 16, from Burshaw. All said that they'd been at the recent 'Cricket Day', and that they'd recognised Marius when he walked into the Local Assessor's office earlier. Zeke also added that he'd played for Stowly Heath in their game against Burshaw.

Marius returned home at around one o'clock, and was greeted by his mother.

"Ah, there you are, Marius, I'm so glad you're home! Your father says that you have something to tell me, and I'm dying to know what it is."

Marius grinned, and related the morning's events. Della stared at him, wide-eyed, and then hugged him. "Whatever else are you going to come up with?" she yelped. "Well done, well done, my darling!... Er... you are pleased, aren't you?"

Marius said that, yes, he was delighted, and that he'd felt very humbled by the news.

"I suppose, as you've recently been made a Thinker, this shouldn't really come as a surprise to me, but, nonetheless, I'm so very, very proud of you."

She gave him a hug and a kiss, and then, suddenly serious, added, "Your father's in the kitchen."

Marius raised his eyebrows. His father wasn't normally home at this hour.

He walked through to the kitchen, and found Uri sitting at the table, staring into a drink, apparently deep in thought.

"Hello, father," he began cheerily, "I wasn't expecting you to be here."

Uri looked up, and gave a half-smile. "I came home to congratulate you, son," he said. "I wanted to tell you that I believe your new status is good for you, and for the community."

He then looked back at his drink, and Marius realised that something was definitely wrong. "Thank you, father," he replied. "Er…are you all right? You seem a little…preoccupied."

Uri didn't look up, but began to speak – slowly and evenly.

"Every day at midday, as a matter of routine, I receive a list of the latest personal grading amendments for all of the residents of our LGU. Today was no exception, but it was the first I knew of your new status.

"I suppose I was hurt that Clement hadn't told me, so I asked him why. Apparently, Sir Grindon Blane has said that, in future, he requires all Worthy Council business to be confidential to those directly involved, and that detail should only be given to others on a 'need to know basis'. I said that, surely, other Worthies do need to know. His reply was, 'Yes they do, and that's why I transcreen the full list of all grading changes to you daily.' "

He sighed and continued.

"It simply isn't Clement's style. Our conversation wasn't the usual discussion between old friends and colleagues. It was cold. Almost like he was granting me an audience. He was just feeding me the official line. I can only assume that our new Archworthy has got to him, and is now starting to make his presence felt. Maybe this is how things are going to be in future.

"Of course, from what Clement says, I'm already falling foul of the new instructions by telling you this. However, as Blane hasn't yet spoken to me on the subject, I don't consider myself bound by it – not that I would dream of leaking anything sensitive to anyone anyway.

"Actually, there is another change that the new Archworthy has brought about. You may have noticed that five of the six to be trained as Worthies are sixteen or seventeen years old, whereas one, Hayden Burcher, is thirty. It wouldn't be unreasonable to wonder why he hadn't been selected for Worthy training when he was much younger. The answer is that Sir Bedford Coote, our previous Archworthy, would not allow, as a matter of principle, any member of an existing Worthy's family to be selected for high office. Sir Grindon clearly doesn't hold the same view, and Sir Clement has obviously convinced him that, although Hayden is his son, he deserves a place on the team, which, incidently, I wouldn't dispute. It's also true, of course, that if there hadn't been a change of Archworthy you wouldn't have been included either."

He paused before finally looking up. "So that bit's good, anyway. Sorry to bore you with my other problems. I expect I'm just having a bad day. I'm sure everything'll be fine. Congratulations on your new grading, my boy."

Marius said, "Thank you, father," but decided, at least for the moment, not to pursue Uri's worries any further. He already harboured his own concerns privately about recent political events, and suggestions of a harsher approach from the authorities did nothing to allay them.

Marius rose early the following morning. He was excited, and wanted to ensure that he was ready – both physically and mentally – for the start of his Worthy training. He was looking forward to it immensely.

His mother greeted him cheerfully when he walked into the kitchen, "Hello – you're up good and early! There must be something in the air today. When I awoke this morning, your father had already gone out. He left a message on my IDS saying he was in Stowly Heath, at the Council Chamber."

At about eight o'clock – one hour before the training was due to start – Marius was alerted by his IDS to an urgent message from the Local Assessor's Office. It read simply, "DUE TO AN EMERGENCY COUNCIL MEETING, WORTHY TRAINING IS POSTPONED UNTIL FURTHER NOTICE."

His initial surprise was quickly followed by deflation, and then by puzzlement.

"What's going on now?" he said out loud.

His mother heard him and, when shown the message, said, "I wonder what that's all about. It must be important though, to drag your father from his bed in the early hours."

Marius straightaway called up Stin by IDS, who confirmed that he'd received the same message. Soon, each of the trainees had made contact, exchanged theories and speculations, and expressed disappointment and frustration. Zeke and Glebba had walked to the Worthy Hall in Stowly Heath, and were able to confirm that the Council was indeed in closed session, and that it had been sitting since before seven, and was still going on.

At about 5.30 that morning, Uri and the other Worthies had been called from their beds by personal IDS attention-pulse. By 6.45am, they were all sitting in silence in the Council Chamber in Stowly Heath waiting for the Archworthy. Having been summoned with such urgency, and at such an early hour, Uri, for one, wasn't in the best of spirits. In truth, he wasn't yet fully awake, either.

They didn't have long to wait. A grim-faced Grindon Blane entered the chamber from the ante-room and began to speak without preamble.

"I've received a communication from Regional Administration, and I'll read it to you in its entirety." He took a deep breath and read from his IDS:

INSTRUCTION TO WORTHY COUNCIL. IDS monitoring, carried out for Central Government by Regional Administrations, indicates insufficient interaction between newly-merged communities. Even at this early stage, it is evident that the appropriate degree of encouragement and persuasion is not being applied at Worthy Council level.

For this reason, and to ensure consistency across the BFF, the names of the three area entities that make up each LGU will cease to exist with immediate effect. They will be replaced by a single designation, to be agreed today and announced by the Worthy Council. From tomorrow at noon, it will be an offence to refer to any former area entity by its previous name. Reference to those parts will in future be by geographical location within the LGU – for example "North District." Local Culturists will be provided with details of action to be taken in the event of any breach of the new regulations, which have been made in order to retain all essential features of Dunstan Heathfield's Revolution.

In addition to deciding the new designation of its LGU, the Worthy Council will make the necessary arrangements for all key functions to be centralised within the LGU by the end of March 2467. Key functions to be centralised must include the following: Education Facility; Medical Facility; Food Storage, Processing & Distribution; Non-Food Storage, Processing & Distribution; Machine Maintenance and all Council establishments – including the Local Service Centre and Clarification Facility.

In addition to the above, the Worthy Council will identify further ways in which the integration of the LGU will be encouraged at local level."

Blane looked up. "That's the end of the communication. I'm now having it transcreened to you in full."

He waited for a reaction, but for a long time no one said anything.

Each Worthy re-read the instruction with incredulity.

Eventually, Uri broke the silence. In a slightly uneven voice, he said, "I'd like to request an off-the-record discussion."

The Archworthy agreed immediately, and signalled for the roomscriber to be de-activated.

As soon as he was satisfied that he could speak freely, Uri continued in as measured a tone as he could manage.

"I've requested an off-the-record discussion because, having only had the briefest of time to digest this instruction, there's probably a danger that either I've misunderstood something, or that I'll say something that I'll later come to regret.

"However, my understanding is that we're being told that the names of our three area entities – Drayling, Stowly Heath and Burshaw – are now not only defunct, but outlawed, and that, irrespective of any view that we may hold to the contrary based upon our local knowledge, all key functions are to be centralised.

"The communication tells us that this is to aid integration, and that the measures are being taken...," he referred to his IDS to ensure that he quoted accurately, "...in order to retain all essential features of Dunstan Heathfield's Revolution."

He looked around at the other Worthies.

"I don't know if I'm alone on this Council in my reaction to these instructions, but I feel I must make a number of points to you.

"Firstly, we're told that these instructions have been prompted following IDS monitoring for Central Government. One of two things is therefore true. Either the statement is a lie...," again he looked around at the other members of the Council, "...or the degree of surveillance of the daily lives of individuals is far greater than I, for one, have ever been led to believe.

"Now, I'm the Local Historian. I venture to suggest that, if I wasn't aware, then the vast majority of the residents of our LGU – and, I suggest, this Council – weren't aware either.

"Dunstan Heathfield's Revolution was based on trust. Without trust, none of the monumental, but necessary, changes would ever have been made.

"Am I alone in wondering whether that trust is now under threat?"

He raised his hand to stop any of the others seeking to answer the question before he'd finished what he wanted to say.

"People generally don't like change. I believe it's simply unreasonable to expect people – particularly older people – to cease to use the traditional name of their home district overnight on someone else's whim, whatever that someone's status. It'll be second-nature to them to use the names without even thinking.

"I note also that the Local Culturist hasn't yet been informed what action to take in the event of a breach of this new regulation." He turned briefly to face the councillor concerned. "I urge him to consider the position very carefully.

"The communication says that we, the Worthy Council, have not applied "the appropriate degree of encouragement and persuasion..." What does that mean? It's clearly far too early to take a reasonable view that integration isn't working, and this unhelpful intervention by central government – quite possibly instigated by this new Archwitan "Tujo" – effectively overrides any sensible and considered actions that we may have taken in the interests of our LGU, whether specifically to facilitate integration or for any other reason.

"The same applies to the instruction to centralise key functions. This may or may not be an appropriate move, but we, the Worthy Council, are clearly in the best position to see what would work most effectively locally. The system works very well at present. Why make ill-considered changes to something that's working perfectly well? Obviously, we would, as a matter of course, consider the new options available to us as a result of our new LGU amalgamation and, if we identified that a function could be made more efficient, we'd make the necessary changes, including managing the most appropriate rate of change."

He paused and took a deep breath.

"This approach – in fact the whole instruction from Regional Administration – is destructive, positively anti smooth integration and, frankly, downright stupid."

At this, the Archworthy intervened. "That's enough, Sir Uri. I now give notice that the Council will return to formal session."

Immediately two other councillors leapt to their feet to object that they hadn't had the opportunity to contribute to the off-the-record discussion, but Sir Grindon stood firm.

"The roomscriber will now be re-activated."

The remainder of the meeting was kept on a tight rein by the Archworthy, and he ensured that it applied itself to the business of carrying out the new instructions. It was decided that the new name of their LGU should incorporate an element of all three previous names, and after much discussion they settled upon 'Drayshaw Heath'. The individual entities of Drayling, Stowly Heath and Burshaw would henceforth be referred to as West District, North District and East District respectively.

The Archworthy instructed the Local Culturist to announce the new LGU and district names by IDS as soon as he'd received the promised details of the action to be taken in the event of any breach of the new regulations. He then said that he felt a period of reflection would benefit them all, and that the meeting would reconvene, still in closed session, "at 10.30 tomorrow morning."

Uri was still angry when he got home. He didn't often lose his temper, but on the rare occasions that he did, it was spectacular. He hadn't quite worked himself up to that point yet, but Della knew the signs, and warned Marius and Urania that "something serious must have happened at the Council meeting," and that they needed to tread warily.

The more Uri thought of the events of the morning, the more upset, and bewildered, he became. He reached for his IDS and called the Local Assessor.

"Clement, we need to talk. Are you doing anything important?"

Burcher agreed immediately that a discussion would be useful and, twenty minutes later, they were sitting together in Uri's house.

"Clement, I don't know where to start," moaned Uri, clearly troubled. He began to talk to his friend and, as he talked, his words came faster and faster until they were a torrent. "So many things have happened…so many things are up in the air…I don't feel I know where I am…to say I'm uncomfortable doesn't begin to describe how I feel...things are happening that are not right…but I'm really not sure that I know exactly what's happening…it's as if…"

"Uri, please stop," intervened Burcher. "Calm down. We're all very stressed at the moment…"

"Stop?" spluttered Uri. "Stop? Is that all you can say?"

"Uri," retorted Burcher in a slightly raised, yet ultimately calming voice, "you're not alone. What you said in the Chamber was absolutely right. And yes, you're correct that many things have happened, and wrong things are still happening. But we can't discuss anything rationally unless you calm down. We need to talk about many things – yes, many things."

He touched his friend and colleague on the arm and looked into his eyes. "Uri, there's far more to this – and we must talk about it all. …But we've got all afternoon. So, first, I think we both need to relax and have a drink."

Uri knew he was right, and they forced themselves to talk, albeit rather mechanically, about trivial matters.

But they couldn't keep it up for long.

It was Clement who broached the subject first.

"Uri, I have something to tell you that will surprise you, and which may perhaps begin to paint a picture of what's going on.

"A few days ago, Sir Grindon Blane called me to his office and told me something in absolute confidence. He said he was speaking to me with the Witan's authority, and that…"

Uri interrupted him. "So you shouldn't be telling me of the conversation. If anyone found out, the consequences would be extremely severe for you."

Burcher smiled grimly.

"You're absolutely right, of course. However, I'm telling you because I think it's the right thing to do. You must judge for yourself when I've finished.

"Blane told me that he'd been specifically instructed by Regional Administration – and you and I both know that that means the Witan – to "sort out" this district. He said he'd been told that Drayling and Burshaw had been "inefficiently run" for some time, and that he was being given a mandate to take whatever action he sees fit to "bring them up to standard." He said that the "inbreeding story" was a cover for the merging of poorly run districts with more robust ones to "facilitate the necessary improvements." He told me that he needed to work closely with the Local Culturist and Local Assessor – in complete secrecy.

"When I asked why those two, he replied that he couldn't do it alone, and that the minimum he needed was the Assessor's involvement for necessary action in the areas of Grading and Clarification, and the Culturist's in the areas of Public Order and Published Information. He emphasised that the existence and activities of this 'inner group' needed to be kept absolutely confidential.

"You can appreciate, therefore, the gravity of the personal decision that I've taken to be telling you this, but I've come to the view that the implications of what he said could be so great that I, as a mere pawn, am simply not important in the overall picture.

"He went on to tell me that I shouldn't trust any information given to me by any of the other Worthies – with the exception of the Culturist – as it may be based on false information which has been provided to them.

"I couldn't believe what I was hearing. I said I couldn't understand why anyone should suggest that Drayling had been "inefficiently run," and that I was certainly not prepared to become involved in some kind of conspiracy against my fellow Worthies.

"He responded by saying that he "fully understood my initial reaction," but that I should "go home and consider my position." He said he felt sure that, as the instructions were specific, and coming direct from Regional Administration, I would, on reflection, realise – as he had – where my duty lay.

"Since he spoke to me, I've been agonising over that very question. Where does my duty lay?…To my family?…Do I need to "succeed" as a Worthy for the sake of my family?…What is "success" anyway? Is my duty to my friends?…To the Archworthy?…To my country? Under what circumstances can it be right to contemplate betrayal of old friends and colleagues, and maybe also my principles? At what point should I call a halt and say that what I'm being ordered to do is wrong? What if I don't believe that what I'm being instructed to do is in the best interests of the people of our new Drayshaw Heath?

"The only conclusion I've come to so far is that both this and the instructions the Council received this morning appear to herald a new approach from our "Government of National Unity" – and that presumably means Tujo, our new Archwitan."

Uri stared wide-eyed at Burcher.

"I – I've noticed you've been a bit distant of late," he stammered, "but, Clement…I had no idea…"

He stopped speaking as the full extent of the issues confronting them began to dawn on him. He realised also that, by telling him these things, his friend had already betrayed the new Archworthy. "What on earth are we going to do?"

Burcher spoke in a calm voice. "Well, as I said, I've been wrestling with my conscience for a while now. You'll need time to think about it too. I think we both need to be absolutely sure what our priorities are, and then we can decide what to do. I believe that hasty action of any kind would be a mistake. In the meanwhile, I think we should just carry on as usual, and be seen to be doing so."

Uri nodded in solemn agreement, and Burcher went home.

For the remainder of the day, and despite the fact that his mind was racing, Uri made a huge effort to appear as normal as possible to his family, to avoid any probing questions that he wasn't yet ready to answer.

That evening, when he was sitting alone with his thoughts, however, his logic was cool and clinical. He'd known, and worked closely with, Clement Burcher for many years. He knew he could trust him and that he wouldn't lie to him. He knew therefore that the conversation with the Archworthy had taken place precisely as Clement had described it.

That meant that he also knew – without any question – that he was being undermined deliberately by the new Archworthy, that the Worthy Council was being cynically manipulated for some reason, and that, almost certainly, it was with the authority of Regional Administration – which effectively meant the Witan itself. The recent instructions were dictatorial, certain to cause unrest, and showed clearly that the Worthy Council was neither trusted nor respected.

Although his fierce patriotism and strong sense of duty urged otherwise, his intellect and innate objectivity forced him to the conclusion that radical changes were taking place. Convinced that they were not for the better, and that it was distinctly possible that something far more sinister was afoot, he felt physically sick.

Despite all his natural loyalties, nurtured over many years, he realised with alarm that he had no alternative but to take action – and that the action he was going to have to take would almost certainly amount to nothing less than treason.

The mere idea appalled him.

9

The Council meeting resumed at 10.30 the following morning as planned.

Blane began by saying that he hadn't yet seen the Local Culturist's announcement of the new district names, or, more importantly, the notification of the new offence of using the old names. The Culturist replied that he hadn't yet made the announcement because he hadn't yet received the promised details of the action to be taken in the event of breach of the regulation.

This precipitated a heated exchange in which the Archworthy pointed out that the new offence came into force at noon, and that "presumably the Local Culturist would agree that it would be a good idea for people to know about it prior to that?" and the Culturist responded by shouting back that the Archworthy's clear instruction had been to make the announcement when he'd received details of the action to be taken in the event of breach of the regulation – and that he hadn't yet received them.

At this, an apoplectic Archworthy leapt to his feet and spluttered something to the effect that he expected a degree of common sense from Worthies, and that the Culturist should get on to Regional Administration "Now!…Right now!…This minute!…" – and get it sorted out.

In fact, the people of Drayshaw Heath received IDS notification of their new LGU and district names, together with a bland statement of the new regulation banning use of the old ones, at around 11.25am. No mention was made of what action would be taken in the event of a breach of the regulation.

Uri made a mental note of this further example of an approach that was patently unbeneficial to the residents of Drayling, Stowly Heath and Burshaw.

He endured the remainder of the meeting with as much grace and apparent cooperation as he could muster. In fact, despite the anger still fermenting inside him, he was able to make two suggestions that he genuinely felt would be helpful to the integration process. The first was that there be a series of cricket matches between the Districts "given the success of our recent games," and the second that a public transport system of some kind be introduced to assist the movement of people "between our three districts." He took the opportunity to observe that it was "one of life's little enigmas" that, whilst incredible advances in technology of all kinds had been made prior to Dunstan Heathfield's Revolution, and undoubtedly since, it was still an accepted and normal part of their culture for all able-bodied people to move around on foot.

He continued, "That is so because area entities are…were…, by definition, small. Now that we're an LGU, I believe we should consider the introduction of a suitable method of transport – due to the greater distances that people will be able to travel. Of course, we all know that many years ago the cessation of the use of fossil-fuels was one key factor in this evolutionary process, but it's a fact, nonetheless, that modern technological aids such as machines and computers are available to us, despite the fact that they're generally used now only as labour-saving devices in areas such as production and medicine rather than for transport. I propose that we look into the possibility of utilising any suitable technology – or, failing that, consider using animal-drawn vehicles as were used to great effect by our ancestors."

As the meeting progressed, he mused to himself that, in an ideal world, there would always be a prescribed procedure to follow to deal with any problem, no matter how huge.

With great foreboding, however, he realised that, in the situation in which they now found themselves, no such mechanism was available.

The proceedings were eventually brought to a close by the Archworthy in mid-afternoon.

In an irritated voice, he observed, "This Council is not making the progress I was expecting. The meeting is therefore adjourned to give members more time for reflection. In the meantime, I shall give further consideration to the matters before us, and contact you as appropriate."

When they were alone later that evening, Uri spoke grimly to his friend and colleague of many years.

"Clement, we must act. I don't think we have any alternative. We have to take some kind of positive action and fight for what's right."

Burcher agreed immediately, so Uri continued, "…But let's be absolutely clear. What we're saying is that we believe that recent events are not just some trivial irritation, but nothing short of a fundamental attack on our way of life – the way of life that has served us so well since the days of Dunstan Heathfield – and which we now feel we have no alternative but to defend."

"Yes, that's it," responded Clement, "…that's exactly it."

"Right, then the question is what to do now," said Uri. "The first thing to say is that it's obviously important that Grindon Blane remains unaware that you've told me of his plans – and, for that reason alone, I don't believe we can afford to take the other members of the Council into our confidence.

"At the same time, however – and assuming we're going to take the kind of action that I believe is necessary – we're not going to be able to act alone. We don't know to what extent things might escalate, or indeed in which direction they may go, but I do believe we're going to need people around us that we can trust."

He looked straight at Burcher.

"And I think those people are Hayden and Marius...do you agree?"

"Yes, I do," replied his friend without hesitation. "...I'd come to the same conclusion."

He paused for a moment and returned Uri's gaze.

"...But be under no illusion. The kind of action we're contemplating will almost certainly be against the law, and therefore highly dangerous. We'll be putting ourselves – and them – at great risk."

"But, as you say, we have no choice," replied Uri quietly.

They each called up their son by IDS, and about half an hour later Marius and Hayden were sitting with them in stunned silence.

"It goes without saying that this conversation must remain absolutely secret," said Uri. "For the moment, at least, I don't even propose to say anything to Della or Urania. I hope you agree with that approach, Clement."

Burcher nodded in concurrence.

The ensuing discussion enabled each of the four, in his own time, to conclude that, despite the extreme risks involved, radical action was indeed necessary, and that they were the people in the best position to take it.

Marius, like his father, was naturally logical.

"One thought occurs to me," he said. "Whilst it seems probable that the Archworthy is acting under the instructions of the Witan, the fact is that we only have his word for it. We know he's prepared to lie – he told Sir Clement that he proposed to feed false information to members of the Worthy Council – but it is possible that he's either acting alone or with one or more others – say, for example, with a dissident individual in South Country Regional Administration.

"It would be helpful if we could ascertain whether similar things are happening elsewhere in the country...whether other Archworthies have received similar instructions...whether other Worthy Councils have received similar name-change and centralisation orders…and, indeed, whether the merger of area entities has also occurred elsewhere."

His words served to underline the enormity of what they were discussing. What he'd said made perfect sense, but they could see no easy way of finding the answers.

"Since the abolition of inter-district communications, brought about by Dunstan Heathfield's Revolution, the means to make such contact has inevitably disappeared," observed Uri. "What you're proposing not only breaks the law, but the very spirit of Dunstan's Revolution. We need to be very sure that we're doing the right thing before we embark on something like this."

"Uri," said Clement, putting a consoling hand on his shoulder, "…ever since Dunstan's Revolution, the whole country has had to trust that the rest of the BFF has been operating in the same way and, indeed, been enjoying the same peaceful and well-ordered way of life that we've enjoyed in Drayling. The key word is trust. You've extolled the virtues of DHR to countless people over the years, and what you've said is that Dunstan Heathfield convinced people that the many changes to the pieces of jigsaw were vital for the good of the overall picture. But the fact is that the whole thing depended on trust. The people trusted Dunstan Heathfield, and allowed him to make what were exceptionally far-reaching changes – all based on trust.

"That trust is now under threat. In fact, more than that, I'd say we have grounds to believe that our trust has been misplaced – that it's already been broken – and that means that the spirit of Dunstan's Revolution has been broken also.

"That's why we have to act, and why, as Marius suggests, our first move must be to ascertain the scale of what's happening."

Uri shrugged, but nodded resignedly. He knew his colleague was right, but the mere thought made him feel physically sick, and very afraid for them all.

"Could identiscreens help us?" queried Hayden. "We contact each other with them, and everyone uses them to access the national database for information, so logically there ought to be some way that we could use them to make contact with other parts of the country."

"Yes, I was wondering that too," said Marius, "but because of the ban on inter-district communications, there must, presumably, be some means by which their use is confined to the local area. The obvious assumption is that computer technology is involved in some way."

"I'm sure that's right," agreed Sir Clement. "However, although inter-district communication is generally restricted, identiscreens are used regularly by the Worthy Council for administrative communication with Regional Administration, and, if we're to believe what we're told, they may also have been used by the authorities to monitor the movements of our citizens too. Does anyone know anything about this type of technology?"

They all shook their heads.

After a pause, Marius said, "There is, of course, someone who does know about computers, and may well be prepared to help us – Stin Goodman."

"How does he know about computers?" asked Sir Clement.

Marius recounted what Stin had told him of his studies, and they agreed that his knowledge might well be useful to them. Uri, however, did not react positively.

"Look, we can't just go around recruiting people willy-nilly. What we're talking about here is treason…insurrection. There's a very good chance that, if we're discovered, we'll be put to death or taken away for life, or something like that. It really is that serious. How do we know that we can trust Stin Goodman? If we increase our number, we multiply the risk of detection hugely. Is that really what we want?"

At that point, Sir Clement intervened and said, "No. We don't want to increase the dangers unnecessarily, and neither do we wish to take any actions until we've considered them properly. Let's call a halt to the discussions today, and talk again tomorrow."

"Just one more thing before we finish," said Hayden, "...and I hope I'm not scare-mongering without good reason, but if the people of Drayling really are being monitored by IDS as you were told, then would it not be a good idea to meet somewhere else tomorrow, and perhaps only for a short time?"

The implications of his words chilled them all, but Sir Clement once again came to the rescue.

"Yes. Good idea, Hayden. Uri, why don't you and Marius come to our house tomorrow for a men's evening? Say seven o'clock?"

With that agreed, they said their goodbyes, and Uri and Marius were left to act as normally as they could for the benefit of Della and Urania, before going to bed to try to sleep.

Whilst walking home, Clement expressed concern to Hayden.

"I'm a little worried about Uri," he said. "I wonder if this may all be too much for him. I'm really not sure he's going to be able to cope."

"It's not an easy situation for anyone," replied Hayden, "...particularly if you're as passionate about your heritage as Sir Uri is. It's not surprising he's uncomfortable."

"No, it isn't, but, in addition, he also has a particularly strong sense of loyalty and duty," said Sir Clement, "...and he's now being forced to question their validity. I think he's going to find it very hard."

"Well, I was going to make a suggestion which, by coincidence, may make things a bit easier for Sir Uri at the same time," said Hayden.

"Whilst feelings in the Worthy Council are running high, and we're also concerned about possible surveillance, it might be better if you and Sir Uri stay away from our new activities for the moment. Both of you, as Worthies, are likely to be watched closely by Sir Grindon, so I suggest it would be beneficial that you be seen to be carrying on as normal.

"We've already agreed that our first priority is to ascertain the scale of the problem. Marius and I can address that, whilst keeping you and Sir Uri informed of course. I do agree with Marius that we should approach Stin Goodman, though. Whilst I believe Sir Uri is right to be cautious, I think a knowledge of computers is our overriding need, and Stin appears to have that.

"Although Marius has only known him for a short time, he's got on extremely well with him, to the extent that, intuitively, he feels confident he's trustworthy...and it doesn't seem very likely to me that he's a security risk either, as he doesn't have any emotional ties to Drayling...er, Drayshaw Heath.

"Also, he has knowledge of another area entity elsewhere in the country. I think that could be helpful to us, too.

"With Marius, Stin and me doing the work, and you and Sir Uri staying at arm's length, things should be a little more comfortable for both of you, at least for the time being."

Sir Clement nodded slightly as he thought.

"Hmm...it's certainly true that Sir Uri and I will have plenty of Council work to do as a result of recent developments...and I could suggest that you and Marius be given the joint task of arranging forthcoming cricket games – that would provide additional protection from the surveillance point of view. Yes, I think it makes a lot of sense. I'll speak to Sir Uri tomorrow and seek his agreement."

At approximately eleven o'clock the following morning, all members of the Worthy Council received the following IDS communication from Sir Grindon Blane:

DRAYSHAW HEATH WORTHY COUNCIL

Action to be taken following recent Central Government Directives

Further to the Worthy Council meeting which ended yesterday, and following further assistance from South Country Regional Administration, I clarify below the action to be taken by each member of the Council as a result of the Central Government directives recently received.

For the sake of good order, I set these alongside a summary of the individual responsibilities of each Worthy Councillor.

LOCAL HISTORIAN

Responsibilities
To: Run education facility / Teach history at education facility / Look after local historical records accessible on IDS / Keep local mapping up-to-date / Co-ordinate local events which have historical significance / Provide one-to-one tuition as required by Local Assessor or Local Culturist.

Action Required
1.   Incorporate the designations Drayshaw Heath, West District, North District and East District into all history lessons to be given to children and other citizens.
2.   Expunge all references to Drayling, Burshaw and Stowly Heath from all maps and records available on IDS.
3.   Draft proposals for the centralisation of the education facility.
4.   Assume responsibility for a series of cricket games between districts.

LOCAL CULTURIST

Responsibilities
To: Teach literacy at education facility / Provide one-to-one tuition as required by Local Assessor / Provide citizens

with daily information by IDS / Look after public gardens and recreational areas / Take responsibility for public order, entertainment and leisure (other than events with historical significance and cricket).

Action Required
1.   Announce action to be taken in the event of breach of new regulation.
2.   Establish monitoring system for new regulation.
3.   Liaise with Local Assessor on draft proposal for the centralisation of clarification facilities.

LOCAL ASSESSOR

Responsibilities
To: Teach citizenship at the education facility / Provide one-to-one tuition as appropriate / Run grading system / Run Local Service Centre and clarification facility.

Action Required
1.   Increase contribution of individuals through grading system.
2.   Draft proposals for centralisation of Council buildings, Local Service Centre and clarification facilities.
3.   Increase size of clarification facility in liaison with Local Culturist.
4.   Review Local Worthy training programme.

LOCAL PROVIDER

Responsibilities
To: Take responsibility for the provision, storage, processing and distribution of all food and non-food products including water / Look after all livestock / Run agricultural operations.

1.   Liaise with Local Assessor to achieve significant increase in output.

2.   Draft proposals for the centralisation of food and non-food storage, processing and distribution.

LOCAL GENWORTHY

Responsibilities

To: Run medical facility / Run machine maintenance facility / Take reponsibility for all building erection and maintenance.

Action Required

1.   Remove/replace as appropriate all signs in LGU making reference to Drayling, Burshaw or Stowly Heath.

2.   Draft proposals for introduction and ongoing provision of public transport facility.

3.   Draft proposals for the centralisation of medical facility and machine maintenance facilities.

ALL WORTHY COUNCILLORS

Responsibilities

To: Carry out instructions received from Regional Administration and Archworthy / Accept collective responsibility for all Worthy Council decisions and actions.

Action Required

1.   Confirm progress on all above matters by IDS report daily.

Within minutes of receiving the IDS communication, Sir Clement Burcher was summoned to the Archworthy's office.

When he arrived, Blane was already in conversation with the Local Culturist.

86

"Ah, Burcher," he said, "the Local Culturist is just announcing what action will be taken in the event of a breach of the new regulation."

Sir Clement looked at his IDS.

The communication read:

To all citizens of Drayshaw Heath.

As notified by IDS previously, the Area Entity names Burshaw, Drayling and Stowly Heath ceased to exist at noon on 14th September 2466.

*These names have been replaced by **East District, West District** and **North District** respectively.*

It is now an offence to refer to a former area entity by its previous name.

Anyone breaching this regulation will be named in IDS daily information.

Any further breach will require attendance at the clarification facility, where appropriate action will be taken.

Burcher could not disguise his disgust.

"What appropriate action?" he queried. "It just sounds like a threat.

"Do you honestly think this is a reasonable approach? Do you really believe that treating people like this will encourage smooth integration?"

"What I think doesn't matter," retorted Blane. "I have clear instructions, and I'm carrying them out."

He looked Sir Clement straight in the eye. "And I expect you to do the same."

The Local Assessor opened his mouth to reply, but didn't. He decided, at least for the moment, that there was nothing to be gained by further antagonising the Archworthy.

Blane continued, "I've asked the Local Culturist to set up a monitoring network to hear and report any breaches of the new regulation. It's important, as I'm sure you'll agree, that we're seen to be taking the matter seriously. He'll need your assistance to put together a team of listeners – through the usual grading system, of course. You'll need to incorporate estimated results into your draft proposals for the centralisation of the clarification facilities."

He paused, and then said, "One last thing, gentlemen. I'm sure I don't need to keep repeating that the activities of this little group must remain strictly between ourselves. We've been given the task of making historic advances for our country in this community. It's a responsibility which cannot be shirked."

With that, he looked at both of them in turn and said, "Thank you. That is all."

10

The events of recent days had induced a strange feeling of hopelessness into Sir Clement Burcher. Things had occurred that were so out of step with how he thought life should be, that he, like Uri, had simply not been best equipped to deal with them. Decisions had been taken that were so far removed from any reasonable concept of common sense, that there had been no obvious points of reference to dictate how he should react.

However, the Local Culturist's announcement had been the critical point. He now knew what he had to do. It was clear that the old way of life was gone, and that a new, and uncertain, era was beginning.

He went straight to Uri's house from his meeting with the Archworthy.

He'd hardly had time to select a drink from the drinksmade before Della walked in from the back of the house and said to Uri, "I think you have some more visitors, dear," and nodded towards the day screen.

As she spoke, the front entrance sensor buzzed.

"It looks like a delegation," observed Clement.

Uri pulled a face.

"Yes," he sighed, "...and I'm not really surprised, are you?"

He looked at his friend searchingly.

"What can we say?"

"Well...I suggest we listen first, and then be very careful. Last time we spoke, we agreed that we'd not act quickly, but consider carefully what we're going to do. I think that applies here. I think we should try to buy time."

Uri nodded and went to the front door to find a group of about a dozen local residents. He looked around at them. He knew them all, and considered them all to be his friends.

Their spokesman was Sefton Dobbs, whose son, Gil, had helped Marius with his archaeological dig.

"Hello, Sefton," said Uri cheerily, "what can I do for you?"

"Oh…Good morning, Sir Uri," began Dobbs a little uncertainly, "I hope you don't mind us all coming along to see you like this, only…well, we're not happy about this announcement what's just been made. Er…in fact, if truth be told, we're not very happy about quite a lot of things lately. It's not the same as it used to be. We don't mind the folks of…the other districts and that, and we can sort of understand why we have to join up with them – you know, inbreeding and all that – but this latest thing about the names of the places…well, it isn't right. 'Drayling' – he articulated the word clearly and with emphasis – is our home. It's where we live. It's not right to be told to forget all about it…and we don't want to…Sir.

"We've come to you because we think you'll listen to us. We know all you councillors will have talked about it all already, before the announcement and that, and, well, you've always been approachable, and we thought you might be able to do something about it for us, Sir."

Uri didn't reply straight away. He was moved by the little speech, and immediately in a quandary. However, he marshalled his thoughts quickly and, being an experienced Worthy, called upon political skills honed over many years.

"My friends, of course I don't mind you coming to see me, and I'm sure that Sir Clement here would say the same. At this time of change – as you say, the merger with our new friends in the other districts, and, of course, the sad passing of Spencer Curtis – there are indeed matters of concern that we must all share. The BFF has a new Archwitan, and we wish him well. The Worthy Council is now learning of the approach that he, together with the rest of the Witan, proposes to adopt, and of course we'll continue to take time and care to ensure that we do our best for the people of Drayshaw Heath.

"The particular concern that you raise, Sefton, is likely to be an issue for many of us in the LGU, and I fully understand what you say. I'm grateful to you for letting me know the extent of your feelings, and I'll report back to the Council. Whilst I ask that you give me the time to do that, I'd be failing in my duty if I did not remind you that the new regulation is already in force, and is binding in law. However, the nature of your approach to me is such that I can fully accept that the one-off use of the old name of our area entity was essential, on this occasion, to enable you to convey the proper message to the Worthy Council."

Dobbs looked around at his fellow residents. There were a few mutterings, but he turned back to Uri and said, "We've all known you for a long time, Sir Uri, and you've always been fair and straightforward and that. We're happy to leave it to you to make our feelings known to the Worthy Council."

One added, "Thank you, Sir Uri," and a number of others nodded. The group then turned and left.

Uri and Clement returned to their hospitality chairs, where Della was waiting for them.

"Right. What's going on?" she demanded. "Obviously there are some strange decisions being made, and your behaviour tells me there's a lot more to it than just this ridiculous new regulation. I'll sit down and you can both tell me all about it."

With that, she deposited herself in a vacant chair and made a selection from the drinksmade.

"I'm not sure what you mean…" attempted Uri.

"Oh, I think you do," responded Della. "I've not been married to the Local Historian for all this time to not be able to read the signs. You're both deeply concerned about something, and I want to know what it is."

With that, she fixed a defiant stare on Uri.

Uri looked at Clement, and the latter shrugged. "You may as well tell her," he said, "she'll need to be told at some point anyway. I'll leave you to it."

He got up.

"No, sit down, Clement," said Uri, "I think perhaps the right time has come. Is Sara at home? It would be better if your wife was here too."

Clement shook his head.

"No, you tell Della. I'll go home and tell Sara."

He paused for a moment, and then added, "Della may wish to join us this evening. That'll be fine – we'll see you at seven."

With that, he left them alone.

When Uri had told Della the full story, she was extremely alarmed. The implications of what they were discussing were far-reaching and highly dangerous. If it was all true, then their whole way of life could be crumbling around them.

She could see that they had to do something, but nonetheless blanched at the suggestion that Marius should be involved.

It didn't take long, however, for her to accept that, if their concerns proved to be well-founded, then they would all inevitably be drawn in anyway, and it would make little difference.

Irrespective of that, they still agreed that they would say nothing to Urania, at least for the moment.

"Is there anything more you haven't told me?" she asked, already emotionally frayed. "I realise I haven't had long to come to terms with all of this, but despite the huge implications of what you've said, and the obvious dangers to all of us, what concerns me most is that you've considered dealing with it all without telling me. I want your promise that there's nothing else you haven't told me."

Not for the first time, Uri marvelled at his wife's ability to surprise him.

He walked to her and put his arm around her.

"I did what I thought was right," he said. "But I can see now that I was wrong. We're all in this together, and that is indeed how it should be. Your strength, and your love, are the most important things in the world to me, and everything else – however immense – is only secondary."

He kissed her, and she looked deep into his eyes.

He half-shrugged and half-smiled.

"I think, if you don't mind, I'd like to lie down for a while to reflect," he said, and left the room.

Della stayed where she was and watched him go, churning everything over in her mind, and wondering where it was all going to lead them.

As arranged, they reconvened later at Clement's house – and, by the early hours of the following morning, they'd agreed a list of facts, concerns and action points. Hayden had recorded them all carefully – by handpen rather than IDS to reduce the risk of surveillance – and, at Clement's request, was reading them out.

"<u>Facts:</u>

1. The Archworthy has said that false information may be fed to members of the Worthy Council.

2. Regional Administration has admitted IDS surveillance of citizens in its communication to the Worthy Council.

3. The Archworthy claims that the 'inbreeding story' was a cover, and that the real reason for the merger of area entities was to 'sort out Worthy Councils which had been inefficiently run'.

4. A dictatorial approach is being taken by the authorities. Examples: Area entity merger, district name changes, new law banning reference to traditional names, centralisation instruction, latest IDS communication from the Archworthy to Worthy Councillors, and the instruction to

'expunge all reference to previous names in maps and records'.

5. The Worthy Council is clearly not trusted to do the job required.

<u>Concerns:</u>

1. The Archworthy claims that Regional Administration told him that Drayling and Burshaw were 'inefficiently run'. This implies either that he's lying or that further radical changes can be expected.

2. The Archworthy predicts an increased need for the clarification facilities. This implies further radical changes.

3. The Archworthy said he needed the assistance of the Local Assessor and Local Culturist in the areas of grading, clarification, public order and published information. This implies an expectation of increased activity in all these areas.

4. The views of people, both citizens and Worthies, appear to have been subjugated.

5. The Archworthy's IDS communication incorporates subtle changes to councillors' responsibilities. For example, the Local Historian's are widened to include 'one-to-one tuition required by the Local Culturist', and under 'All Worthy Councillors', the first responsibility has been changed from '…carry out instructions received from Regional Administration <u>via</u> Archworthy' to '…carry out instructions received from RA <u>and</u> Archworthy'.

6. The instruction to expunge all reference to previous names from IDS records appears to be an attempt to rewrite history.

7. The proposed network of 'listeners to hear and report breaches of the new regulation' could be said to be a re-introduction of a policing system that was discontinued in this country many years ago.

8. The extent to which each citizen's contribution is to be increased 'through the grading system' – and exactly what that means – is unknown at present, but may be a matter for concern.

9. Many of these points imply the existence of a hidden agenda. The Archworthy appears to be prepared to carry out his rôle in its implementation.

Action points:

1. Sir Clement and Sir Uri to continue their duties as normally as possible. They're likely to be watched closely.

2. Marius and Hayden to ascertain if similar things are happening elsewhere in the country.

3. Marius to make a tentative approach to Stin Goodman to seek his help.

4. Marius and Hayden to organise cricket matches between districts. This will give them a good excuse for regular meetings."

Hayden stopped reading and looked up.

"Well, that's it so far."

"Yes, and it's quite enough to be going on with," said his father. "Obviously, it doesn't really need saying that this discussion must be kept strictly between ourselves – and Stin Goodman, of course, depending on your conversation with him, Marius – but I feel I should say 'Good luck everyone'. May good fortune accompany our quest for what's right."

Uri, Della and Marius were silent as they made their way home, partly because it was the middle of the night, and partly because they were each locked in their own thoughts. None of them knew what the future had in store.

When Marius sent Stin an IDS message a few hours later asking him to make contact when convenient, he received a voice-reply almost immediately.

"Good morning Marius. Stin Goodman at your service. I trust you're well this sunny morning?"

"Yes, I'm fine, and thanks for coming back so quickly," said Marius. "You certainly sound full of the joys of spring. Are you doing anything important?"

"Nothing that can't be done at some other time," replied Goodman. "Actually, I'm exploring deepest East District. There's some beautiful countryside around here, although I have to say I haven't seen much evidence of the joys of spring. Possibly because it's the sixteenth of September."

Marius laughed. "Purely a figure of speech. However, I must remember to take greater care when I next speak to a wordsmith!"

"Indeed you should," chuckled Stin. "What can I do for you?"

"There's something I'd like to discuss with you," replied Marius. "Could you come to my home? We could have something to eat."

"Ah! Eat! The magic word! Yes, of course I'll come. Let's see now…What time is it?…He consulted his IDS – just after eleven. It'll take me about an hour to get home, and then I ought to wash. If I get to you at, say, one o'clock or shortly after, would that be all right?"

"That'll be fine," said Marius. "I'll see you then."

In fact, Stin arrived at about five past one. Marius saw him coming on the day-screen, and went to the entrance to greet him.

"Thanks for coming, Stin," he said, "I hope I haven't disrupted your plans too much."

"Not at all," replied his visitor, "I have all the time in the world. What's the problem?"

Marius started cautiously. Whilst he was intuitively confident that Stin would be sympathetic to their concerns, the stakes were too high to take unnecessary risks.

He talked first about the merging of area entities, and asked how the creation of the new LGUs had been received in Stin's home district.

Stin's reply was that it hadn't been very popular initially.

"I suspect that's been the case throughout the country," he conjectured. "People generally don't like change, no matter where they live. However, by the time I left – which was only a couple of weeks after the announcement – I think most people were becoming reconciled to the fact that the inbreeding issue needed to be dealt with in one way or another."

Marius nodded his understanding.

"What do you think about the new regulation banning any mention of the names of the old area entities?" he asked, still treading carefully.

"Well now, I think I need to be a little tactful in my answer to that question. After all, I'm being entertained in the home of one of the members of the Worthy Council that announced the measure. In such circumstances, it would be a little churlish of me to be too colourful in my condemnation of it, wouldn't it?"

"Can I assume that that means you don't like it?" persisted Marius gently, looking straight into his eyes. "Actually, I understand that most of the Worthies don't like it either, including my father. I don't think it originated from our council. I think the order came from much higher than that."

"Well, in that case, no, I don't like it," responded Stin. "It's ridiculous, isn't it? As we've just agreed, people don't like change. They need time to adapt. They've been asked to accept the district mergers, and, over time, they could come to terms with that, and learn how to get along with their new neighbours.

"To my mind, the new law is insensitive and misguided. It does nothing at all to help the situation, and is quite simply unnecessary. In fact, if anything, it's more likely to hinder the process of community integration than help it.

"But, listen, I'm new to the district. Even if the order did come from central government, I really oughtn't to be shouting my mouth off about anything – at least until I've been around for a while. But I must say that I do feel that such a dictatorial approach can only have the effect of stirring people up."

The vehemence of Stin's reply was sufficient to convince Marius that his intuition had not been misplaced, and that he should proceed. Despite all the risks they'd discussed, and the fact that he'd only known the newcomer for a short while, he decided to place his trust firmly in his own instinct, and told him the full story – from the Archworthy's approach to Sir Clement Burcher right through to their plan to ascertain if similar things were happening elsewhere.

He breathed a huge sigh of relief when Stin readily agreed to help.

"To be frank, I find it encouraging that someone's trying to do something," said Stin, "because, from what you say, there's no doubt that something does need to be done. I appreciate that the situation's very dangerous, and I can see that your decision to approach me has probably, in itself, been of some concern to you – after all, you haven't known me for very long. However, all I can say is that I'm glad – and flattered – that you've asked me, and you can rest assured that I'll do my very best to assist in any way I can."

"Thanks, Stin," replied a now more relaxed Marius. "I'll speak to Hayden, and get back to you. Now, to more important things. Let's have something to eat."

Uri was buoyed when he heard, later that afternoon, of Stin's readiness to join them. Despite his initial misgivings, he was reassured that, even in one so young, the reaction to the new regulation had been very similar to his own.

As he composed his IDS progress report to Grindon Blane, he felt a strange sense of affirmation that what they were doing was right.

However, for the moment at least, he knew he needed to be seen to be continuing as normal.

His report read:

To: Sir Grindon Blane,
Archworthy, Drayshaw Heath.
From: Local Historian.

Daily progress report as requested.

The designations Drayshaw Heath, West District, North District and East District will, as requested, be incorporated into all history lessons to be given to children and other citizens.

At this point, I'm unsure how to expunge all references to the previous area entity names from all maps and records available on IDS. I'm looking into the matter, but any help would be appreciated.

I anticipate that considered proposals for the centralisation of the education facilities will take several weeks to formulate. As part of the process, I plan to revisit the facilities in North District and East District. Obviously, I already know the facility in West District well. When I have a better idea of the estimated date of delivery of my proposals, I'll report accordingly.

I've asked my son, Marius, and Hayden Burcher to organise a series of cricket games between districts. I shall, of course, retain overall responsibility.

Whilst at home yesterday afternoon (15th September), I received an unsolicited visit from a delegation of around a dozen local citizens. They expressed their deep unhappiness at the new regulation banning reference to the previous names of our three districts. I undertook to make their feelings known to the Worthy Council.

UG, 16th September 2466.

Clement Burcher's report, by contrast, was somewhat shorter:

Citizenship training, grading system, Local Service Centre and clarification facilities are all operating well. Requests for increased productivity will need to be more specific.

CB.

Although he proposed to go through each of them in detail in the morning, Grindon Blane had a cursory look at the Worthies' IDS reports later that evening. His initial feeling was that only one was likely to give him any major reason for concern. The most important, the Culturist, was definitely no problem – he'd already fallen into line. And the Genworthy, Provider and Historian all sounded reasonable on the face of it.

That left the Assessor...hmm...the Assessor...what to do about the Assessor.....

11

Marius and Stin went to see Hayden at his home the following day. As soon as they were seated comfortably in hospitality chairs, Hayden said to Stin, "Marius tells me that he's outlined our concerns to you, and explained what we're planning to do. He says that you've indicated your readiness to help us, and that you fully understand the risks involved. I feel, nonetheless, that I should re-emphasise the potential dangers to you. At this stage, we don't know in which direction our activities will take us, but it's almost inevitable that we'll be breaking the law – and maybe even committing treason…at least in the eyes of the authorities.

"I can guarantee you one thing, however, and that is that we shall only ever do what we consider to be right. Our sole intention is to resist what we believe to be wrong.

"If you join us, it's important that you understand all these things."

Stin replied that he did, indeed, understand the dangers, and that he was "getting involved entirely by his own choice."

They then went through the list of concerns that the group had identified two nights previously.

"I certainly agree that there's enough here to warrant concern," observed Stin, "although it is still possible, albeit unlikely, that it's all just the aggregate effect of a rogue new Archworthy and an insensitive new Archwitan."

"Yes, but even if that were true, there'd still be grounds for serious concern," pointed out Marius. "…And that's why we need to determine the scale – and thence the nature – of the problems. That's why we want to find out if similar things are happening elsewhere in the country. We need to know if other Archworthies have been given similar instructions, whether other Worthy Councils have received similar name-change and centralisation orders, and even whether the merger of area entities has occurred nationwide...although I do recall you saying in our conversation yesterday that the latter has occurred in at least one other place – your previous home.

"We made the assumption that computer technology was being used to ensure that inter-district communication did not take place. We therefore assumed that, if we are to find the answers we seek, we'll need to utilise that kind of technology in some way...and that's what led us to you. We don't have the necessary knowledge, but we think it's likely that you do – from your studies on the subject.

"Would you say that that's the case?"

"I could certainly give it a shot," accepted Stin. "My initial thoughts are that, whilst it's undoubtedly possible in some way to use identiscreens, it would also probably be the most dangerous route. You said that Sir Clement confirmed that the Worthy Council regularly contacts Regional Administration by IDS, and also that Regional Administration had admitted IDS surveillance – presumably from outside the district. I think that simply confirms that the technology is indeed already in place, and that, as you say, computer technology would be used to ensure that the facility is only used by those who are authorised to use it. That makes it highly likely that any unauthorised traffic would very quickly be detected.

"No, I have the feeling that we need to be a little more creative than that ...I'll see what I can do."

He looked at Marius and Hayden, and grinned.

"And don't look so worried! I promise I'll be careful – I'll be implicating myself in this as well you know!"

They nodded their acceptance, and Stin left them.

To the relief of all, the next few days passed relatively normally. Stin went off to consider the computer options, and Marius and Hayden turned their attention to the far more relaxing, and infinitely safer, question of cricket.

After some discussion, they decided that the establishment of regular games between the districts would be a better way forward than infrequent 'one-offs'. They therefore sent an IDS message to the other two captains from the previous month's games, and invited them to "a meeting to discuss the organisation of regular cricket."

Griff Davey, from North District (Stowly Heath), replied immediately that he thought it was an excellent idea, and that he'd be delighted to attend.

Norton Greatley, on the other hand, took a little longer to reply, but eventually sent a message saying, "Whilst I thoroughly enjoyed the cricket day a few weeks ago – and certainly support the idea of future games – I really think that it would be more appropriate if someone rather younger could be asked to represent East District."

They sent an acknowledgement to Greatley and, after a few moments' thought, Marius said, "What about Gordy Wester?"

"Good idea," replied Hayden, and immediately sent an IDS message to their Worthy-training colleague.

About an hour later they received a response from Gordy saying that, although he wasn't sure he was the best person to "carry the flag for our district in the future," he would be very happy to come along to the initial meeting "to help get the idea moving."

They arranged to meet at 10am on the 24th – two days' time – at Marius' home.

The previous few days had seen many discussions between Sir Grindon Blane and his councillors, although no formal council meeting had taken place. Each Worthy had submitted a daily IDS report as requested, and Blane had responded as he felt necessary.

Uri had visited the Archworthy's office on two occasions and, as a result, had learned how to make alterations to official records on IDS – and been given the authorisation to do it. A by-product of the meetings was that he'd surmised that, at the time of sending the instruction, Blane had had no more idea of how to do it than he had. It seemed to Uri that he was indeed acting under direct instructions from above.

Uri's approach to the centralisation issue seemed to be acceptable, at least for the moment, and Blane confirmed that the whole process needed to be completed by the end of March next year.

Uri was far less comfortable, however, with the situation regarding the visit to his home recently by Sefton Dobbs and the other citizens, and asked for a Council meeting to be arranged to debate the issue.

Sir Grindon replied that he did not consider such a meeting to be necessary.

"You undertook to let the Council know their feelings. You've done that, so there's nothing more to do."

"And what should my response be?" persisted Uri, "…they'll certainly be expecting one."

Blane was unmoved. "This is a nationwide decision, taken by the Witan, our Government of National Unity. It will have been taken for a reason. It's not unusual for the full rationale behind a decision to be unknown or unavailable to us. Inevitably, as you well know, Sir Uri, some measures will be more popular than others. If they are good citizens, they will understand that."

Uri wasn't happy, but he could see he wasn't going to get anywhere.

He was completely convinced now, though, that the Witan was pulling the strings. It was this new Archwitan – Tujo – who was behind the new dictatorial approach.

By coincidence, Clement Burcher had arrived at the same conclusion by a different route. He'd been told by the Archworthy that his initial daily report had been "neither informative nor helpful," and that more substance was expected in the future.

Sensibly, Clement had accepted that he needed to curb his natural frustrations. Whilst curt one-liners written in a fit of pique may well make him feel better at the time, they didn't sit well with the agreed strategy of carrying on as normal and creating no unnecessary waves.

In his conversations with Sir Grindon concerning the requirement for greater output, he'd ascertained that the Archworthy had had no detailed instructions on the subject. Their discussions had all been about where increased production might be achieved. In fact, it seemed rather paradoxical to Clement that, on this matter, Blane had received no specific instructions, whereas on the subject of the new regulation banning reference to previous district names, his orders had, apparently, been clear and unequivocal.

Nonetheless, the various conversations led Clement to the conclusion that this was indeed the case, and that the Archworthy was certainly acting under orders from above.

When he decided that he had enough to report, Stin contacted Marius and Hayden, and they arranged to meet at Marius' house.

"Have you come up with anything?" asked Hayden as soon as they were seated.

"Well, I've had a few thoughts," replied Stin. "The problem isn't only how to make contact with another district...it's also how to do it without being caught.

"We've already mentioned the feasibility of using IDS as though we were making contact locally – and there's no doubt in my mind that it would be possible to go that route. I think the likelihood of getting through would be high.

"However, as I said before, I also believe that the likelihood of detection would be high. For that reason, I've assumed, at least for the moment, that we'll agree that the risk of going that route is too great."

"Is there an alternative?" asked Marius.

Stin gave a confident smile.

"Well, yes. I think there may be. You may recall that, shortly after we first met, I told you that I'd looked up the details of your archaelogical dig in the Northern Agricultural Area. One of the things that your multitron scan detected was a line running diagonally right across the site. You said that the Regional Historian told you that it was a cable conduit laid during the internet boom of the 21st Century. I think we may be able to use that."

"How?" asked Hayden.

"Well, I reckon we could try to send something called a 'Cumber Pulse' along it…a kind of intelligent message which could make itself known as soon as it detected a suitable recipient along its route. The internet was an extensive network, so there ought to be plenty of potential targets. I could restrict the criteria to relatively safe personal grading categories and levels."

"I've never heard of it," said Marius.

"Neither had I until I stumbled on it whilst I was reading up about the Mark One and Two generation computers," explained Stin. "It was discovered – well, invented I suppose – by a man called Cumber about a hundred and fifty years ago. Like most technological progress since Dunstan Heathfield's Revolution, hardly anyone knows about it, but I've read a lot about it, and I reckon it's got to be worth a try.

"However, there is a word of caution. Whatever method we use to send our message out, it can only be received at the other end – wherever that is – by IDS. That means that the risk of detection will be greater at that end. What I propose to do is try to make the initial message, both method and content, appear to be a chance event rather than a planned one – at least at first glance. Obviously, it wouldn't stand up to detailed scrutiny, but it may at least help in the event of early detection."

He paused, and looked at both of them. "Any thoughts so far?"

Marius and Hayden exchanged glances. Hayden shook his head and Marius half-shrugged.

"I think you've already lost us in terms of technical knowledge," said Hayden. "We'll have to be guided by you. It all sounds good though. If you think it's the best way to go, then let's do it. What exactly does it entail?"

"Well, once again we need to balance the method with the degree of risk. If I had access to multitronic technology, I could probably send a pulse without disturbing the soil. However, such aditronic activity would almost certainly be detected. The alternative is to dig down to the conduit, and launch the pulse by physically attaching an emitter to it. The obvious means of doing that is a metrographic earthworker, which would do the job in seconds, but, there again, the technology it uses to reach its target is so readily detectable that it makes that unfeasible also."

"OK, stop!" interrupted Marius. "I think I know exactly where you're going. You're going to say that, despite all the wonderful technology available to us, you want us to dig down to the conduit with our bare hands – or at least with trowels or something."

Stin smiled. "Yes, I'm afraid so – it would be the safest route. Although, having said that, it would take time, so there'd still be a risk of detection by being seen or heard."

"It's also extremely primitive," observed Hayden. "But I can see the logic – and, of course, Marius and I do have the necessary experience of manual excavation!"

They all laughed.

"I promise I'll do my share," grinned Stin.

"In all seriousness, I do really think it's the best answer. I suggest we dig at night. It's quite remote in the Northern Agricultural Area, so with reasonable care we ought to be able to do it without alerting anyone."

"When do you want to do it?" asked Marius.

"I'll just need a couple of days to get the stuff together. I think I can adapt my IDS to act as an emitter, and, provided it's actually in contact with the conduit when it's activated, I reckon it would be pretty difficult to detect from any distance away.

"It's Thursday today…I need to recheck the geomitron map from your dig to select the safest point… and then I'll need…hmm…I reckon we could do it on, say, Saturday night. How does that sound?"

Marius looked enquiringly at Hayden, who shrugged and nodded.

"I guess it's as good as any other time," he said.

"Right. I'll get some digging tools together in the meantime," volunteered Marius.

Then, apparently as an afterthought, he added, "…But we need to be very careful. We don't want to excite anyone's interest at all."

12

The following day was 24th September – the day of the cricket meeting – and Gordy Wester walked up to the Graves' house at ten o'clock on the dot. Marius was at the door to meet him.

"Good morning, Gordy – thanks for coming," greeted Marius.

"No problem," replied the young visitor. "Am I the last?"

"No. Hayden's here, but Griff Davey, North District's captain, hasn't arrived yet. He'll be along shortly. There's no hurry…go through and get yourself a drink."

In fact, Davey didn't appear until nearly eleven o'clock, by which time the others were beginning to wonder what had become of him.

When he did arrive, he had a face like thunder.

"Griff, is something the matter?" enquired Marius as soon as he saw him.

"Sorry I'm late," he replied in a voice which suggested to Marius that he was having difficulty controlling his temper.

They walked through to join the others.

"Yes there's something wrong. Have you seen the daily bulletin this morning?"

They all shook their heads.

"Then read it," said Davey.

They all looked at their IDS. In addition to a couple of trivial items, there was an announcement that three people had been "referred to the clarification facility for repeatedly flouting new district designation regulations."

One of the names was Varna Davey, Griff's mother.

"She's ninety eight years old," snarled Griff through his teeth. He was shaking and staring resolutely at the wall.

"She's lived in a place called Stowly Heath all her life, and she's never hurt anyone. To my knowledge she's never even upset anyone. She's now worried sick, and I'm very, very angry. I've tried to calm her down by saying that I'll sort it out – that there's been a mistake – but I don't know what I can do."

"I think I might know," volunteered Gordy. "I've been thinking about it ever since it was announced.

"What could they do if everyone in the LGU went around openly saying the names every five minutes? Take everyone to the clarification facility?"

The others all looked at each other.

"That's an exceptionally good idea," said Davey, "...and I have to do something. I'm not going to let them victimise my mother." He turned to Marius. "Sorry about the cricket meeting. I'll go along with whatever you decide, but right now, I need to go."

"Hold on," said Hayden, who'd been listening to the conversation, but hadn't contributed up to that point. "I also think it's an excellent idea – and I suspect our fathers would too, Marius."

Marius nodded his agreement.

"Sometimes," continued Hayden, "decisions need to be taken and acted upon straightaway. I think this is one of those times. If we split up and go to our respective districts right now, we could get most of the citizens on board and shouting within an hour. I reckon the feeling will be so strong that it's almost not a gamble. Come on – let's do it."

Hayden was absolutely right. Within three hours, there were over a thousand disgruntled local residents chanting "Stowly Heath, Stowly Heath..." outside the Worthy Hall.

Sir Grindon Blane, who was working in his office inside the building, became aware of what sounded like a disturbance outside. An aide requested entry, and Blane released the security array.

"What's going on?" asked the Archworthy.

"Sir, there's a large crowd of citizens milling outside the building chanting Stow...er...the former name of this district...Sir."

Blane stood up. "What the...?"

"Er...I'm told that the same is also happening outside the old Worthy Halls in the other two districts, Sir. It appears to be orchestrated. Some of our Listeners have reported a few names, but they've been overwhelmed by the numbers, and have now stopped trying. In fact, I think some of them are now chanting with the crowd...Sir. And, look, I'm sorry Sir...but I'm afraid I'm going to join them."

He turned and left.

"What? Come back here! You can't do that! This is anarchy!..." His voice tailed off as he realised that there was no one there to hear him.

He thought quickly. He'd been in difficult spots before. So we have civil disobedience, do we? His eyes narrowed as he contemplated the options open to him. Obviously, he couldn't send every citizen to the clarification facilities.

"All right then, if that's the way they want it, we'll only send three," he resolved. "And I'll select them. One from each district. That'll make examples of them. We'll make it clear that their fate has been brought about by the ill-judged actions of their peers."

He went to his IDS and summoned Sir Clement Burcher and the Local Culturist by personal attention-pulse. The latter arrived within minutes, but the Local Assessor took a little longer.

"You took your time," observed Blane when he finally arrived. "Where were you?"

"In West District."

"Doing what?"

"Council business,"

"What Council business?"

"Observation. A crowd of residents of West District had gathered outside the old Worthy Hall to indicate their dissatisfaction with the regulation banning the use of the previous area entity designations. As a result, I've formed the view that the Listener system is insufficient for the purpose for which it was designed. I propose to express this view formally to the Local Culturist, whose responsibility it is. Also, I propose to look into how the clarification facility operations might be rapidly expanded to accommodate what appears to be a much heavier potential workload than was initially estimated. It may be possible to create a kind of 'mobile clarification facility', which visits all the homes in the district to dispense its services and benefits to everyone. To that end, I've selected one person in North District, a lady called Varna Davey, and informed her that I'll use her case as a trial run. I've told her to ignore Friday's daily bulletin, that we may have made an error, and that I'll be visiting her shortly to discuss how we might develop the concept in a fair and reasonable way. Overall, I've been fortunate enough to have had the opportunity…"

"Enough!" interrupted Blane, realising that his Local Assessor was getting the better of him. "To business. I've called you here because immediate action is obviously necessary. I have instructions for you."

He told them what he wanted them to do.

Burcher responded straightaway.

"Before we go any further, I feel I should point out that this proposal is a new approach, and therefore there ought to be a full Council meeting to discuss it."

"Not so," replied Blane. "I refer you to your responsibilities as a Worthy Councillor. I took the liberty of setting them out in full in my IDS communication dated 15th September, and you'll see that one of them is to carry out instructions received from the Archworthy. I'm the Archworthy, and I'm giving you an instruction."

Sir Clement couldn't help himself. "You know very well that you doctored those responsibilities to suit your purpose. It didn't go unnoticed that you'd made a number of subtle alterations. My responsibilities are, and have always been, to carry out instructions received from Central Government *via* the Archworthy. I accept that you're the Archworthy, but you do not have the right to give me an instruction like this, and you do not have the right to run roughshod over the Worthy Council. I don't believe that this instruction has come from Central Government – from Regional Administration – or from anyone else, and I do not wish to be part of a secret society that is seeking to undermine the established means of administering our local area properly. And whilst we're on the subject, I don't accept that Drayling has been inefficiently run either. It appears to me that you've sold out to a new and unreasonable approach being taken by the new Archwitan who calls himself Tujo. If you had anything about you, you'd be able to see that, and you'd realise that what I'm saying is not only the truth, but that you should be campaigning in whatever is the most appropriate way, to re-establish common sense and fair play for the future."

He stopped speaking, and immediately realised that he'd probably said rather more than was wise.

The three men stood in a rather stunned silence for a few moments, and then the Culturist opened his mouth.

"I...I feel I have to agree with much of that," he stammered.

A rather battered Blane seized the soft target gratefully. "Oh you do, do you? Right, I'd like to speak to you alone. Burcher, I suggest you leave now."

Sir Clement didn't need to be told twice, and left.

He immediately contacted Uri, and, having ascertained that he was at his home, went straight there.

"I've messed things up badly," he told his friend as soon as he arrived, "we agreed that we'd carry on as normal, and not give anyone any cause for concern. I lost my temper with the Archworthy, and now I feel wretched. I really don't know how much damage I've done."

It was Uri's turn to be calm and reassuring.

"Clement, I'm not sure that you've necessarily done much damage at all. Blane was already beleaguered by the peoples' disobedience, and he was already well aware of your feelings, whether you'd actually been quite so forthright previously or not. I doubt if it's changed much.

"However, given the way things are, I suggest it's time for another 'council of war'. Do you agree? Do you know where Sara and Hayden are?"

They called the others by IDS, and soon the six of them, plus Stin, were sitting in Uri's hospitality chairs. The latter assumed the rôle of chairman without discussion.

"Clement and I were chatting earlier, and came to the conclusion that we needed to talk," he said. "A number of things have occurred since our last discussion. Firstly, however, I'd like to thank Stin for agreeing to join us. Marius has, of course, already explained to him that we believe his knowledge will be invaluable to us."

They all looked at Stin, who acknowledged wordlessly with a nod. Uri then continued.

"Hayden, do you have the list of issues from our previous discussion?"

Hayden produced the handpenned record, and they ran through it item by item. From this second discussion, he produced a further list and, once again, read it out in full at the end of the meeting.

"<u>Facts:</u>

1. All our concerns about the new Archworthy have been vindicated.

2. He has a new approach, which we are (so far, at least) finding unacceptable.

3. We're now convinced that the Archworthy is acting on orders from the new Archwitan, Tujo, and that he (and presumably other Archworthies around the country) has been given wide authority to take action if he deems it appropriate.

114

4. The people of Drayshaw Heath have taken unilateral action.

5. The Archworthy is threatening an extreme response.

Action points:

1. Sir Clement and Sir Uri to be seen to be continuing their duties as normally as possible.

2. Sir Clement to "apologise" to the Archworthy for his remarks – as a damage-limitation measure.

3. Stin, Marius and Hayden to report back as soon as possible on their efforts to confirm that similar things are happening elsewhere in the country.

4. Marius and Hayden to continue with the cricket plan."

"Yes, that last action point may sound trivial compared to the others, but, in fact, it's important for two reasons," observed Della. "Firstly, because of the need for life to continue as normally as possible, and secondly, because we believe it will genuinely help the integration process. We shouldn't lose sight of that with all this other stuff going on."

All present agreed with the sentiment, and the discussion ended on a positive note.

The following morning, Saturday, Sir Clement Burcher sent an IDS communication to the Archworthy, which read:

From our conversation yesterday afternoon, you'll realise that I care deeply about our LGU.

On reflection, however, I also realise that you have a job to do, and that outbursts such as mine don't help.

I therefore apologise for my remarks, and ask that they be set aside for the wider benefit of our community.

CB.

At about the same time, Marius was checking that he had everything that the digging party would need later that day. Having kept most of the equipment from the archaeological excavation, it hadn't been difficult for him to find manual digging tools and three pairs of gloves. Hayden had undertaken to find "some discreet illumination," and Stin was, of course, bringing along all the computer stuff.

The day passed all too slowly for Marius, but eventually night fell and he slipped out to meet Hayden and Stin in the Northern Agricultural Area. Thankfully, the weather was fine and the moon not too bright. At around eleven thirty they located the spot that Stin had selected as best for their purpose, and began to dig in silence. The first job was to cut the turf as carefully as they could, so that they could replace it when they'd finished. They didn't want anyone to notice that the ground had been disturbed.

As it hadn't rained for a few days, the ground was dry and quite hard. This meant that progress was slow and not a little tiring. They established a rota of "two on and one off," whereby they each worked for ten minutes and rested for five in every quarter of an hour.

They'd been toiling for over two hours when Stin, who was having his rest turn, suddenly hissed, "Stop digging!"

Hayden and Marius froze. Had they been discovered? They looked up at the silhouette of Stin against the sky.

"Listen!" he breathed.

They listened.

In the still of the night, they could just detect a low, steady hum.

"What is it?" queried Marius.

"Do as I say, and don't ask questions," demanded Stin, in a low and even voice. "Drop the tools and get out of the hole slowly and carefully. I'll explain it to you in a moment."

The urgency in his voice was sufficient to make them do as he asked.

When they were standing beside the hole, he held out his IDS and whispered, "Look at this."

The screen was flashing "IMMINENT DANGER."

"What does that mean?" asked Hayden.

"I've done some checks, and, I think we've just been very, very lucky. According to my calculations, we've got to within six inches of the conduit.

"But that's good, isn't it?" questioned Marius.

"It would be if it was an old internet conduit," conceded Stin. "But it certainly isn't. It's a live power line of some kind. And not just any power line either. My readings are telling me that the power going through this beauty is far, far beyond anything I've ever come across before – by a factor of about twenty. If you'd touched it, you would have been fried to nothing in an instant."

"Wow," exclaimed Hayden.

"Wow, indeed," echoed Stin.

They stood together for a few more moments, collecting their thoughts, and then Marius said, "Well, it seems that the conduit, or whatever it is, is of no use to us now, so we need to fill in the hole."

"We can't use the tools that are in there," warned Stin, "they may be live, even now."

Marius shuddered as he digested the graphic confirmation of how close they'd come to death.

They refilled the hole using Stin's hand digger and the trowels. It took about an hour to complete the job – including the painstaking replacement of the turf – but, shortly before three-thirty, they were sitting in the Burchers' hospitality chairs discussing the night's events.

"We've been extremely fortunate," observed Stin. "The sheer might of that power-route could quite easily have liquidated us. We wouldn't have known a thing. Ironically, I suspect the only reason we were able to get so close to it, yet live to tell the tale, is that the flow was probably being specifically guided along the line of the route using similar technology to the Cumber Pulse that we were going to use."

"Presumably it carries power to the local districts," surmised Marius, "although I don't quite understand why the Regional Historian told us it was an old internet conduit – unless he made a mistake, that is."

"Oh, I don't think he made a mistake," replied Stin. "To my mind, the power going through it is far, far too great for it to be a simple power-feed for the local area, however many districts we might be talking about. No, you were deliberately misled when you were told it was an internet conduit. I think we've discovered another lie."

"All the more reason to continue with our efforts then," commented Hayden. "...But where on earth do we go from here?"

"Well, I'll keep thinking," said Stin. "...But, in the meantime, I suggest we ought to be getting home for some sleep. The night's nearly over."

"No, no...hold on," cautioned Hayden, "I think you both ought to stay here until at least mid-morning. There's no point in going out now and risking unnecessary questions."

The suggestion made obvious good sense, and so Marius and Stin adapted their hospitality chairs for overnight and, within minutes, all was quiet.

As Marius lay awake in the dark, his mind raced. Why would the Regional Historian lie to his father? What could such a massive power-route be needed for? If it was so secret, why had he been allowed to excavate the area in the first place? They must have realised that the route would be detected. Maybe they decided that to refuse permission would have provoked even more difficult questions.

He was still churning things over and over when he finally fell asleep, only to be roused – seemingly just minutes later – by his IDS informing him that 9.30am had arrived.

"It isn't an internet conduit at all. It's a huge power-route," explained Marius to Uri a couple of hours later. "...And, according to Stin, of a magnitude many times greater than would be needed to simply supply a number of districts with their normal power needs. We were extremely lucky that he was so alert to the danger. If he hadn't been, the outcome would almost certainly have been very different indeed.

"However, fortunately, we got out with our lives."

118

Uri raised one eyebrow momentarily, but retained his thoughtful demeanour.

"Your discovery is certainly astonishing – but your final point is the most important. I think we should all remember that, whatever twists and turns our lives may take in the coming weeks and months, we need to stay focussed on what really matters. It's vital that we retain our perspective."

"Why do you think the Regional Historian lied to you?" asked Marius.

"I don't know," replied his father, "but he certainly did. He clearly didn't want us digging up the truth."

"Then why were we allowed to excavate the area in the first place, if it's so sensitive?"

"The permission for the archaeological dig was granted by the Worthy Council – it's within their authority to give it – I simply mentioned it in a report as a matter of routine. I was surprised, and pleased at the time, when the Regional Historian picked it up and showed such interest. Obviously, we now know what his interest really was. It seems that every stone we look under is hiding something. It makes your efforts to find out if this kind of thing is happening all over the country even more important. Does Stin have any other ideas?"

"Well, he hasn't had long to reflect on what we discovered last night, but he's gone away to give it some thought."

"Right, then that gives you the opportunity to get some more sleep. I suspect you need it. I'll tell your mother and the others what happened, and that the three of you are still working on it.

"By the way, it would be helpful to me if you could make an announcement about cricket as soon as possible, so that I can report some progress to the Archworthy, but, please, do get some rest first."

"No problem. I can do that later today," said Marius. "We did have a chat on the subject with representatives of all three districts present, albeit an extremely brief one, so that can now happen…and don't worry about me – I'm fine."

13

In fact, Marius did fall asleep for a couple of hours, and contacted Hayden in mid-afternoon. They very quickly agreed the principles, and Marius issued the following IDS announcement at around four o'clock:

DRAYSHAW HEATH
ANNUAL CRICKET COMPETITION

Following the success of the cricket day in August, it's been suggested that an annual competition should be established. The proposal is that a series of games be arranged between our three districts. In a full summer (starting next year), it's envisaged that six matches will be played – each district playing the other two twice, once in their own district, and once in their opponent's.

However, as this year's summer is already half-over, an initial, shorter competition of three games is proposed. The rules to be the same as for the cricket day – sixteen overs to each team.

Drawn at random, but ensuring there'll be a game played in each district, the games will be:

North District (N.D.) against West District (W.D.)

E.D. against N.D.

W.D against E.D.

Each game will be played in the district named first, and the dates of the games will be announced shortly.

It's also been suggested that there should be ladies' games. The format of these will depend on the level of interest shown.

The results of the games are not felt to be especially important. The main aim is to provide enjoyment for players and watchers. Everyone will be welcome to attend.

District representatives are:

N.D. – Griff Davey

E.D. – Gordy Wester

W.D. – Hayden Burcher.

If you're interested in playing, please contact your district representative. If you'd like to help in some other way (for example as umpire, score recorder, ground preparer, equipment marshal or food helper) please contact me in the first instance.

Marius Graves (Th.) – West District.

At about the same time, Sir Grindon Blane issued the following to all citizens of Drayshaw Heath:

COMMUNICATION FROM

THE WORTHY COUNCIL

As a result of their part in the recent civil disobedience, and the events leading up to it, the following have received personal orders to attend the clarification facility in North District immediately. In addition to their own conduct, each will be held responsible for the ill-judged actions of their fellow citizens.

Griff Davey (North District), Sefton Dobbs (West District), Norton Greatley (East District).

DHWC."

Clement Burcher also received the following personal communication (required status):

"Attend clarification facility in North District immediately.

GB."

When he arrived at the clarification facility, there was a small crowd – made up mainly of younger men, he noticed – just outside the entrance. The mood was clearly highly charged, and the men were shouting abuse into the building, whilst being kept at bay by two burly men unknown to Clement.

He pushed himself to the front of the mob, and walked towards the open door. Immediately, one of the two men planted himself in front of him. As he moved to one side to avoid him, the man moved with him.

"Young man, I don't know who you are, but I'm the Local Assessor. Kindly get out of my way."

"It's all right, Stefan, let him through," said Blane's voice from inside the building.

As the man stepped aside, Burcher looked hard into his face. In previous visits to each of the clarification facilities, he'd made a point of speaking to every official, yet he couldn't recall ever having seen this one before.

When he got inside, he found the Archworthy standing in the centre of the hospitality area. Seated in three of the chairs were Griff Davey, Sefton Dobbs and Norton Greatley. Behind each of them was yet another large gentleman, and once again he didn't recognise any of them.

"Ah, Burcher, these three citizens are guilty of deliberate transgression of government regulations," said Blane with a wave of his hand. "They're also instigators of unrest in our LGU, and have been brought here for correction. I required you to witness their attendance. You've now done so. You may go."

"I beg your pardon?" reacted the Local Assessor. "What do you mean, 'I may go'?"

"Just that," said Blane. "I'll take it from here. Thank you. Good afternoon."

He motioned to one of the 'attendants', who moved to usher Sir Clement towards the door.

Shocked by the peremptory treatment, and unsure what was going on, he allowed himself to be edged out.

As they reached the main entrance, he turned and shouted, "I'm the Local Assessor! I run these facilities! I didn't send for these three men, and this is a clarification facility, not a correction facility! You've taken these actions without the authority of the Worthy Council. You're acting independently because you know very well that the Council would not approve!"

He looked around him and then shouted again.

"And where did these men come from?"

Blane barked back from inside the building. "As Archworthy, I'm exercising my right to make decisions in the best interests of the LGU. Stefan! Escort Sir Clement home. That mob out there seems a little volatile – I wouldn't want any harm to come to him!"

Clement then heard Sefton Dobbs' voice clearly. "You've got to help us, Sir Clement. We're being treated like prisoners. We haven't done anything that others haven't done, Sir, and we haven't..."

His voice was abruptly muffled.

Burcher was helpless. He turned to Stefan and scowled, "I don't need you," and strode away.

He headed straight for Uri's house. En route, he was accosted verbally by a number of citizens who wished to vent their displeasure at the recent actions of the Worthy Council...but he was barely aware of them. He neither acknowledged nor answered them. Keeping his eyes fixed resolutely to the front, he just kept walking.

When he arrived, Uri was ready for him. News had travelled quickly, and although a few people were standing outside, they moved quietly aside to allow him to pass.

"Come in, Clement," said Uri, and put a consoling hand on his shoulder. "I know roughly what's happened, and I've asked the others to join us. We obviously need to talk...but first of all, I think you need a drink."

Clement stared at him, his eyes blazing. He opened his mouth to speak, but nothing came out. Uri could see that he was shaking. In all the years that they'd known each other, he'd never seen Clement quite like this. This was more than anger. His friend was incensed almost to the point of collapse.

It took more than an hour for Clement to recover sufficiently to speak in any way rationally about what had occurred, and by that time the others had joined them.

The whole area was buzzing with news of the events, and each one of them had already heard a variety of versions of exactly what had taken place. As is usual with these things, conflicting rumours were rife.

Eventually, Uri called the meeting to order.

"My friends, I think we've now reached the point at which open conflict has been declared. Blane's made it clear that he has no intention of following established procedures, and more than that, it seems to me that he's shown scant respect for the citizens of Drayling, Stowly Heath and Burshaw. However, before we consider where we go from here, I would like to ask Clement to run through the events of today, to ensure that we discuss truth and not just rumour."

There was general agreement with this approach, and Sir Clement gave them an emotionally charged account of all that had happened. He emphasised particularly the rude nature of his summons to the clarification facility, and the sheer contempt displayed in his dismissal from it.

"I'm the Local Assessor," he bewailed. "The clarification facilities are my responsibility. He has no right to do what he's doing. He's abusing his position. He's..."

"OK, old friend," interjected Uri, "no one here will disagree with that, I'm sure. I should also tell you that, since Blane's IDS announcement – which he carefully worded as coming from the Worthy Council as a whole – a number of local citizens have been standing outside our house, and some of the things they've been shouting have been rather less than complimentary. I understand that the other Worthies have also had similar experiences.

"However, the verbal exchange you had with Blane as you left the clarification facility was witnessed by the crowd outside, and the news has spread quickly by IDS that he was acting independently of the Council. That's why you had no problems when you arrived here. By that time, the mood had changed, and they were shouting that they knew it wasn't our fault, and that they would support any action we can take against the Archworthy. In fact, I got the distinct impression that it was all being orchestrated in some way. They were certainly in direct contact with others."

"May I say something, Sir Uri?" interrupted Stin.

"Of course."

"Although a lot of things have happened in a very short time, I think already there'll be great sympathy throughout the district for the whole Worthy Council – with the exception of the Archworthy, of course. Everybody knows that you, Sir Uri, and you, Sir Clement, are fine examples of officers who've served the local citizens diligently and responsibly for years, and to suddenly have it ripped away from you must be very hard – not to mention the adverse effects on the district as a whole. People will be aware of that, I'm sure."

"Well said, Stin," said Della. "I entirely agree."

There were assenting nods all round, and Sir Clement said, "Thank you, Stin. That's much appreciated."

"Right," said Uri, "what do we do now?"

"We should start by looking at the list of issues from last time," said Hayden, and produced the handpenned record.

They ran through the list, and from it agreed that there was no longer any point in maintaining the illusion of normality.

"I still think we need to confirm that similar stuff is happening elsewhere," observed Marius, "although I think it's becoming more and more obvious that it must be. What might be helpful to us now is to know exactly how districts are reacting to the changes, particularly in neighbouring LGUs."

"I do have a possible way forward on that one," said Stin. "The Cipherslider."

"What?" exclaimed Uri, "the antique computer? How could that help us?"

"Well, I'm not a hundred per cent certain, but I can see no reason why it shouldn't be made to work – assuming it's all there. Computer obsolescence is not normally as a result of wearing out or breaking down, it's just that technological advances are often so rapid that they tend to be cast aside very quickly for more powerful or capable models. The reason that I discounted it previously in favour of the conduit was that I felt it carried a much greater risk of detection. However, if we now agree that that's become less of an issue, then I think we should give it a try."

"If risk of detection is no longer important, why don't we reconsider using IDS?" reasoned Hayden.

"Well, it's a matter of degree, isn't it?" replied Stin. "Whilst I'm sure it would work, I believe that detection would be inevitable using IDS, because that's the route that will have been automatically monitored ever since inter-district communication was abolished. Whilst risky, the use of the Cipherslider would not be expected, so detection ought to be less likely."

Hayden nodded. "OK, yes, I can see that."

"Do you have a plan, Stin?" asked Uri.

"Not in detail yet," said Stin, "but as it's housed in the building that I live in, it ought to be possible to come up with something. It's not just a question of making it work, though. There's also the question of security, not only of the computer itself, but also of the various entrances and rooms of the old Worthy Hall."

"I should be able to find out the extent of the security as Local Historian," offered Uri.

"And I ought to be able to find out the extent of the security specific to the computer itself, as I'm officially its guardian," added Marius.

"Right, that's an action point then," said Hayden. "If the two of you can give us that information by, say, Wednesday, then Stin, Marius and I should be able to do something by the end of the week."

"Is there anything we can do about Griff Davey, Sefton Dobbs and Norton Greatley?" asked Sara, who had listened quietly up to that point.

"I can't help thinking that that's part of a rather bigger issue," said Marius. "As you said earlier, father, Grindon Blane has now declared his position.

"He appears to have abandoned the 'gang of three' approach that he mooted to Sir Clement – presumably because Sir Clement made it fairly obvious that he didn't share his view of the way forward for our LGU.

"In response to the civil disobedience, he did his homework, and identified three citizens who would be well-known to everyone. Griff Davey and Norton Greatley were captains of their district's cricket teams only a few weeks ago, and Sefton Dobbs headed the delegation that came here to express concerns about the new regulation. It wouldn't have been difficult for him to obtain that information with a few discreet enquiries.

"It's by no means certain, but it seems to me likely that the guards he employed at the clarification facility have been brought in from outside. If that's so, then it strengthens our belief that he's operating with the approval of the Witan. It also begs the question – where did they come from? I think it's worth noting also that, under normal circumstances, each of the three detainees would have attended the clarification facility in their own district – the facilities have yet to be centralised. Blane must have taken them all to the same one because he expected trouble and could be present to deal with it personally.

"However, as I said, I believe there's now a much bigger issue. It's a fact that Grindon Blane has lost the confidence of the local citizens. He's also lost the confidence of the Worthy Council. That means that Drayshaw Heath is presented with a stark choice. Either it sits back and accepts that it's governed by Grindon Blane – and all that goes with that – or it simply ignores him and replaces him with its Worthy Council, a system it's been happy with for many years."

Marius' proposal drew a gasp from Sara and stunned silence from everyone else.

"Why not?" he persisted. "It's got to happen sooner or later. Why not now? What's he going to do? Even if his reaction is one of extreme violence, if it's going to happen, it's going to happen. It's a simple choice. Either we decide to defend our district and its way of life, or we decide that we don't think it's worth defending."

He looked around the room.

"Well?"

Uri looked at Della. Clement looked at Sara, and then at Hayden. The enormity of the proposal was evident to all of them, but none of them leapt to disagree.

"Wow, Marius," breathed Hayden slowly, "I really didn't see that one coming."

He paused, and then continued, "…and, given the radical nature of the proposal, I suggest we adjourn – for an hour, say – to allow ourselves time to think about it."

No one disagreed with that, either.

A little while later, at around midnight, the meeting resumed more or less of its own volition.

Having carefully considered their own feelings, and having sought the thoughts and advice of those close to them, they'd arrived at a consensus. They decided that Marius was right.

It wasn't long before an IDS exchange with the other Worthies enabled Uri and Clement to compose and issue the following IDS announcement:

TO ALL CITIZENS OF DRAYLING,
STOWLY HEATH AND BURSHAW
We, the loyal Worthies of our three districts, give notice that there will be a Worthy Council meeting at the Worthy Hall in Stowly Heath at 11am today, Monday 27th September.

This meeting seeks to re-establish normality following unacceptable recent events.

SIR CLEMENT BURCHER (Local Assessor and Acting Chairman)
SIR URI GRAVES (Local Historian and representative for Drayling)
SIR GARTH WELDON (Local Provider and representative for Burshaw)
SIR ROMFORD TESTER (Local Genworthy and representative for Stowly Heath).

"It's a shame our Local Culturist doesn't feel able to join us," observed Clement, "but I guess it's understandable."

14

None of them got much sleep in what remained of the night.

At breakfast, having decided that the time was now right, Della took time to explain to Urania all that had occurred. She emphasised the dangers involved, and asked her to promise not to discuss matters with anyone outside the family. The thirteen-year-old, sensing that her mother was rather more worried than she was prepared to admit, sought to reassure her.

"Mother, it's been obvious for some time that something very strange is going on – but you really don't need to worry about me. I know that you and father will know what to do – you always do."

Della smiled and kissed her on the forehead. "Thank you my darling," she said.

At approximately 10.30am, Hayden joined around two hundred residents of Stowly Heath who had already assembled outside their Worthy Hall. About twenty yards in front of them, and barring their way to the entrance, were a dozen uniformed guards, none of whom anyone recognised.

He studied the guard nearest to him. He was wearing a uniform consisting of black tunic, black leggings and black boots. On each shoulder, the letters 'B.F.F.' were clearly visible. In his right hand he was holding a device that Hayden had never seen before. About the size of an IDS, it was black, with three red projections – directed towards the crowd.

"They look a bit like cricket stumps," thought Hayden, "...but, in fact, they're clear evidence that Blane intends that no one will pass. They're armed."

He sent an IDS report to Sir Clement.

Meanwhile, the newly formed Worthy Council was assembling at the old Worthy Hall – but in Drayling, not Stowly Heath. Their IDS announcement had done its job. It had reassured the citizens that something was being done and, having foreseen some kind of radical action by Blane, had also ensured that he didn't thwart their plans.

Earlier, at around ten o'clock, Marius had joined Stin who, of course, was already in the building, and they'd explained their plan to the two resident orderlies. It hadn't been difficult to obtain their whole-hearted cooperation. As a result, all roomscribers and other security devices had been disabled.

The meeting started promptly at eleven.

Sir Clement opened by informing those present of what was happening at Stowly Heath. He transcreened Hayden's report to them. There was much muttering, but no one was really surprised.

"The importance of this meeting is not what we're going to discuss, but the fact that we're meeting at all," he observed. "I therefore propose that we confine ourselves to the broad agreement of general aims and principles."

It was on that basis that they'd drafted and transcreened the following statement:

To all citizens of Drayshaw Heath:

<u>*Matters agreed at meeting of new Worthy Council –*</u>
<u>*Monday 27th September*</u>

1. The regulation prohibiting reference to Burshaw, Drayling and Stowly Heath is hereby cancelled. The traditional names of our three districts are therefore reinstated.

2. In the spirit of community, we see no reason why our combined district should not continue to be referred to as Drayshaw Heath.

3. Every effort should be made to ensure that life in Burshaw, Drayling and Stowly Heath continues as normally as possible.

4. For the time being, Sir Clement Burcher will take on the duties of Acting Chairman of the Council and Local Culturist.

SIR CLEMENT BURCHER (Acting Chairman/ Culturist and Local Assessor)
SIR URI GRAVES (Local Historian and representative for Drayling)
SIR ROMFORD TESTER (Local Genworthy and representative for Stowly Heath)
SIR GARTH WELDON (Local Provider and representative for Burshaw).

That same morning, some ten or fifteen miles north-west of Drayling – in the tiny district of Cowly Warden – a fresh-faced young man by the name of Dane Heele was starting his Local Service. He'd walked the short distance from the Local Assessor's office, having been seconded to the Local Culturist's office for one month, and been given his first task – to use his IDS to "familiarise himself with the rôle of the Local Culturist in the community."

He successfully accessed the relevant section and began to read:

"The responsibilities of the Local Culturist can be summarised as follows – to teach literacy at the education facility, to provide one-to-one tuition as...Is there anybody there? Please respond if you are reading this. It is important that we make contact...required by Local Assessor."

For a moment Dane did not take the words in. Then he re-read them and a realisation of what might be happening began to dawn. He leapt from his chair, and ran to the Culturist's private office. Barely waiting for leave to enter, he dashed in and blurted, "Message on IDS. From outside. Message from outside. Come quickly ...Sir...please."

The Culturist, Sir Denman Fripp, was not a man to be easily flustered. He was well used to dealing with the excitabilities of young people. However, the urgency with which Heele had delivered his message was sufficient to cause him to follow him back to his IDS. The Culturist took the instrument and looked at the screen. "…Please respond. We believe we are getting through. It is important that you respond…Provide citizens with daily information by IDS. Look after public gardens…"

The Worthy caught his breath. The lad was right. Someone from outside was indeed attempting to make contact. He made a quick decision. The events of the past two months were such that things were no longer as they were. If similar things had occurred in other places, then it would be understandable, and rational, to attempt to communicate.

He keyed in the words, "You've made contact. Who are you?"

He didn't know if the simple act of inputting the words would be sufficient to transmit the reply. He could only hope, and wait.

Sure enough, the words on the screen continued, "…and recreational areas. Take responsibility for public order, entertainment and…we're in Drayling. We're trying to find out if similar things are happening in your area as are happening in ours. We're breaking non-communication regulations because we believe our way of life is under threat. Can you confirm similar? Suggest end specific access to what appears to be a summary of Local Culturist's responsibilities…"

Sir Denman smiled with comprehension and excitement. He terminated the specific information enquiry that Heele had made, and then keyed, "I'm Local Culturist in Cowly Warden, not far from you. Yes, way of life could be said to be under threat. If similar events in Drayling, can understand desire to communicate."

"You've done it!" exclaimed Marius excitedly as the words came through. "Well done, Stin, well done! Go on –

tell him what's happened here! Ask him if the same things are happening there!"

Stin was a little more cautious.

"I suggest we still need to be careful," he said. "There's no point in taking unnecessary risks. Now that a link has been established with one particular IDS, I can ensure that our messages are not easily read by any others. Also, I think we should keep a duplicate record of our exchanges so that we can review them later. I'll put all that in place. It won't take long – then we can re-establish contact."

He keyed the words, "Now that contact made, will formulate method of encryption of communications for greater security. Will revert shortly. Good to talk to you. Best wishes."

As he sent the message, the Council's communication came through on their identiscreens, and Marius said, "The Council meeting must be over. Whilst you're working on that, I'll go and find my father, and tell him our news."

Stin nodded and got to work.

Marius found Sir Uri and Sir Clement in the hospitality area. As soon as he saw them, it was apparent to him that events were weighing heavily upon them. Their faces were ashen.

With some concern, therefore, he asked, "Father, is everything OK?"

Uri responded with no more than a half-smile. "Well, it's all going according to plan so far, but the implications of what we're doing are profound, to say the least. Our actions are certainly not giving us any pleasure."

Marius swallowed hard at this reminder of the depth of emotional turmoil that the momentous events were inevitably stirring in traditionalists like his father and Sir Clement.

He paused for a few moments before continuing, "I've got some good news for you. Stin's made contact with Cowly Warden. In fact, we've just exchanged messages with their Local Culturist!"

Uri and Clement stared at each other, and followed Marius through to the main hall.

Stin looked up and smiled when they appeared.

"Well, it worked," he grinned, "and we found the Local Culturist, no less. Would you like to go through now? I've scrambled the transmission matrix, so it'll only be readable on the IDS we made contact with earlier. Also, I can make a full record of the exchange, and take it off the Cipherslider as soon as you've finished and put it on to your IDS."

The two Worthies were stunned momentarily, and didn't reply.

Eventually, Uri spoke.

"Despite everything that's happening to us at this time, I think we should all be aware that this is an historic moment. For two districts to speak to each other after so long is a truly momentous thing. I sincerely hope that we'll remember it in the future as a key step on the road back to reason and natural order."

There was a period of silence as his observation touched them all.

"Well said, my friend," said Clement, "and I think it only appropriate, therefore, that it be our Local Historian who takes that step."

It was a huge gesture, and Uri appreciated it.

"Thank you, Clement," he replied.

He turned to Stin. "What do I do?"

Stin waved his hand towards the Cipherslider.

"Just compose the words. You're through."

Uri thought for a moment, and then keyed, "This is Uri Graves, Local Historian of Drayling. To whom am I speaking?"

The reply was immediate.

"My name is Denman Fripp, Local Culturist of Cowly Warden. It's an honour to communicate with you, Sir Uri. I understand you feel your way of life is under threat."

"Yes, and I believe you've confirmed the same. That's why we've taken the illegal step of making contact. Things have reached a point here that some kind of radical action seemed necessary. I'd like to list the events that have led us to this point, and then compare your situation. Are you happy with that approach?"

"I'm very happy to talk to you. However, I believe it would be more appropriate for our Archworthy, Sir Enwick Frawton, to represent us in the detailed exchange of information. I've already informed him that you've made contact. He'd very much like to talk to you. He's on his way here now. I'm afraid I don't know how to call you on this IDS. Can you re-establish contact in, say, one hour?"

Uri visibly recoiled from the screen. There were sharp intakes of breath behind him.

"The Archworthy? He wants the Archworthy to talk to us?"

Clement stayed cool. "Don't keep him holding on. Say we'll contact them again in an hour. We've nothing to lose now."

Uri nodded, and turned to Stin, who keyed "Agreed," and severed the link.

"What now?" said Uri.

"Carry on as we intended," replied Clement. "One of two things is true. Either their Archworthy'll be sympathetic to our situation, or he won't. If he is, there's no problem. If he isn't, it won't change anything to any great degree anyway. Just another black mark against us. We've already got a collection of those, so one more won't make much difference!"

Marius, as was often the case, was thoughtful. "I don't think we should jump to any conclusions anyway. People are all different. I think we should proceed as planned until we know we have a problem."

At that moment, one of the orderlies ran into the hall.

"Sir Clement, something terrible is happening in Stowly Heath..."

As he spoke, all their identiscreens pulsed simultaneously. It was a message from Hayden.

It read: "Carnage here. Blane was waiting behind the barrier of armed guards. Nothing happened until the report of your meeting came through on IDS. He was clearly incandescent with rage when he realised he'd been deceived. People cheered, and then started shouting abuse at him. A young lad ran towards the guards and was killed outright. Blane ordered the people to go home, and then instructed the guards to escort him to Drayling. As they were forming into a column, fifty or sixty citizens rushed them. I saw Blane run back into the building. I estimate about fifteen citizens dead. Some reached the Worthy Hall. Someone has just told me that the Archworthy is also dead, but I can't confirm that. Guards have disappeared. I don't believe they're on their way to Drayling. Danger of further violence appears to have passed for the moment. H."

Their shock was palpable.

No one spoke for some time. They just stared at their identiscreens.

Eventually, Clement muttered, "Oh, no...no... please...no...whatever have we come to?"

He staggered backwards slightly, and Marius instinctively put his arm around him and guided him to a chair.

Again, no one spoke for some minutes – each struggling to come to terms with the terrible news – until Uri sat bolt upright and, looking determinedly straight ahead, said, "It's happened, old friend, and now we need to be strong."

He took a deep breath and continued, "there'll be time for regrets later. Right now the new Council must take the lead. The other Worthies are almost certainly still in the building. I suggest you call an emergency meeting here and now."

Sir Clement looked at him and knew he was right. He nodded, and within twenty-five minutes the Council had agreed a crisis plan. Sir Romford Tester, the representative for Stowly Heath, was despatched immediately to join Hayden at the scene, with the authority to make whatever on-the-spot decisions he considered necessary. As Local Genworthy, he would also be available to his medical facility staff, who would already be on site attending to the dead and injured. Sir Clement, in his capacity as Local Assessor, sent an IDS message to a dozen suitably graded citizens in Burshaw and Drayling asking them to stand by in case Sir Romford called for further assistance. As acting Local Culturist, he also issued a brief general communication to all citizens informing them of the tragic events, based on Hayden's report. He assured them that appropriate action was being taken.

15

Despite having had no time at all to come to terms with the truly dreadful events in Stowly Heath, they regathered around Cipherslider at 12.45pm precisely, as promised, and Stin re-established the link with Cowly Warden.

Uri took a deep breath, and opened with, "Greetings, Cowly Warden, this is Drayling again. Are you there?"

"Hello, Drayling," came the immediate response, "Yes, we're here. I'm Enwick Frawton, Archworthy of Cowly Warden, and I'm delighted to speak with you. Denman has told me that you, like us, are having problems with our new Archwitan Tujo."

The directness of the statement took Uri by surprise. He looked up at Clement and the others.

"Go for it," said Clement in determined monotone.

Uri went for it.

"Sir Enwick, it's an honour to speak to you. I'm Uri Graves, Local Historian. As I said to Sir Denman earlier, I'd like to tell you of the events that have led us to make this illegal communication. I'd then like to learn if you've had similar experiences.

Firstly, however – and I hope you won't take offence at this – there's something I need to clarify. Bluntly, I have to establish your goodwill. The Archworthy here is not sympathetic to our situation. In fact, quite the reverse. And we know that, by making this contact, we're probably committing treason. That's how desperate we are. Can we trust you?"

He sat back in his chair and waited.

Once again, the response came straight away.

"Sir Uri, I appreciate your situation and your candour. Obviously, if I were hostile, I could lie to you. Frankly, I think you've probably already done enough to enable me to make your life very uncomfortable if I were so minded! I can only tell you that I'm not hostile, and repeat that there are real concerns here too about the future. I agree that contact between us may help us to protect it. Please tell us your story."

Uri accepted the truth of his words, and pressed on cautiously.

"About two months ago, we were instructed to amalgamate Drayling with Stowly Heath and Burshaw to form one larger unit to be called a Local Geographical Unit. Did that happen to you?"

"Yes, on the 25th of July, to be specific. We were told to merge with Great Stanside and Sherbet Ridge. We didn't like the idea initially."

"That's the same date as us," whispered Clement.

"What do you call your LGU?" keyed Uri.

"Well, that's slightly embarrassing, actually. The other Worthies and Archworthies all got together and insisted we call it 'Frawton'. I'm very flattered, of course – and indeed honoured – but I must say it does make me feel a little awkward."

This brought a puzzled expression to Uri's face.

"You refer to 'the other Worthies and Archworthies'. Did all the outgoing Worthies take part in the naming decision as well? We didn't discuss our new name until about six weeks after the merger."

"There were no outgoing Worthies," replied Frawton.

"Then your situation is very different from ours," responded Uri. "...And the fact that your Worthies wanted to name their LGU after you speaks volumes in itself. We were led to believe that our Archworthy was instructed to form a single Worthy Council, made up of the most appropriate candidates from the three area entity Councils. I think the three Archworthies were originally contacted by Regional Administration. We were simply told who our Archworthy was going to be – Sir Grindon Blane from Stowly Heath. Our Archworthy here in Drayling said that he'd decided, of his own volition, to stand down."

"I think the latter's unlikely," replied Frawton. "Yes, I was contacted by Regional Administration and told much the same. I was informed that I was going to be Archworthy of the LGU. I told them that no one was going to lose his job. Simply adding the three areas together doesn't make the job any easier in my view. We still have a Worthy Council for each district, made up as before. The only minor change is that the other two Archworthies now call themselves District Archworthies. I rejoice in the title of Prime Archworthy. Basically, we carry on much as we've always done."

"Phew!" exclaimed Clement, "why didn't we do that?"

"Sounds easy, doesn't it?" said Uri, "but I bet there's more to it than that. He said earlier that they were worried about the future."

"When you were instructed to agree a name for your LGU, were you also ordered to centralise all main functions?"

"Yes. I told them that I was in the best place to decide whether centralisation would be beneficial or not, and that I'd therefore consider it in due course – through normal Council processes, obviously. They also tried to impose some ill-thought-out regulation about doing away with the district names, or something like that. I told them to concentrate on what they were good at, and leave us to do what we're good at. Unfortunately, however, I don't think that'll be the end of it.

"Before I go any further, could we please have a break for a couple of minutes? I'll tell you more shortly."

Uri responded, "OK," and Stin cut the connection.

"It appears he's had exactly the same orders as Blane, but reacted in a completely different way," observed Uri.

"And from what we've learned so far, I can't imagine awful things like we've had today happening in Frawton," said Clement.

Uri nodded and sighed.

"He does sound impressive, doesn't he?" said Marius. "…And he's obviously got the support of the other Worthies. Do you have any observations, Stin?"

"Well, on the face of it, it would appear that the way to deal with Regional Administration is by presenting a strong front," replied Stin thoughtfully. "However, I'm interested to hear what else he's going to say. As Sir Uri pointed out, he's already told us that he's worried about the future. That wouldn't seem to follow from what he's said so far, so there must be more to come."

"Yes, I agree," said Uri. "Let's see what else he has to tell us."

Stin re-established the connection.

"I'm still here," confirmed Frawton. "I'm now alone at this end. I want to speak freely to you, but there are a few things that my colleagues here are not aware of. Frankly, Regional Administration's response to my refusal to implement their new district designation regulations – or adopt their centralisation programme – hasn't been quite as understanding as I've so far indicated to the three Councils. Obviously, all the Worthies are aware of the Witan's instructions, and because of the apparent change of approach, they're all concerned about the future. However, the fact is that I've been told bluntly by Regional Administration that if I refuse to implement the instructions, I'll be removed.

"That's bad enough, but it gets worse. They also told me that the main reason for the district mergers had nothing to do with inbreeding. They say that the real reason is that some entities were being 'inefficiently run', and that I've been given the job in this one of 'shaking them up'. I pointed out that, even if it were true that some Councils were ineffective

143

(and frankly, I think it's a fabrication), then there are better ways of addressing the problem than by abandoning the principles of Dunstan Heathfield's Revolution.

"Their response was simply to repeat that it wasn't my decision.

"Furthermore, I've now been approached with a proposal that I find so unacceptable that, prior to your communication, I had no idea what to do.

"I've been told that the Witan (which, presumably, means our new Archwitan Tujo) believes that the Worthy Council system is too unwieldy to be able to deliver 'the advances that are necessary', and that I must therefore select an 'inner group' of three – to include myself – to operate, in complete secrecy, to make them happen. Meanwhile, the other Worthies will be fed false information in an elaborate ruse to maintain the illusion of traditional local government as espoused by Dunstan Heathfield.

"I haven't told all this to anyone else yet, but it's clear to me now that the fabric of our way of life is being knowingly broken down, and that's a deep worry. However, it'll explain to you why I too am concerned about our future. Over to you."

Uri responded with, "It appears you've received similar orders to our Archworthy, but have reacted very differently. Our Local Assessor, Sir Clement Burcher, is with me, and I think it would be appropriate at this point to pass over to him."

Clement put his hand on his friend's arm, and squeezed gently. Uri moved from the seat, and Clement took his place.

"Good afternoon, Sir Enwick," he began. "It seems likely from what you say that Archworthies all over the BFF have received similar instructions from our new Archwitan. I can confirm that our Archworthy tried to recruit me into an inner group of three. Everything you've said fits with what we believe has happened here. I'll list some of the key events:

Our Archworthy's approach has been one of total compliance with the orders received.

Our LGU has been named Drayshaw Heath (there's no opposition to this).

The three Councils became one, so twelve Worthies were either downgraded or retired.

The new regulation banning reference to the previous area entity names was implemented with much discontent.

'Listeners' (a new grading) were introduced to report breaches of the new regulation.

Worthies were instructed to formulate plans for the centralisation of all main functions by the end of March next year.

There's general agreement that the new approach is uncaring and unlikely to create harmony.

Many citizens took part in civil disobedience action – openly chanting prohibited designations.

Unrest and distrust of the Archworthy reached the point that four members of the Council (Assessor, Historian, Genworthy and Provider) have formed a new Worthy Council unilaterally. We had our first meeting earlier today. The Archworthy tried to stop us by force of arms (apparently with manpower from outside). Sixteen of our citizens have been killed. I don't yet know how many have been injured. I've just been informed that our Archworthy is also dead, although that's not yet verified.

From the above, I think you'll understand why we've sought to make contact. Over to you."

"I'm saddened by your news," replied Sir Enwick, "and I think we must try to work together. I suggest we take some time now to consider how we might do that. In the meantime, your experiences have convinced me that the first thing I must do is to tell everything to the Worthies here. What appears to be happening in our country is so extreme that they need to know. Could you make contact again at, say, 4pm tomorrow?"

Clement responded with "Agreed. Best wishes. Good afternoon," and then leapt to his feet. "What's happening is scandalous! Up until the death of Spencer Curtis, we enjoyed a peaceful, well-ordered and contented existence. As soon as one misguided man – this 'Tujo' – comes along, it all starts to fall apart around us! Violence, illegality, mistrust – all suddenly appear from nowhere. One man shouldn't be allowed to do that."

"That's true, Clement, and we now have the will, and quite possibly the means as well, to do something about it," replied Uri.

"Er...can I make an observation?" asked Stin cautiously.

"Yes, of course," replied Clement.

"A change of approach by the new Archwitan may explain much of what's happened, but it certainly doesn't explain all of it. For example, where did the armed guards come from – and where did they get their weapons? And it doesn't explain the purpose of that massive power conduit either.

"It seems to me that the unreasonableness of Tujo is only one of the issues. There are other elements here that we're only just beginning to uncover, and if they were there all along, then the 'peaceful, well-ordered and contented existence' to which Sir Clement has referred starts to look a little different, doesn't it?"

"Yes – yes, it does," agreed Marius, "and, as Sir Enwick suggested, I think we now need to work together to get to the truth."

"Absolutely right," confirmed Sir Clement in a confident voice. "But first, Uri, you and I will make contact with Romford in Stowly Heath to see what the situation is there. Marius, would you please join us? – we may need you.

"Stin, would it be feasible for you to try to make contact with your former home district on the Cipherslider in the meanwhile? Any further information you can get would be useful.

"In view of the exceptional sequence of events that has led us to this point, I propose that our 'council of war' group should meet later today with the new Worthy Council, to discuss how we might proceed. It's a little unusual, I know, but, in the circumstances, I think it's appropriate. I'll contact everyone in due course, after I've learned the full story of what's happened in Stowly Heath.

"Any questions or problems for the moment?"

Clement had taken on the demeanour of the leader of the Worthy Council, and Uri was impressed and pleased. It was good – and reassuring – to see him operating again at his effective best.

They contacted Sir Romford by IDS, and, having ensured that things were now calm, decided it was appropriate to visit the scene.

When they arrived, they found draftees still clearing up – although some two hours had elapsed since the violence. The dead and injured had already been removed to the Stowly Heath medical facility, and the Local Genworthy and Hayden were talking to a small group of citizens standing nearby.

"Seventeen people have died," confirmed Tester, "the Archworthy and sixteen residents of Stowly Heath. The citizens were all killed outright by hand weapons carried by Blane's guards. Blane appears to have been suffocated in some way."

"Good riddance to him," said one of the by-standers. "His kind belong to ancient history, not to a civilised modern society."

"I suspect that's not an isolated view," thought Uri, but said nothing.

"Sir Romford, could I ask you to walk us around, and tell us in detail what took place here, please?" requested Clement. He then turned to the small crowd and said, in a sombre tone, "Please excuse us. This has been a terrible tragedy, and we must learn as much as we can. It must never, ever, be allowed to happen again."

With that, the three Worthies moved off, and Marius took the opportunity to pull Hayden to one side.

"Who killed Blane?" he asked. "Any idea?"

"Only speculation," replied Hayden in a low voice. "There are plenty of rumours flying around, though. Some say it was one of the guards, but I reckon that, if that were the case, he'd have used a hand weapon. Another suggestion is that it was one of the detainees – Griff Davey perhaps – or maybe Gil Dobbs, Sefton's son – who I know was here. Others are saying that it was probably a family member of one of the citizens who were killed. One thing's for sure, though – I haven't spoken to a single person who regrets the passing of our Archworthy. This community will mourn the deaths of the sixteen for a long time to come, but don't expect even insincere lip-service to the memory of Sir Grindon Blane."

"It almost sounds like there's a general feeling that justice has been done in that respect," commented Marius.

"I think that's true," replied Hayden, "...and I have to say it's pretty close to my own view too."

"How many were injured?" asked Marius.

"Surprisingly, only four," said Hayden. "The theory is that the technology employed by the hand weapons is so efficient that mere injury is unlikely if death is intended. The medical facility staff told me that the injuries were very minor, and resulted from simple things like stumbling and trampling. I know that one of them just tripped over and hit his head."

As they talked, the stark reality of what had occurred came home to Marius, and, at one point, he was almost physically sick. The incident was so alien to the culture in which he'd grown up, that he was simply not prepared for the mental anguish involved in dealing with it. He realised that the same must apply to every single member of the community, and that it would undoubtedly be a long time before they would all be able come to terms with the emotional upheaval of it all. He knew also, however, that this was just one of a series of events only now starting to unfold. Where was it all going to lead them? He became aware of a new fear – an unpleasant nagging in the pit of his stomach. He supposed that things had occurred so fast up to this point that he really hadn't had time to reflect on the full implications of it all. For the first time, he could see, and comprehend now with crystal clarity, that everything – yes, everything – that he held dear – his family, his home, his country – were all under a direct threat.

However, he was also aware that the decisions they'd taken to date were all based on sound reason, and that they would continue to take such a rational approach to whatever occurred.

This new understanding simply served to strengthen his resolve.

By the time Sir Clement and Sir Romford had concluded their tour of the disaster scene, it had started to drizzle.

"We'd better get back to Drayling," said the former, "...or we'll get wet. It's now twenty-five to four, so we can meet at five."

He transmitted the information to the others by IDS, and they then set off together at a steady pace.

They walked in silence for some time – each with his own thoughts – until, eventually, Tester said, "You know, now that Blane's dead, it's vital that the new Worthy Council regains the confidence of the citizens quickly – to start the process of re-establishing stability and normality for the sake of us all in Drayshaw Heath."

"Yes, indeed. I absolutely agree," concurred Burcher.

"...and for that reason," continued Tester, "I have a suggestion to make. I suggest that the Council and – let's call it the 'project team' – be kept separate, to enable each to focus properly on its task, and to give each the best chance of success. You and Sir Uri are involved in both, so would be the essential link between the two, and thus in a position to ensure that all necessary communication and support is maintained."

Clement thought for a moment, and then replied, "Yes, I can see your point, and I think it makes sense. The meeting we're about to have is unofficial, of course, but under the circumstances I don't think it would be unreasonable to raise it. Let's see what the others have to say."

The mood of the assembly was inevitably sombre.

In the event, not only did everyone agree that Sir Romford's proposal made sense, but Della and Sara also took the opportunity to say that 'as things were now formalising', they felt that the project team would probably function better without their direct involvement.

Having said that, however, Della then turned straight to Uri and added, "Obviously, whilst we would prefer not to be directly involved, we'll still expect our husbands to keep us suitably informed."

With that, the two of them got up and left.

As the meeting was informal, no records were kept. Clement said that he proposed to add "some suitable words to tomorrow's daily IDS bulletin" concerning the day's tragic events, and that he would be contacting Regional Administration to inform them officially of what had occurred. He also said that he would call a formal meeting of the Council in the near future.

As the remaining points for discussion were all project team related, Sir Romford Tester and Sir Garth Weldon took their leave.

"Stin, did you manage to get through to your old home district?" asked Clement.

"Yes Sir, I did," replied Stin, "although not without difficulty. I had a problem with the encryption matrix. However, I managed to make contact with a friend whose father is the Local Culturist in Feardleigh-in-the-Vale. He was shocked to receive my communication, but confirmed that things are not running smoothly there either. He said that the Council's introduced new district names, but has refused to ban reference to the old ones. They're apparently still arguing with their Regional Administration about centralisation. Feardleigh-in-the-Vale has become West District, Rother-On-Stay is now South District, and Kilrane's East District. For the overall LGU, they've adopted the same approach as you and incorporated an element of the name of each area entity. They've called it 'Rotherane-in-the-Vale'."

"It'll be interesting to listen to that communication in full later," remarked Uri.

"Unfortunately, that won't be possible, Sir Uri," replied Stin. "The problem with the encryption matrix meant that I had to delete each part of the signal as I sent it. As a result, the computer wasn't able to retain a record. What I must now do is try to sort the problem out before tomorrow's planned contact with Sir Enwick Frawton."

"Yes, indeed," said Sir Clement, "that's very important."

"I think we can now assume that similar things are happening right across the BFF," concluded Hayden. "And that means we can consider involving others in whatever action we decide to take from now on."

"So what are we going to suggest to Frawton tomorrow?" asked Uri.

"I think I'd like some thinking time before answering that question," said Clement. "I'm a little weary. A lot has happened in our LGU today, and we'll all have been emotionally affected by it. We're experiencing things we've never seen before – Hayden, you've had a particularly traumatic day. I think we'd all benefit from a period of rest and reflection."

He paused and took a deep breath.

"However…having said that, we also know that we need to move forward, and that we've undertaken to make further contact with Sir Enwick tomorrow afternoon. I suggest, therefore, that we meet to discuss it further at ten o'clock tomorrow morning."

"You could come to our house," suggested Uri.

"All right – thanks," replied Clement. "Ten o'clock at your house it is."

With that, they all went their separate ways – each dealing with the memories and emotions of a day that none of them would ever forget.

16

When they reassembled at ten o'clock the following morning as arranged, Hayden told them that he'd been really quite ill during the night, but was pleased to say that he was feeling much better now. Both Uri and Clement reported that they'd had very little sleep.

After making himself comfortable in a hospitality chair and selecting a drink, Clement waited for a few moments for the others to settle down, and then called the meeting to order.

"Right, gentlemen, first things first. Stin, have you managed to sort out the problem with the computer?"

"Yes, Sir, I think so," replied Stin. "I'm pretty sure that it was a time-trip device – a security feature in quite common usage at the time Cipherslider was first conceived. Obviously, the acid test'll be when we try to make contact, but I think – I hope – that I've succeeded in disabling it. It's actually quite primitive by today's standards, so I'm fairly confident that there won't be any knock-on problems."

"Good. Well done. Now...we need to agree what we're going to say to Sir Enwick. Whilst I was lying awake last night, I did a lot of thinking, and there are two key points I'd like us to consider. They're both issues we've alluded to previously by implication, but haven't yet put clearly into words. I think the time is now right to come out and say them.

"The first concerns our objective. What should it be? To change the government's approach? To return to Dunstan Heathfield's values? Of course, we'd all like both of those things...but it seems to me that neither is going to happen under this new Archwitan.

"...And, if that's true, then nothing less than the removal of Tujo will achieve our aims.

"Extreme as it may sound, therefore, our number one objective must be to get rid of Tujo."

He quickly raised his hand to prevent any interruption, and continued, "The other point we've hitherto not said out loud is that we have clear grounds for suspecting that the Witan's been lying to us in a number of ways – quite probably for years. Those guards with BFF uniforms – where did they come from? Who trained them? How long has the force existed...and why?

"The power conduit – if it's not for carrying power to communities for normal usage, then what is it for? The Regional Historian clearly lied to you, Uri, when Marius and Hayden were excavating the Northern Agricultural Area.

"So, our second objective must be to get to the bottom of those questions.

"I must say that it comes hard, after so many years of stability and belief in the values espoused by Dunstan Heathfield, to bring myself to say it, but it seems to me that the very thing that DHR relies on – trust – may not be warranted. And, if that proves to be the case, then how many falsehoods have we all been fed?

"Am I fantasising? The mere thoughts are surreal...and I keep telling myself I must be wrong...but then I think again of the hard evidence we already have..."

He paused and sighed.

"But what we must *not* do, friends," – he emphasised the word 'not' – "is ignore the evidence of our own eyes in favour of some emotional desire to cling on to a discredited illusion of comfort.

"For those reasons, I would now like to buy some time. If we're to achieve our objectives, then time is our first need. I therefore propose to report Blane's death to Regional Administration, and tell them that I'm the new Archworthy. I'll then ask for some leeway, in view of recent events, on the reintroduction of the names regulation, and undertake to re-establish it by 31st March next year – in line with the requested centralisations. Given what we're trying to do, other events are likely to have overtaken us before any of that becomes a problem. Also, if they agree, a welcome by-product will be that the citizens of Drayshaw Heath will have a period of relative calm to recover from the horrors of yesterday, and the new Worthy Council will be able to concentrate on doing a proper job of integrating the three districts."

When he stopped speaking, he quite expected someone to respond immediately, but for some time no one said a word.

Eventually, Marius added, "…And then we can agree with Frawton what happens next."

Burcher smiled and nodded.

Soon, a full discussion developed but, significantly, no one expressed fundamental disagreement with any aspect of what Sir Clement had said.

At one point, Marius became aware that his father was unusually quiet, and walked over to him. Uri looked up at him and, with tears in his eyes, bemoaned, "Son, I'm the Local Historian. I've been evangelising on behalf of Dunstan Heathfield for many years. To hear the mantra being openly challenged – and, furthermore, to now be questioning it myself – is…very, very hard. I really don't know what to think. My head's telling me one thing, and my heart something completely different. I do so hope we're doing the right thing."

Marius swallowed, and then smiled. Looking him in the eye, he replied, "We're doing what has to be done, father…and we're doing it together."

Uri gazed at his son, and returned his smile without a trace of humour. He just nodded wordlessly.

"Right then, has anyone got anything else to say before we make contact with Frawton again at four o'clock?" asked Sir Clement.

"Just one further thought," added Stin. "Communicating with identiscreens in other districts is dangerous. Even with encrypted signals, there's a high risk of detection. If we continuously contact the same IDS, I reckon we're significantly increasing that risk. Currently, we're contacting the IDS of the person we first encountered in Frawton – which, as an aside, may well also be causing a security issue for Sir Enwick. If we could ask him to send an agreed message to that IDS from his, or from any other IDS of his choice, then I think I could identify the route back to it. If so, we can then use that one next time. Thereafter, I would suggest that we change to a new one at agreed intervals."

"Good thinking," concurred Sir Clement, "we'll do that…anything else, anyone?" He looked around. "No? OK, we'll meet again at Cipherslider at 3.45pm. Now, I suggest you all go home and relax for a while."

With that, he got up and left.

At 4pm, they called up Frawton as arranged.

"Good afternoon, Sir Enwick, this is Clement Burcher."

"Good afternoon, Sir Clement. If you don't mind, I'd like to start by informing you of developments here. Please confirm."

"Go ahead," replied Clement.

"I've told the Worthies everything that's happened – including your contact and RA's secret approach to form an inner group of three. As a result, there's a unanimous desire to work with you to protect our future. I have with me our two District Archworthies, Sir Wesden Gatt and Sir Greg Boon. Please feel free to speak openly."

"Good afternoon, Sir Wesden and Sir Greg," keyed Clement. "Before we proceed, our expert here has made a security suggestion. Despite encrypting the signals that we send, communicating with identiscreens is risky. To provide greater protection to both of us, we'd like to change the IDS we're in contact with at your end. If you would send an agreed message to that IDS from your own – or another, if you prefer – we can use the message to identify the new receiver. It would be prudent to then make a similar change, from time to time, in future. If you agree, we can do it now. End."

"Understood," said Frawton. "Message will be 'New Friends'. End."

He sent the message, and the change was completed in minutes.

He then continued on his own IDS.

"I propose to go to RA with 'a change of heart'. I'll say that we three shall be our 'inner group', and that we'll centralise all main functions by 31st March 2467 as requested. I'll also say that we propose to bring in the names regulation in due course, but in any event by the same date. I'll express fears that there'll be 'violent reaction' when it's introduced, and ask if they're able to assist with that in any way. Presumably they'll then introduce me to your armed guards. Assuming that's the case, I'll try to find out as much as I can about them. Also, I'll take any opportunity to learn more about Archwitan Tujo. End."

"I too want to buy time," replied Clement. "I'll report to RA that our Archworthy has died, and that I've replaced him. 'In view of events', I'll ask for some leeway on the re-introduction of the names regulation, and – like you – will propose to have introduced both that and full centralisation by the end of March. We've now concluded that our clear objective is the removal of Tujo. We believe that anything less is unlikely to bring the necessary safeguards for the future of our people. Whilst you're seeking information about the armed guards and Tujo, we'll try to explain an underground power conduit which we've discovered crossing our district – which, incidentally, crosses yours also. We believe it's carrying far more power than would be necessary to supply any normal needs, and we've evidence that RA's lied to us about it, which is why we believe it's significant. I suggest we contact you again in one week. Please confirm."

This time, response was not immediate.

"They're probably debating what you've said," observed Uri.

There was no reaction for five or six minutes, which felt like an eternity to the waiting group. Eventually, Frawton's reply came through.

"I apologise for the slight delay. We needed to consider our position in view of what you've said. We'll have further discussions with our other Worthies, of course, but we're prepared to say at this point that we'll work with you, as best we can, to try to bring about the removal of Tujo. We're sad that things have come to this, but agree that there appears to be no other appropriate course of action.

"There's one more thing. We have no means of contacting you. Is there any way we could call you in an emergency? End."

Everyone looked at Stin, who shrugged slightly, pulled a face, and said, "I'm sure IDS to IDS is conceivable, but my immediate reaction is that the risk of detection – and consequent monitoring of the content of the communications – would be so great that we should consider it unacceptable, at least at this stage. Could we say for the moment that we'll look into it?"

"Agreed," said Clement, and keyed, "Unsure of answer to that at present. Will give it thought. Meanwhile, I suggest we contact you in one week – Tuesday, 5th October at 4pm. Please confirm."

"Confirmed. Best wishes. End."

The following day, Clement made his report to Regional Administration, and was mildly surprised to receive a prompt response that his proposals were acceptable.

158

Following the recent events, the general mood in the LGU was a mixture of calm and sorrow, although Della was pleased to report to Uri that a number of people had made a point of asking her to pass on to him that the efforts of the loyal Worthies were very much appreciated, and that they knew they could trust the new Worthy Council.

Clement called a formal meeting of the Council for ten o'clock on the Friday morning, at Drayling Worthy Hall.

At five minutes to ten, Clement walked into the hall to an amazing scene. The area set aside for the public was overflowing with people, and the noise and chatter was deafening. He caught the eye of an orderly. "What's going on?" he mouthed.

"They all want to be here for the first official meeting of the new Worthy Council, Sir Clement. I suppose they want to witness local history being made."

Suddenly, someone shouted, "Sir Clement! Could I have a word, Sir?"

Clement turned abruptly and spotted Sefton Dobbs waving to him from the nearest group of citizens. He walked over to him and smiled.

"Good morning, Sefton, I'm glad to see you appear to have recovered well from your recent ordeal! What on earth is going on?"

"We've come to support you, Sir. Now that we all know the full story an' that, we've realised how lucky we are to have loyal Worthies like you, Sir. We've come to demonstrate to you that we're all behind you. Er...sorry if we've sort of overrun the place – I'm afraid there aren't enough seats for us all."

Clement thought quickly, and turned back to the orderly. "Is the Assembly Hall free?"

"Yes, Sir," was the reply.

"Right."

With that, he walked to the address system, and activated the attention signal.

There was instant quiet.

"Ladies and gentlemen, good morning. You're all very welcome. As there are so many of us here today, our meeting will be in the Assembly Hall next door. If you would kindly walk through and find yourself a seat in there, the meeting will commence in about fifteen minutes."

With that, he turned to the orderly, and asked him to arrange for a simple table and four seats to be placed on the stage for the Worthies.

The other three members of the Council were nearby, and joined him.

"Let's go into the office for a moment," said Clement, and walked through the nearby door. As soon as they were alone, he said, "Sorry to spring that on you. I hope you're all happy to sit on the stage at a simple table. I know it's all a bit primitive, but I think we have an opportunity to give our LGU a welcome boost."

No one demurred.

"It's encouraging to see so much interest," observed Romford Tester.

In view of the situation, Clement opened the meeting with a short impromptu speech.

"Ladies and gentlemen, this is the first formal meeting of Drayshaw Heath's new Worthy Council. I won't pretend that it's a happy occasion, because of the tragic events that have led to it. However, we know we must learn from our experiences, and look to the future. Let's get on with the meeting."

About an hour and a half later, the Council had agreed the following, and had transcreened it in full to every resident:

1.   The new Worthy Council will be based in Drayling Worthy Hall – the move away from Stowly Heath symbolising a new start.

2. *The declared intention of the new Worthy Council is that Drayshaw Heath will return to its previous peaceful and ordered way of life. Positive steps to assist this process will be considered and announced as appropriate.*

3. *A memorial to the citizens who died in the recent tragedy will be erected in Stowly Heath. Sir Romford Tester will be seeking the views of local citizens as to what form it might take, and will make an announcement as soon as possible.*

4. *The forthcoming cricket games will be dedicated to our collective desire to celebrate the integration of our three districts.*

5. *The Council registers its regret that the previous Local Culturist has taken up permanent residence at the medical facility following a severe breakdown. A new Local Culturist will be appointed in due course.*

6. *Any citizen wishing to express a view on any of the matters discussed should contact his/her district representative.*

7. *The new Worthy Council is:*

SIR CLEMENT BURCHER (Archworthy and Acting Local Assessor/Culturist)
SIR URI GRAVES (Local Historian and representative for Drayling)
SIR ROMFORD TESTER (Local Genworthy and representative for Stowly Heath)
SIR GARTH WELDON (Local Provider and representative for Burshaw).

After the meeting, it took a concerted effort to get away. Everyone seemed to want to stay behind to assure the Worthies that they had their trust and support. Clement remarked later that it had seemed 'almost like a ritual exorcism of some collective guilt'. "However," he added, "it's certainly encouraging to know that we have their confidence."

Later that day, when the project team assembled at Uri's house, Clement took immediate control.

"We have a lot to do, and we need to stay focussed on our task. We've agreed that our main objective is to oust Tujo, and the question therefore is – how do we do it?

"We're not likely to be able to achieve it on our own, so we'll need help. If Frawton is anything to go by, we'll not find it difficult to find allies once we've made contact. Our first priority, therefore, is to make those contacts. Once we've established links with a reasonable number, and confirmed that we have their support, we'll be in a much better position to agree a way forward. Stin – is there any reason why we can't make a concerted, constant effort to contact as many areas as possible – concentrating, say, on South Country initially?"

Stin shook his head.

"Right. Good. Uri and Marius, would you please get together and come up with a form of words telling our full story. It'll be better to have a standard script, so that each contact receives precisely the same message. Obviously, we want to know their story also. Whilst we believe they'll have been told all the same stuff as us, we've already discovered that different districts can react in different ways.

"Stin, we've undertaken to investigate the power-route. We believe it's likely to be important, so would you please concentrate your efforts on how we're going to do that…will you need Cipherslider?"

"Um…no, probably not," replied Stin.

"Right. In that case, would you please teach Marius how to use it to make the contacts. That way, we should be able to make progress more quickly."

He then turned to Hayden and, mindful of the truly shocking events that his son had witnessed only a few days previously, said, "Hayden, for the same reason, and not forgetting that we must make progress here in our normal world as well, I'd like you, please, to take responsibility for arranging the next cricket game. I realise it's perhaps not quite so exciting, but it's still important to the people of Drayshaw Heath. I'd like it to take place as soon as possible. Can you see any reason why it shouldn't take place within the next seven days?"

Hayden looked a little disappointed, but responded, "No, no reason at all."

"OK, good," continued his father, "and don't feel you're losing out. There'll be plenty more opportunities to get involved in other stuff later on.

"Uri, you and I are the link between this team and the Council. It's already obvious that responsibilities will overlap. We need to keep our minds clear at all times as to what our priorities are, and what will be of greatest benefit to the people of Drayshaw Heath and, ultimately, to all the citizens of the BFF. It really is that crucial. We therefore need to stay positive and focussed. Please don't hesitate to tell me if I need telling – anything at all."

Uri knew exactly what he meant. He'd known Clement for many years, and their relationship was based on a deep understanding and trust. For his part, he was delighted to see his friend functioning at his effective best – in control, as someone needed to be. He'd be glad to provide the counsel and support that he was asking for.

"Rest assured," smiled Uri.

That evening, on Della's insistance, both Uri and Marius were banned from doing any work relating to either the Worthy Council or the project team. Instead, the whole family sat together, in their favourite chairs, and talked. Inevitably, the conversation turned to the events in Stowly Heath, and to the many other things that had happened to their community both before and since.

The discussion went on into the small hours, which – as Della pointed out to Uri when they finally retired for the night – clearly showed the need that they'd all had to try to make some sense out of the emotional onslaught they were all facing.

"It's good to talk about it as a family," she asserted. "It's good for the family, and it's good for us all as individuals."

Uri looked at her, and knew she was right. "I love you," he said, and kissed her.

"Good night, my love."

17

The next forty-eight hours saw plenty of activity. Marius hammered out some words with his father, and learned from Stin the basics of using Cipherslider to search for contacts. He then keyed the words into the computer – taking great care – so that Drayling's full story could be transmitted, simply and consistently, at the touch of a button.

After helping Marius, Stin retreated to his living accommodation to give his full attention to the proposed power-route investigation, and Hayden, true to his word, arranged for the cricket game between Stowly Heath and Drayling to take place on Thursday next – 7th October. Out of courtesy, he also asked Sir Romford Tester if he'd like to make the public announcement of the event. Tester appreciated the thought, and sent an IDS message to all residents emphasising 'this celebration of the integration of our three districts', and telling them that there would also be a ladies' game 'prior to the gentlemens' performance'. He informed Hayden that, as he was receiving plenty of ideas, he hoped also that he might be in a position, by then, to use the occasion to announce details of the memorial to be erected in Stowly Heath.

By the time Monday arrived, Marius had become more confident on Cipherslider, and had grown accustomed to its constant interventions – usually in the form of a question such as "Shall I make an observation?" or "Would you like me to try that again?"

However, he hadn't yet succeeded in getting through to anyone, and was still taking things slowly – one step at a time – to ensure that he understood what was happening at each stage of the process.

He was therefore somewhat taken aback when the machine suddenly flashed up, "You're clearly seeking to make contact with other districts, and appear to be concentrating on South Country. As you're apparently an inexperienced operator, would you like me to take over?"

His jaw dropped. What should he do now? He was tempted for a split-second to simply throw caution to the wind and key "Yes," but prudence hurriedly intervened, and he decided to seek out Stin and ask for his advice.

Stin laughed out loud when he heard what had happened.

"I told you it was clever! You're in co-operation with the first computer to have an element of cognitive capability. It'll use every scrap of information it has to try to help, by suggesting better ways of doing things that you've attempted more than once, making observational comments,…that sort of thing. Don't be frightened by it, though. It's on your side! I suggest you tell it to go ahead, but re-emphasise the need for encryption, so that it gives security a high priority."

So that was what Marius did.

By two o'clock that afternoon, Cipherslider had made contact with three other districts, and Marius had exchanged stories with a Worthy in each. He reported his successes to Sir Clement, who then formally introduced himself to them and shared views and experiences in greater detail. Unhappiness with the new Archwitan's approach was a common feature of all three, and each of them welcomed the communication and understood the need to make it. In one of the districts, Choperton, there had been actual armed conflict. Soldiers – whom Sir Clement took to be Blane's guards – had clashed with a gang of young male citizens who had managed to acquire some of their hand weapons. Because of their ignorance of the technology involved, however, all of the youths – ten in all – had perished.

Whilst the stories from the various districts differed in the detail, the underlying elements were always the same. For that reason, Sir Clement didn't find it difficult, even in this initial communication, to establish an alliance, at least in spirit, with each of them.

At four o'clock, Clement called up Sir Enwick Frawton as arranged, and informed him of their progress. In his turn, Frawton confirmed that he'd been in contact with Regional Administration, and had, as expected, been offered a company of guards to "see them through any difficulties."

"I told them I'd be in touch," he said. "I also asked for more information about Tujo 'so that I could tell our citizens more about their Archwitan'. I was given short shrift on that one. 'You've been told all you need to know', was all they'd say."

Sir Clement observed that this was in line with everything they'd discovered to date, and promised to get in touch again when there was more to report.

Frawton signed off with "Acknowledged. Look forward to hearing if a way of contacting you can be devised. Regards. EF."

As things were moving so quickly, Clement decided to call a project team meeting for seven o'clock that evening at his home.

As soon as they were all settled into his hospitality chairs, Clement wasted no time.

"Right, Stin. What's the plan for the power-route?"

His brisk tone prompted Stin to jump to his feet.

"Well, as I see it, there's only one way to find out what it's for, and that's to follow it. We already know five things about it. One, it's carrying a massive amount of power. Two, it's therefore extremely dangerous. Three, it's using Cumber Pulse directional technology. Four, the power is flowing in a South-Easterly direction, and five, whatever its purpose is, the Regional Historian felt it was worth lying to Sir Uri about it.

"I've come up with a plan, but I must emphasise that it involves great risk – quite apart from the fact that we'll also be breaking the non-travel laws."

"Yes, the stakes are high," interjected Sir Clement, "but I think we must all now accept that every aspect of what we're trying to do will be hazardous in one way or another. What's your plan?"

Stin accepted with a nod, and swallowed.

"Along the border of each district is a barrier, which takes the form of an invisible, and apparently impenetrable, fence," said Stin. "You may remember, Marius, that I was exploring Burshaw a couple of weeks ago when you contacted me and asked me to your home, to invite me to join the project team. I was actually exploring where the border barrier might be. The technology involved intrigues me. In fact, everything about the barriers intrigues me. Even after so many years of non-travel, you never seem to hear anyone talking about them. Why is that? Presumably everyone here is aware of their existence?"

He looked around.

Sir Uri spoke first.

"I think we all more or less knew there was something," he said, "but it's a subject that is, shall we say, pushed to the back of our minds. I've been asked about alleged 'barriers' on a number of occasions, and in each case I've simply explained that national issues are for the government to concern itself with, not us. We all know that Dunstan's jigsaw has many parts, and that each part is integral to the whole picture."

"No more than a myth then?" said Stin.

Uri shrugged.

"I've made a bit of a study of them," continued Stin, "and you're right – no one seems able to talk authoritatively about them, despite the fact that they've presumably been a feature of every district in the country for over a hundred years. So I asked myself why that might be?

"We know that technological progress allows all sorts of things to be achieved, and it's reasonable to assume that there's been a lot of progress over the years of which we're unaware. What if, for example, the barrier can identify anyone who attempts to cross it – or simply comes into contact with it – by recognising, say, their IDS?...Or what if it's even more sophisticated than that, and can in some way target the brain of the illegal travellers – maybe their memory cells – so that no one can ever remember anything definitive? It's a frightening thought, I know, but I submit we'd be naïve to underestimate what might be possible, and indeed what some powerful people might be prepared to do."

"What are you proposing?" asked Clement, trying to keep the discussion moving forward.

"Well, it seems reasonable to assume that the border barrier must leave a gap underground to allow the power-route through. If that's so, and the gap's wide enough, then there ought to be a way of getting through without being detected. Bearing in mind how close Marius, Hayden and I were able to get to the conduit when we were digging down to it, I think the Cumber technology makes it feasible. Risky, but feasible."

"And the barrier wouldn't identify us?" queried Hayden.

"Not if my assumptions are correct," replied Stin. "We wouldn't be affecting it in any way. We'd pass through the space between it and the power-route.

"I think we should be realistic, though. This whole thing's fraught with danger. Frankly, I think we need to face up to the possibility that, once through, we may never return. The fact is, we don't know what we're going to find. Even what I've said so far is littered with speculation and risk. At every stage, we'll simply be playing the odds. The reality is that it could all very easily go wrong."

Clement cut in. "Look, as I've already said, we all know the stakes are high. We've accepted that what we're embarking upon is hazardous. Of course it is. However, I don't think we're going to help ourselves by constantly reminding ourselves of the fact. Plan carefully, yes, but let's not talk ourselves out of what we know we have to do."

They were all quiet for a few moments, and then Uri said, "Yes, it's hard. The whole thing is hard. But we mustn't let ourselves forget the big picture. This has to be done."

"Good," said Clement. "So let's get to the plan. Who goes, and when? I suggest that Stin, Marius and Hayden should all go. Does anyone disagree?"

Uri, Hayden and Marius shook their heads, and Stin said, "No, that would've been my proposal too."

"Right. When?" said Clement, still pushing.

"I suggest Friday evening," replied Stin. "I think we should cross districts at night to avoid being seen. Even friendly contact with innocent bystanders could potentially lead us into trouble.

"We'll need quite a lot of equipment – digging tools, gloves, food, clothing, personal accommodation kits and so on for, say, two weeks – all of which must be small enough to pass through the gaps once we've identified them. We'll also require a multitron scanner to follow the power-route. I've adapted a directional sensor to fit on to it, which I hope will enable me to locate precisely where the border barriers are, or more particularly, where they're not.

"I've also looked at the question of how we might stay in contact with base once we're through.

"Part of my computer studies related to IDS technology. I reckon that, if we bury an active IDS in the space at the point where we pass through a border barrier, it should still be able to send and receive signals from both sides of the barrier as though it were a local screen. Therefore, if we pass through, say, three barriers, we'd need to leave three screens. In theory, they could then act as relay points for our communications. They'd need to be de-designated so that they couldn't be traced back to their original owners in the event of discovery. Assuming it works, we'd be able to send regular progress reports – all encrypted, of course.

170

"As an aside, and once again provided all my assumptions are correct, this method could also be used by Frawton to communicate with Drayshaw Heath. In that case, just the one relay point would be necessary."

"You've clearly given it a lot of thought," commented Clement. "Does anyone have any observations?"

"It sounds to me like the chanciest part is the risk of being seen as we pass through the other districts," said Hayden. "Whilst there are obvious physical dangers when we're actually in close proximity to the conduit and barriers, we're at least in full control of our own safety at those points. When we're actually following the power-route across open country, we'll need a degree of good fortune – even if we travel at night."

"Yes, I agree," said Stin. "Are we likely to go through any of the districts we've already established contact with?"

"No – not unless the power-route does a U-turn," replied Clement. "They're all to the North or West of us. However, even if it were likely, I'd still say that I think you'd be best advised to assume that every district is potentially hostile. These are early days, and it would only take one unsympathetic individual to blow the whole thing. Does anyone want to make any other comment?"

"I can get the identiscreens," volunteered Uri. "How many do you think we'll need?"

"Well, there are only four or five area entities between here and the coast," said Clement, "and there's a good chance that some of those will now have merged. So, assuming the route continues to run in a generally southerly direction, you shouldn't need more than, say, eight at absolute tops. Don't forget you're going to have to carry everything you take with you."

There was a general murmur of agreement, but as no one had anything meaningful to add, Stin said, "Right, in that case, I suggest that Marius, Hayden and I sit down and make a complete list of what we want to take, and set about putting it all together."

"But not until tomorrow morning," cut in Uri. "It's still only Monday, so you have plenty of time. I know we keep saying it, but we must guard against making hurried decisions for the sake of it. The odd few hours won't adversely affect the potential success of the project, but may well enable our brains to add something useful."

"Agreed," said Clement. "For the moment, let's rest them."

"Fair enough," smiled Stin, "but can I just say that we still need to be aware that there's work to do. If the three of us meet at my living quarters at, say, ten o'clock tomorrow morning, we can agree who's going to do what and start putting it into practice. I then suggest that we go to Burshaw in the afternoon to locate the point at which the route leaves Drayshaw Heath, to test the scanner. On Wednesday, I want to test the IDS relay theory, so I'd appreciate having the screens by then, if that's possible, Sir Uri.

"Thursday is of course cricket day, so presumably we'll all be in Stowly Heath. I don't know if you still need to spend any time on anything related to that before then, Hayden?

"Anyway, I think you'll all agree that there really isn't that much time between now and Friday evening... and, by the way, I'd love to play cricket!"

Everyone laughed, and the atmosphere eased noticeably.

"You do make a fair point," acknowledged Clement thoughtfully, "but the fact is, there's no special reason why your journey has to commence on Friday night. It's far more important to do it right. Let's go ahead as you suggest, and then review the situation on Friday morning."

They continued chatting for nearly two hours before parting – pensive, concerned, but with renewed confidence.

The following morning, Marius and Hayden joined Stin at his living quarters in the Drayling Worthy Hall.

By eleven o'clock, they'd made a list of what they considered to be the necessary items for their expedition, and by two o'clock, almost all were in a pile in the middle of the floor.

"Apart from the screens and the last-minute food items, that's it, isn't it?" said Marius.

"Yes, I think so," agreed Stin.

"This isn't going to be a doddle, is it?" observed Hayden darkly. "There's a whole lot of stuff here. We certainly aren't going to be able to move very quickly."

Stin nodded, but was keen to get on. "Mmm...yes, it'll be a lot to carry. But we've considered every item, and agreed that we need it all, so that's how it's going to be.

"OK? Right. Let's go and make sure the scanner works."

It was one of those beautiful sunny days when everything feels right with the world, and the three friends were soon in good spirits as they strolled southwards together.

"Assuming the power-route continues on a roughly straight course, it should cut across the corner of Burshaw's Southern Agricultural Area," reasoned Stin.

"...And there must be a good chance that most of the route'll be across agricultural land," replied Marius. "If it was laid after Heathfield's Revolution, they'd almost certainly have avoided the areas of greatest settlement."

"Yes, that may well be true," said Stin, "and that would make it safer for us."

Marius nodded as Hayden stopped suddenly, raised his hand and whispered, "Just listen to the birds and insects! Doesn't that sound just put everything back into some kind of sensible perspective? At least some of the residents of Drayshaw Heath don't seem to have a care in the world! And look at those swallows – their aerial dance is truly something to behold."

"I'm not sure if you're aware, Stin," explained Marius with mock solemnity, "that our Mister Burcher is a wildlife enthusiast."

"Mmm. Yes, it's true. I am…but I make no apology. Nature really is a thing of beauty," he cooed. "It just keeps on and on evolving. I mean, just look at that! Amazing patterns being drawn in the sky!"

He pointed at the expert flyers as they fed on the wing all around them.

"And they need to be jolly careful," commented Stin, "because they're getting extremely close to the barrier."

His remark changed the mood in an instant.

Marius looked around. They were in the middle of a large field. He'd always assumed that the edge of a district would be in dense woodland, or at least appear impenetrable in some natural way.

He looked at Stin, who was holding the multitron scanner in front of him and moving it from side to side.

"I reckon we're about thirty yards from the barrier," he announced.

"But that doesn't seem right," queried Hayden. "How can it be, if we're standing in the middle of a field that has obviously been cared for in a consistent way, right the way across?"

"I don't pretend to know the answer to that," replied Stin, "but what I do know is that there are a lot of things we don't know, so why shouldn't this be one of them?"

"Maybe it's a subject for another time," said Marius. "I think, when I've got time, I'll speak to the Local Provider. He has to be involved in some way."

"And that suggests all sorts of interesting thoughts like brain-washing," observed Hayden.

"Come on chaps. All very intriguing, but let's stick with the job in hand," urged Stin. "We're definitely close to the barrier."

"In that case, let's talk about the wildlife," said Hayden.

"What?" snapped Stin.

"No, bear with me. Do you see that slightly worn line going across from left to right in front of us, and then curving around to the left?"

Stin and Marius nodded.

"That's a spoor – a track habitually used by wild animals."

"I'm ahead of you," cut in Stin. "I see what you're saying. Just give me a moment to identify the exact course of the power-route."

A couple of minutes later he chuckled, "That short straight part of the spoor follows the power-route precisely."

Marius put their thoughts into words. "Which means that, at least sometimes, there's a route through the barrier…above ground."

"And it's there now!" exclaimed Hayden. "…And it's a fair size! Look at those birds!"

They stood in awe as, every few seconds, a swallow would swoop down, follow the spoor for a few yards, and then soar aloft again.

"Yahoo!" he whooped. "Evolution in action!"

Marius was more cautious. "Are you absolutely sure that that's the precise point that the conduit goes through the border barrier?"

"Yes, but I'll check it again," replied Stin.

He edged closer, and reactivated the sensor.

"The gap above ground is roughly semi-circular. It's about three feet wide, and just a little over two feet high – easily large enough for us to get ourselves, and our gear, through. I estimate that the barrier's about six feet thick."

"But how do we know there'll be a gap like that at every barrier? And how can we be sure it's permanent?" queried Marius.

Stin thought for a moment, and then replied, "Well, it's true we can't be a hundred per cent certain, but I reckon it's reasonable to assume that the same conditions will apply at each crossing."

"Yes, I do too," said Hayden, "…and if we can all agree on that, we can significantly lighten our load by not taking most of the digging equipment. We'll need one tool for burying an identiscreen at each crossing point, though."

Marius accepted the point. "OK, sounds good to me," he said. "Is that it, then?"

The other two nodded.

They walked back to Drayling, well pleased with their afternoon's work.

That evening, Uri gave Marius eight unattributed identiscreens, and asked how the sensor check had gone.

He marvelled when he heard how wild animals and birds had led them to discover the gap above ground, and was fascinated too by the thought that the border barrier could cross apparently open ground.

"I really wonder how that can be," he said. "As Local Historian, I've always taken the view that I have a loyal responsibility to encourage disinterest – a kind of 'healthy ignorance' of such matters. Yet now that we've begun to ask questions, I'm forced to conclude that we may be about to discover something quite, quite incredible."

Marius could see that he was still struggling with his emotions.

"Father, we've already agreed that our trust has almost certainly been misplaced. What we're doing here is all part of trying to change things for the better."

He smiled at his father, and Uri grinned back sheepishly.

"Sorry, Marius. You're right, of course. Too many years of blind compliance, I suppose."

Marius nodded his understanding, put his hand on his shoulder, and said, "Thanks for the screens. We'll test them tomorrow."

With that, he went to bed.

"To test the theory properly, I propose we do it in three parts," said Stin the following morning. "Firstly, here in my living quarters, send a simple message through a chain of screens to confirm that the basic principle's correct. Secondly, assuming the initial test's successful, go to the Northern Agricultural Area, and do it again over, say, four hundred yards – but this time burying the intermediate screens.

Then – assuming that's successful – repeat it yet again, but this time right across the district. By introducing a new feature each time, we'll have the best chance of isolating any problems as we go along."

"Sounds good to me," said Marius.

"Yes, sounds fine to me too," agreed Hayden, "but, as you rightly pointed out the other evening, Stin, I really must disappear at some point to ensure that the preparations for the cricket tomorrow are all on track. It sounds daft, I know, bearing in mind the importance of what we're doing here – and I must admit I did consider ducking out and getting someone else to look after the cricket – but, well, having been specifically detailed by the Archworthy, who also happens to be my father, I thought maybe it would be sensible to be seen to be doing as I was told!"

Stin grinned. "I think you're absolutely right. I reckon we should be able to complete the first two stages by early afternoon. Would that be early enough for you to go and sort out the cricket? Marius and I could ask your fathers to help with the third test – they may well like to see it for themselves anyway – and if you think you need to leave before we've completed the first two tests, don't worry. As Sir Clement said, the timing isn't really critical at the end of the day – it's far more important that we do the job properly."

With that, they got down to the first test. They placed three of the unattributed screens in three corners of the room, and then Stin input the words 'Test One' into his own IDS.

"Screen three is pre-set to receive from screen two and to send on to your IDS, Marius. Two is set to receive from one, and send to three, and so on. All I'm doing is sending a message to screen one in the usual way."

"It works!" whooped Marius as the message appeared on his screen.

"Well done, Stin!" applauded Hayden.

Stin just grinned. "Phase One completed – let's do phase two."

They wasted no time. Taking two digging tools and four screens, they set off for the Northern Agricultural Area.

When they arrived, Marius was pensive. "It feels sort of appropriate that we're doing this in the place that we first discovered the power-line, doesn't it? Although we didn't know what it was then, of course."

"They didn't make you a 'Thinker' for nothing, did they?" observed Hayden, "...but you're absolutely right – there's a kind of symmetry to it, isn't there?"

"When you two have finished philosophising, we'll do the test," said Stin. "Hayden, would you please take this screen about four hundred yards in that direction and conceal it just underneath the turf. Remember, the ground must appear to be undisturbed."

He pointed.

"Marius, you take this one and do the same over there. Give me a wave when you're ready, and please keep your ears open. I also want to check that they can't be heard."

They walked off at an angle of approximately ninety degrees to each other, each with an IDS and a digging tool.

The ground was relatively soft, but it still took Marius a few attempts before he'd deduced the best way to remove and replace the turf. Once he'd buried the screen, he waved at Stin, and looked across at Hayden, who was waving also.

Stin keyed the words 'Test two' into his screen, and the same words appeared immediately on his other screen.

He punched the sky, and exclaimed, "Message received! Did you hear anything?"

Both Marius and Hayden shook their heads.

"Excellent! Please leave your screens, and come back here."

As they walked back towards him, Stin sidled a few yards from where he'd been standing, in an attempt to disorientate them.

When they were standing together, he asked them to find each other's screen.

In fact, it didn't take very long – mainly because Hayden and Marius' initial attempts at turfing hadn't been particularly successful. However, they both agreed that they wouldn't have noticed the place in which the screen had finally been hidden if they hadn't had the benefit of the adjacent disturbed area – and the knowledge that the screen was there in the first place.

All-in-all, then, a very successful test.

As it was now past noon, Hayden left them to attend to his cricketing responsibilities, and Marius and Stin sought out Uri at home. They found him relaxing in his favourite chair, chatting to Sir Clement.

"Ah, there you are," he said as they entered, "we wondered where you were. Where do you want us?"

Marius hesitated momentarily and then laughed.

"You've obviously already realised that we're here to ask if you'd like to help us with the screen testing," he said.

"Indeed we would," interjected Clement, "and we've planned our day accordingly. How did it go this morning?"

Stin outlined to them the pleasing results of the two tests so far, and explained what he wanted to do next.

"We now know that the basic premise works, so we're ready to introduce distance into the equation," he said. "What I'd like to do is bury two screens in Stowly Heath and one in Burshaw, and use here as the base – if that's OK, Sir Uri."

"Yes, that's fine," replied Uri, "and as there's three of us, we can each take a screen."

"Well, actually, I think it would be better if one of you – either you or Sir Clement – stayed here with me," ventured Stin. "When Marius, Hayden and I embark on the expedition itself, you'll be at this end. If we can simulate the real thing as closely as possible now, we stand the best chance of getting the most out of it."

"Or, to put it another way, one of you two old timers is going to have to learn what to do, and you may take some time to catch on, so let's start that process as soon as possible," chuckled Clement.

"Oh, no, I…"

"Don't worry, Stin. I think you're absolutely right…and I applaud your clear thinking. Uri, I suggest you remain here. I'm meeting Sir Romford in Stowly Heath later on today anyway, so perhaps I could take a screen there."

"I'll go to Burshaw then," said Marius. "I can bury two there. Presumably it won't compromise the test to have two in Burshaw and one in Stowly Heath, rather than the other way round?"

"No, that's fine," agreed Stin, "and we can stay in contact in the usual way with our own identiscreens, so that we all know what's going on."

They then agreed rough locations for the test, and, just under two hours later, Clement had buried his screen near the cricket field in Stowly Heath, and Marius had hidden one near the barrier in Burshaw's Southern Agricultural Area, and the other just under a mile away on the edge of the Public Gardens and Recreational Facility.

As soon as he'd received confirmation that the three screens were in place, Stin sent messages to Marius and Sir Clement on their personal IDS saying simply 'testing now', and then keyed 'Test Three' into screen one. He and Uri turned to see the same words appear on screen five.

But they didn't.

Stin frowned. "Now why's that?" he murmured to himself.

Uri said nothing.

Stin thought for a moment, and then sent a further message to Marius and Clement. "First attempt failed. Trying again." He then re-keyed 'Test 3 / Attempt 2'.

Still nothing appeared on screen five.

"Shall I tell the others what's happening whilst you concentrate on the test?" asked Uri.

"Yes...yes...please," replied Stin in a voice which reflected that he was already trawling his brain for a reason for the failure of the test. "Er...and could you ask them to check that the three screens are still active please...umm ...and I guess apologise to Marius especially...it's a good thing he's fit."

Uri contacted Clement and Marius whilst Stin reapplied himself to the problem.

He stared into space as he sifted the various stages of the tests through his mind. "We know the principle works – the first two tests have shown that...we know that burying the screens isn't a problem...why, as soon as we increase the size of the circle, should the test fail?"

"Marius wants a verbal word," said Uri, turning up the volume on his IDS.

Marius' voice came through clearly. It was obvious from his uneven breathing that he was walking as he talked. "What's powering these screens, Stin?" he asked. "How does an IDS work if it isn't designated to one particular person? My understanding is that identiscreens work by proximetry – by recognising and drawing from their owner's innate ambium – and that's one of the reasons why we must always be within fifty yards of our IDS. Is that not correct? What happens in this case?"

Stin's face lit up.

"Yes! Well done, Marius! I think you may well be right!"

He paused for a moment to think, and then continued, "In fact, because these screens are unattributed, they should work – as you say, by proximetry – provided *any* person is within their sensor range. They're not dependent on any one individual. Theoretically at least, they ought to be able to utilise any innate ambium, provided it's within range. However, if there's nobody at all within whatever the exact distance is – and it's obviously more than fifty yards – then you're right – they couldn't work. It's probably the screen that's up in the Agricultural Area that's the culprit. I should've thought of that."

He paused again, and said, "Is Sir Clement also listening?"

Uri confirmed that he was, so he went on, "We've proved the value of logical and meticulous testing, but we've identified a problem. We can't guarantee there'll always be someone within proximetry range of the screens we hide. There are some obvious options. We could go ahead and trust to luck – sometimes the screens would work and sometimes they wouldn't. We could consider trying to ensure that we bury them in places that are always likely to be close to people, but that would involve increased risk."

Sir Clement's voice cut in from the IDS that Uri was holding. "Well done with the testing, Stin. As you say, we've discovered a problem – which is, of course, precisely what testing is for. Now, I suggest we need time to reflect. We've already agreed to meet and take stock on Friday morning, so we can leave it there for the moment. The cricket game here in Stowly Heath is all set for tomorrow. Let's take the time to enjoy that. Hayden's standing beside me, and he tells me that Marius and Stin are two of his star players, so we can discuss their performances on Friday morning as well! Meanwhile, have a good evening, and we'll see you tomorrow."

With that, he signed off. Marius, Uri and Stin chatted briefly, and then Stin went home.

About three hours later, at around seven o'clock, as he was lazing in his chair, Marius was summoned by his IDS.

"I've done it! The screens work! I've made them work!" screamed a jubilant Stin. "I had a sudden flash of inspiration – and it works!"

"Whoa…steady there…slow down," cried Marius. "You've made the screens work? How?"

"Yes! There's a thing called 'capillimetry', which I read about in a completely different context some time ago. It's a phenomenon which sometimes arises when two computers are in contact with each other. If one happens to be significantly more powerful than the other, there can be a sort of 'uneven distribution of responsibility' – a kind of sharing of the work in proportion to the capabilities of each. Because of its significant superiority in terms of capability, the stronger of the two can take more than its share of the load – do more than half of the work, if you like – so that the transaction, whatever it happens to be, has a better chance of success. Well, I started to think about Cipherslider. We know it's extremely powerful. Now, obviously, it only utilises minimal energy when performing most of its functions, just like any other machine, but I wondered what would happen if I asked it specifically to concentrate more of its capability – its power – when put in contact with an unattributed IDS – or three or four or more. So I tried it, and…tarra! It works!…er…with one minor reservation, that is."

"Reservation?" queried Marius.

"At this moment, I can't be one hundred per cent sure that there isn't at least one person within range of each of our three buried screens – although it isn't likely. Therefore, I'll test it again in the small hours just to be sure. But I'm pretty sure they're working by capillimetry and not proximetry. One point to bear in mind, though – for the chain to work by proximetry, there would need to be someone within range of every screen. If any one of them goes out of range, then the whole chain would have to be powered by capillimetry, and that means *all* of the power would have to come from Cipherslider.

"Because the key factor is always the difference in power between each unit and its immediate neighbour, it means that every time an additional IDS is added to the chain, a reduced amount of energy would be available to it. The strength becomes more and more diluted as the chain gets longer.

"Sir Clement suggested we take a maximum of eight screens with us, so I'll test that many tomorrow. I'm pretty confident it'll work though – Cipherslider is a mighty beast."

"Sounds good," said Marius. "I'll come over early and help you. In the meantime, don't forget we're playing cricket tomorrow – so don't miss too much sleep!"

"I won't," chuckled Stin. "It's important we show those Stowlies a thing or two!"

"Absolutely," agreed Marius. "See you tomorrow. Good night."

Before Marius had finished his breakfast the following morning, Stin had called him up.

"Good morning, Marius – I've done it, and it works fine!"

Marius finished chewing a mouthful of food, swallowed, and replied, "That's good news. So we now know that your…er…capillimetry?…theory works. Shall I come over to help with the eight-screen test?"

"No, no need. I've done that too," said Stin. "There didn't seem a lot of point in stopping. I re-ran the first check at around 3.00am, and it worked fine. Having confirmed that the chain was working by capillimetry, I carried on. As I'm already in the Worthy Hall, and therefore have plenty of space, I put another five screens in various places around the building, linked them with the other three, and then sent the message 'Chain Reaction'…and that's exactly what I got.

"Interestingly, there was a delay of about four seconds, but I'm sure we can live with that! Also, of course, only three of the screens were actually buried, but I don't believe that's significant either."

"Great stuff, Stin! Brilliant work! Your knowledge of computers is proving really useful…I assume you haven't told the others yet?"

"No, I'll do that now – and I'll see you at the cricket."

"OK. See you there."

18

That afternoon, as expected, almost everyone in the LGU was in Stowly Heath. At 2.00pm on the dot, Sir Romford Tester stood up and activated the attention signal on his IDS. There was a sudden hush, and every face turned towards him.

"Citizens of Drayshaw Heath," he began in a clear and practised tone, "...following the success of our previous cricket occasions, you'll already be aware that, starting next summer, there will be an annual series of six games, featuring teams representing each of our three districts.

"This year, by way of an introduction, there are to be three cricket days. Today is the first, and, as you know, it's been dedicated to the celebration of our newly-integrated LGU. I urge you all to take this ideal opportunity to make new friends, and to exchange memories and experiences with your new neighbours.

"In actual fact, our event today will consist of two games. The first will be a ladies' game, which I'll tell you more about in a moment, and that will be followed by a gentlemens' match between Stowly Heath and Drayling."

He then stopped speaking for some seconds – and sighed. He looked at the ground in front of him, and then around at the faces of those listening to him.

"Firstly, however, I wish to take this opportunity to address a much more serious matter.

"Following the recent appalling events in Stowly Heath, and after consultation with local residents, it's been decided that a tree will be planted on the spot where sixteen of our young men were murdered.

"It will be known as 'The Sixteen Tree', and will act as a living memorial to those who fell – and also as a symbol of a new and better future for their families, their friends and for all the residents of Drayshaw Heath. There'll be a planting ceremony in a few days' time, and details of that will be provided shortly."

He turned and had a brief whispered conversation with Hayden Burcher before continuing.

"Right. To start proceedings, there'll now be a ladies' cricket game. Apparently, it was originally intended that the two teams would be 'the under 25s' and 'the over 25s' – but I'm told that some of the players were a little reticent about which team they ought to be playing in, so it's been decided to call them 'Della's team' and 'Urania's team'!"

There was a ripple of laughter around the audience, and then suitable applause.

The ladies' game took a while to get going, with the umpires constantly adapting the rules – and sometimes ignoring them altogether – in an effort to keep the game moving. The standard of play was, perhaps unsurprisingly for this first attempt, not high. However, the mood was light, and the players thoroughly enjoyed themselves.

"It's nice to hear people laughing and joking, after all that's happened," observed Marius to Hayden, "it must be a welcome change for some."

Hayden nodded. "Yes, indeed, and very difficult for others, I expect. I must say, I like the idea of a memorial tree…and the name's clever too – it neatly excludes Grindon Blane."

"So it does," responded Marius, and changed the subject.

"Look, there's Caleb Mob. He's playing today, isn't he? Let's go and say hello."

They wandered over to a small group of people who were half talking and half watching the cricket.

"Hi, Caleb," said Marius. "Good to see you. Are you fit and ready for the fray?"

"Hello, Marius...Hayden..." replied Caleb. "Yes, I'm fine – and raring to go – thanks." He turned and inclined his head towards the man standing next to him. "Do you know my father? Dad, this is Marius Graves...and Hayden Burcher."

"Hello, Marius...Hayden," responded the older man, and held out his hand. "Brace Mob. Yes, I know who you are, although we've probably not spoken before. I understand you know this gentleman, though." He referred to a man standing a couple of yards away. It was Norton Greatley.

"Ah, yes, we do," said Hayden. "Hello, Norton. Are you a friend of Brace and Caleb?"

"Well, no...or, at least, we haven't met before today," replied Greatley, "...but we're taking the opportunity – as Sir Romford's suggested – to get acquainted. Caleb tells me he helped with your archaeological dig back in May."

"Yes, that's right," said Hayden, "...and it turned out to be the origin of the cricket idea. Actually, we wouldn't be here today without Marius' inspiration...and the hard work they all put in. How are your hands, Caleb?"

Caleb laughed. "They're just about OK now, thanks, but I must say they were a bit raw at the time!"

"Yes, he did suffer a bit," said Brace, "but it's a source of great pride for me that he was able to be a part of it. And now, as Norton says, we're all getting to know each other. We haven't been talking for very long, but it's already pretty clear that, even though our two districts have only just been merged, there are great similarities between us, both in terms of our approach to life and also in things that have happened to us. For example, Norton says that two Burshaw lads who were seconded to the Channel Dredging Project were tragically killed in an unfortunate accident. Well, as you know, two of our Drayling boys were killed as well – probably in the same incident."

At that point, a man standing not far away interrupted. "I'm sorry to be rude," he said, "...but I couldn't help overhearing what you were saying. I live here in Stowly Heath. We lost two of our young men in that tragedy too — about eighteen months ago it was."

"Oh, it can't have been the same accident, then," said Brace. The Drayling boys were killed, oh, it must be all of three years ago now."

"No, it wasn't anywhere near as long ago as that," declared Norton emphatically. "Certainly no more than a year."

Marius was immediately intrigued by what was being said, but decided for the moment to try to guide the conversation back to the events of the day.

"The ladies' game seems to be coming to an end," he observed. "Does anyone know the score?"

"Well, judging by the grin on Urania's face, I'd say her team must have won," chuckled Caleb.

And, indeed, Urania's team had won — by 42 runs to 31 — and all the players were now in an informal group, shaking hands and chattering excitedly.

Hayden returned to his responsibilities. "Right, that means we need to get the gentlemen together for their game now. Excuse us please Norton...Brace...good to talk to you. Enjoy the rest of the day. Come on Caleb...Marius...we've got important work to do." So saying, he walked over to Griff Davey, the captain of the Stowly Heath team, who was standing about thirty yards away.

"Is your team ready for its drubbing, Griff?" he chirped.

Davey gave a half-smile, and said, "Yes, we're ready, Hayden. Although I have to confess I'm finding all this a bit hard. I can't speak for the others, but — well, you see, five of the sixteen who died were in our team last time. Today, we've decided to replace each one with a member of his immediate family — and, in at least one case, that's with no expectation of any kind of cricketing ability at all. They're playing out of respect. I don't think you're going to find us too difficult."

Hayden swallowed. "Oh, I'm sorry, Griff. I wasn't aware of that."

"No, no, you weren't to know," replied Davey, and patted him on the arm. "C'mon let's get the game started."

As captains, they walked out towards the centre of the field to toss a specially-made metal disc to see who had the choice of batting or bowling first. As soon as they were out of earshot of everyone else, Griff said, "Look, Hayden, I hope you don't mind, but, as there's an obvious imbalance between our two teams today, can I suggest that we pretend to toss the disc, but agree now, before we do, that Drayling'll bat first? If Stowly bats first, the likelihood is we'll be bowled out very quickly. Then you'll hit off the runs, and the game'll be over. It would be better for everyone if we can stretch the day out a little."

Hayden could see that Griff's proposal made sense, and agreed. The game had suddenly taken on a completely different complexion, and he wasn't sure now that he wanted Drayling to win it.

It was, of course, only a game and it didn't really matter who won – they'd always emphasised that enjoyment was the prime reason for playing – but when you're out there, well, you do have to be competitive, out of respect for your opponents, if nothing else.

In the event, the game panned out much as Griff had said it would. Drayling were much the superior side, and made over 150 runs in their sixteen overs. After eight overs of their innings, Stowly Heath were 29 for seven, and the game was drifting towards the inevitable victory for Drayling.

It was then that fate took a hand. One of the less able of Stowly Heath's players let go of his bat when attempting a hoik to leg, and it hit Stin on the side of the head. He dropped to the ground, and lay motionless. Members of the medical team – already in attendance because of their responsibility to be wherever their presence was most likely to be needed – ran straight onto the field.

Having established, within seconds, that he was unconscious, but still alive, they had him transferred with all speed to the Stowly Heath medical facility.

The game was, of course, abandoned immediately by unanimous consent, and the unfortunate batsman – in a state of some distress – was treated for shock.

Della, Urania and Marius went directly to the medical facility, and Clement, Romford, Hayden and Uri followed as soon as all the other citizens had dispersed.

They waited anxiously for news.

"How is he, Romford?" asked Clement when, at long last, the former finally emerged from the treatment room.

"Critical," replied Tester. "He's in a deep coma, so we're going to use the Gushlaam Technique. We'll hold him under for the necessary time – and right now that looks like days – and then bring him out at the key moment. Don't worry, though – we'll save him."

His words came as a great relief to them all, and Clement noted particularly also that he'd said, *"We'll* save him," and not *"They'll* save him." It showed that the Local Genworthy took his responsibilities seriously, and fully accepted them.

Turning to the others, Clement said, "Well, we now know, thankfully, that Stin's going to be OK, that he's being well looked after, and that he's going to take a few days to recover.

"Despite that, I think we should go ahead with our project team meeting tomorrow morning, as planned, and I suggest we hold it at our house. See you at about 10am"

The following morning, after breakfast, Marius and Uri relaxed in their favourite chairs and chatted.

"Sir Romford tells me that Stin's been a very lucky boy," said Uri. "He said that if the bat had hit him an inch or so to the left, he may well have been killed outright. As it is, despite the fact that he's still in a deep coma, they're confident he'll be fine in a couple of days. Apparently, this Gushlaam procedure is now such a precise science that they can tell, even at this early stage, what the outcome should be – always barring the unforeseen, of course."

"That's good," replied Marius. "I must say, I was more than a little worried there for a while. We're lucky to have such good medical facilities available to us."

"Yes, that's certainly true," agreed Uri, "...yes, indeed..."

They each took a sip of their drink and, for a few seconds, neither spoke.

Then Marius, in an altogether different and much more enquiring tone, said, "Father...presumably you can remember people being sent away from Drayling for various reasons in the past...can't you?"

Uri looked at him. He wasn't unduly surprised at the sudden change of subject. Over the years, he'd become accustomed to his son's searching questions – always considered, and frequently unannounced.

"Yes, there've been a few."

"How many can you remember?" enquired Marius.

"Oh, three or four, I suppose."

"Can you remember when and why?"

"Well, the most recent would've been the two young lads who were seconded to the Channel Dredging Project. Sadly, they were killed in an accident."

"When would that have been?" asked Marius.

"Oh, about three, maybe three and a half, years ago now, I suppose."

"Yes, that's what Brace said. He was talking to Norton Greatley and a man from Stowly Heath yesterday. There's something strange about this. Each remembered two young men being sent on the dredging project relatively recently. In all three cases, they were reported killed in an accident, yet the timing of the accident seems to be significantly different in each case. You've confirmed Brace's recollection of the date. Norton says the Burshaw lads' accident was no more than a year ago, and the Stowly Heath man said their accident was about eighteen months ago. I think that suggests that they couldn't all have been the same incident. Now, if that's true, then either there've been a lot of accidents at the dredging project, or we've been lied to – again. And if the latter's indeed the case, then it may well be that these young men weren't killed at all – at least, not in a dredging accident."

"Whoa, slow down," protested Uri, who was being taken along at a pace that was a little too fast for him. "There are a lot of ifs and maybes in there."

"Yes, there are, but you have to admit that, in the climate we now find ourselves in, it starts to make you wonder. It all fits, doesn't it? We're already asking ourselves where those armed guards came from…and it certainly wasn't thin air. OK…what others can you remember?"

Uri was getting uncomfortable now, but he couldn't challenge his son's logic.

"I can remember the Clarification Facility having to send a boy and girl away a few years ago for breaching the illiteracy laws. They had to go to a district which had special facilities to deal with them."

"Did their families expect them to return?" enquired Marius.

"Yes, eventually I think – but, in the event, they received IDS messages from them saying they were getting on very well, and had decided to stay and make their life in their new district. It was a very pleasing thing to hear, although not without regrets for their families, I suppose."

"So, again, we're being told something which may, or may not, be true," pointed out Marius.

"I'm beginning to see a very different, and increasingly cynical, side to you," observed Uri.

"You have to admit that an awful lot of what we've built our lives around is based on trust," said Marius. "We keep coming back to that word – trust. You…especially you…feel understandable discomfort over the uncertainty which now surrounds Dunstan Heathfield's Revolution, but the fact remains that recent events hardly give us grounds to trust that everything we've been told is the truth."

Uri had to accept that what he said made sense. Marius, though conscious that he didn't want to push his father too far, had one more question.

"Can you ever remember *anyone* returning to Drayling after going away, irrespective of the reason?"

Uri had to admit that he could not.

At ten o'clock, the project team, minus Stin, assembled as arranged.

Clement opened by saying that he'd spoken to Sir Romford, and that all was well with Stin. Although still in a controlled coma, he'd be brought out of it on Sunday morning, with no lasting ill effects.

As a result, they quickly agreed that the power-route expedition should be put on hold pending his recovery.

He then asked if there were any other items for discussion.

"Yes, I have a couple of items," said Marius. "Easy one first...the three screens we buried have done their job now, so we ought to retrieve them. I'll go for a walk when we finish here."

"I'll join you," said Hayden.

"In that case, I suggest you two go to Burshaw. I'm going over to see Sir Romford later on, so I can pick up the one in Stowly Heath," said Clement. "What was your second point?"

Marius told them of his conversation with his father earlier that morning, and related, in detail, what he'd heard at the cricket.

"I accept that it's all hearsay, and based on people's memories," he explained, "but it all seems too...well... tidy...to me. People get sent away – for a variety of reasons –

but, apparently, no one ever comes back. Can you remember anyone returning to Drayling, Sir Clement?"

Clement looked at Uri, who shrugged, and shook his head.

Clement accepted that he couldn't either, but made the point – as Uri had done – that, in all cases, valid reasons had been given to explain the non-return. In fact, he was able to recall a further case of illiteracy that he'd been involved in, which had had a similar outcome to the one that Uri had mentioned.

"So no one has ever returned, and the 'reasons' all have to be taken on trust," repeated Marius.

"I'm not aware of any evidence to support a suggestion that the reasons given were anything other than genuine," declared Clement, in a tone which suggested he did not wish to discuss the matter further.

Realising that his friend was becoming a little irritated, Uri decided to step in.

"I think we have to accept that there's a lot of smoke, even if we can't, at this point, prove that there's a fire," he said. "Given everything else that we've discovered – or have come to believe – I don't think it's unreasonable to view the issue with at least some degree of scepticism."

He looked enquiringly at Clement, who conceded with a nod but said nothing.

So Uri continued. "I suggest we make use of our new friends in the other districts. If nothing else, it gives us a reason to recontact them with something to talk about. Let's see what they can remember."

"Yes, that makes sense," acknowledged Clement, "…and we do have some time whilst Stin's recovering. Why don't we all go over to the Worthy Hall now? Marius, you've learned how to operate Cipherslider, so this is probably a good opportunity for you to help your father and me get used to it too. As Stin said…we're the ones who'll have to work it when you're off on your expedition."

"Yes Sir," smiled Marius. "We'll go for our walk after that then."

On their way to the Worthy Hall, Marius and Hayden walked on ahead of their fathers and discussed, amongst other things, their perceptions of the dangers involved in their forthcoming expedition. Clement, meanwhile, was taking the opportunity to admit to Uri that he had indeed become a little fractious during their meeting.

"It's not that Marius wasn't right to make the point, Uri. His observations are valid – or, at least, the questions are worth asking. It's just that...well...I suppose I feel sort of guilty. I mean...if it's logical to ask the questions now, why wasn't it logical for educated adults such as ourselves to ask them years ago? The only thing that's changed is that we now wonder if the things we've been told are the truth. If they're not, then how can we have been so gullible?"

"It's the same for all of us, old friend," said Uri. "Bear in mind that, whether they're true or not, we've lived very happy and contented lives up to now, and whatever happens in the future, the memory of all that can't be taken away, can it?"

Clement shuddered, not for the first time, at the enormity of what was happening to them.

When they arrived at the Worthy Hall, they went straight to Cipherslider.

"I suggest you start by calling up one of our recent contacts, Marius, and talk your father and me through what you're doing as you do it," said Clement. "Come on, Uri, learning caps on now."

Marius did as he was bade, and was soon through to the Choperton Worthy he'd been in touch with four days previously.

"Hello, Drayling. Good to hear from you again," responded the Worthy. "You've picked a good time. May I please take this opportunity to introduce you to our Archworthy, Sir Clifton Easford, who's here with me?"

"Sir Clement Burcher is also with me. Wait please."

Clement took over from Marius, and keyed "Good morning, Sir Clifton. I'm pleased to make your acquaintance. As we said to your colleague a few days ago, these are truly changing, and challenging, times. Our reason for contacting you again today is that we'd like to continue to compare Choperton's story with ours. We established on Monday that your recent experiences have been very similar to our own – even down to the tragic deaths of some of our young people. Are you happy for me to ask you some more questions? Over to you."

"I'm delighted to talk to you, Sir Clement. I believe that friendship and cooperation between us can only be helpful in these difficult times. Please ask your questions. Back to you."

"Thank you. Over the years, a number of citizens have been sent away from Drayling for various reasons. These reasons include, for example, breach of the illiteracy laws and secondment to the Channel Dredging Project. Can you confirm that Choperton has had similar? How many can you remember? Are there other reasons? Were they expected to return? Did they return? Back to you."

"Two young men were seconded to the dredging project about a year ago. Sadly, they were killed in an accident. Wait please."

There was a pause of about five minutes before the message continued.

"We can recall three other instances. A difficult young man was sent away for his own good around fifteen years ago. I don't think he was expected to return. Also, there have been a couple of illiteracy problem cases. There was better news there – they went to a district which was able to help them, and they decided to stay there. Over to you."

"Sound familiar?" muttered Marius.

"Can you recall anyone returning to Choperton for any reason – ever – after going away? Back to you."

There was a brief pause.

"No, we can't. Do you think this is significant? Over to you."

"Not sure. Still gathering information. Will let you know how we get on. Thanks for your help. Regards. End."

Clement snorted. "It's beginning to look like you're right to be sceptical, Marius. Let's get on to the others."

They decided to call up the other recent contacts, and Uri and Clement operated Cipherslider successfully without help from Marius. The story was the same in each case.

"Well, I think that's conclusive," said Clement. "But I think I'd like to give the matter some more thought before we go any further. Can I suggest that you two...," he indicated Hayden and Marius, "go on your walk to Burshaw now, and enjoy the best of the day? We'll call up Sir Enwick and tell him we think we've found a way for him to contact us."

"And then why don't we have drinks at our home and talk further?" suggested Uri.

"Sounds good to me," replied Clement – before remembering that he'd made other plans for the rest of the day. He made a quick decision. "Say five o'clock? I'll tell Romford I'll see him tomorrow."

"About five then," said Hayden with a grin. "Get the picture, Marius? That means you and I have ample time for a full and proper walk, and can pick up all three screens – including the one my father was going to retrieve – and still be back before five."

As soon as Hayden and Marius had gone, Clement called up Frawton.

"Good afternoon, Sir Enwick. I hope I haven't chosen an inconvenient time to make contact? Over to you."

"Not at all, Sir Clement, it's good to hear from you. How are things progressing? Back to you."

"Not as well as they could be, but we certainly have plenty to occupy our minds. There are a number of points I'd like to raise..."

He then went on to ask the questions that they'd already asked the other districts. The replies, as they'd now come to expect, were essentially the same.

"Why do you ask these questions?" queried Frawton. "Are you implying something sinister? Back."

"I suppose I have to admit that I am," replied Burcher. "We've now contacted four other districts with the same questions. All five of us have a history of sending a few people away for illiteracy or behavioural reasons, and all of us have sent two young men to the Channel Dredging Project within the last three years. No one can recall anyone returning, despite the expectation in almost every case that they would. A plausible reason is always received, but no one has actually returned. Also, the dates of the dredging accident vary significantly.

"We're still considering what we think the implications of this are, and many things have already sprung to mind. At this stage, I'd prefer not to comment further until I've better marshalled my thoughts. Back."

"Understood. I'll await the result of your deliberations – and I'll give it some thought also. Has your computer expert made any progress on how we might be able to contact you? Back."

"Yes. It's pleasing to report some good news. He's come up with a method that we've tentatively tested. It involves burying a screen at the point at which the power conduit crosses the barrier between our districts, and using it as a signal relay point. Unfortunately, there's bad news also. He was badly injured yesterday, and is currently in a coma. However, I'm pleased to say that our medical people say he'll be OK in a few days. We'll get back to you as soon as we're in a position to go ahead. Meanwhile, it's also forced us to postpone our planned expedition to follow the power-route. For someone who's only been in our district a short while, he's become quite important to us. Back."

"The progress on a method of communicating is indeed good news. Thank you. Sorry to hear of the injury to your computer expert. Please explain 'only been in our district a short while'. Back."

"He's the additional male who was sent to us as part of the solution to the inbreeding problem – when the new LGUs were created. Back."

"He came in from outside Drayshaw Heath? Back."

Clement creased his brow.

"Yes. He was the 'one healthy male' whom the Witan said would help to strengthen our gene pool. You were sent one also surely? Back."

Again there was a pause before Frawton's response came through.

"It would seem there's a mystery at every turn. No, we've been sent no one. Please explain what you were told. Back."

Uri, who was also watching the screen, gasped.

Clement stared open-mouthed.

"Oh, my thunder…" he whispered, his mind already throwing up all sorts of panic scenarios. "Oh, my life…"

Uri put his hand on his shoulder, and said, "Steady, Clement, let's not overreact. There could be many reasons for this. Let's just apply the same kind of efficient logic that we've applied to everything else so far. For the moment, I suggest we recontact the other districts to see if they were sent anyone."

"Yes…yes, you're right," acknowledged Clement, and took a deep breath. He then keyed his response to Frawton outlining how Stin's arrival had come about. Sir Enwick confirmed that he knew nothing of any such arrangement, and made the same observation that the Drayling Worthies had made when they first learned of the proposal – how can the addition of one male make any significant difference to the gene pool?

Clement needed to close the communication. "I'm going to recontact the other districts to see if they were sent anyone. I'll let you know the outcome. End."

Having signed off, he turned to face Uri.

"You do realise what might be going on here, don't you?" he said. "We've no idea who Stin is. He could be a plant – a mole. He could've been put here to spy on us. He could…"

"Stop!" yelled Uri, and this time put both his hands on his friend's shoulders.

Looking him straight in the eye, and speaking slowly and deliberately, he said, "There's probably a perfectly simple explanation. We just don't know. Now, let's take a break and have a drink. Then we can contact the other districts again."

Realising that this was sound advice, Clement nodded.

Whilst they were sitting in the hospitality chairs, Uri said, "I don't think the idea that Stin could be a spy stands up very well. As I recall it, we were told about the additional male before we did anything that might have caused concern to anyone. There would've been no reason. Recent events have put us all under stress, and we must be careful not to become paranoid. I can think of a number of possible explanations. Maybe only selected districts received an additional male. Maybe the death of Spencer Curtis altered the plans. Maybe the introductions have been phased, and were never intended to all happen at the same time. And I'm sure I could think of a lot more, given time."

He looked at his friend and smiled.

"And that's precisely the kind of level-headed, rational advice to which I was referring when I asked you, a few days ago, to make sure that you tell me – anything – whenever I need telling," replied Clement. "You're truly a good friend, and I'm truly a wise man."

They laughed.

"And we're truly a fine team," grinned Uri. "Let's call the other districts."

They did so, and confirmed what they now feared – that none of them had any knowledge of an additional male.

"As Sir Enwick said – a mystery at every turn," commented Uri.

"Yes," said Clement. "We've many things to ponder. We've agreed to meet at your house at five, so there's some time for reflection. I'm going home now. I'll see you then."

With that, he got up and left.

Uri watched him go and sighed. He and his friend had been in many stressful situations over the years, but never anything like now. The events of recent times were unprecedented, and he had no idea where it was all going to lead.

19

Hayden and Marius returned from their walk at about a quarter to five, and went straight to Marius' house. They collapsed gratefully into hospitality chairs, and selected long, cool drinks from the drinksmade. They were chatting about the Channel Dredging Project when Uri walked in.

Marius sensed immediately that there was something on his mind. "Hello, father. You look thoughtful. What's up?"

"Let's wait until Sir Clement gets here," replied Uri without smiling. "Did you retrieve the screens?"

Marius and Hayden exchanged puzzled glances. Clearly something was wrong.

"Yes, no problems. It was a long walk though. I think I'll sleep well tonight."

"Let's hope so," said Uri. "Ah…here he comes now."

Clement walked in and sat down. He started talking without making prior eye-contact with either Hayden or Marius.

"Right. We've a number of issues to deal with. Hayden, would you make a handpenned record as you did for our earlier meetings please."

"Er…yes…of course. But I don't actually have all the stuff…"

"I have it here," interrupted his father, and held it out.

Hayden took it, and threw a glance at Marius. Whatever it was that they were about to hear, it had clearly had a profound effect on both Sir Clement and Sir Uri.

"Whilst you were collecting the buried screens – and I assume there were no problems with that – Sir Uri and I made a discovery. None of the other districts that we're in contact with have received an additional male, or know anything about any such arrangement."

He stopped to allow Marius and Hayden to digest the information, and a long, stunned silence followed.

Eventually, Hayden said, "Maybe there's some mistake?"

"Seems unlikely," said his father. "Not one of the four knew what we were talking about."

Uri chipped in. "There is the possibility, as I've already said to Sir Clement, that the arrangement may have been restricted to selected districts, or was always intended to be phased over time, or maybe the plans were altered on the death of Spencer Curtis. We just don't know."

"But none of that has the ring of truth, does it?" said Marius, still capable of cool logic and objectivity despite having only just received potentially alarming news.

"It isn't likely to be directly connected with the activities of our project team," he continued, "because Stin joined us before we'd taken any action that might be of interest to the authorities."

"Yes, your father made that point too," said Sir Clement. "Nonetheless, it's apparent from your observation that our minds have all gone in a similar direction. If we've been singled out to be given this additional male, then it would appear that somebody somewhere has an interest in us. It would also appear that we've been lied to, or, at the very least, misled."

"And we don't know whether Stin has misled us, or has also been misled himself," pointed out Marius. He thought quickly. "Did the Worthy Council ever receive any information on screen about the additional male?"

"No, I don't think so," replied Uri. "My recollection is that the Archworthy – Sir Bedford Coote at that time – told us verbally that he'd been informed by Regional

Administration that all new LGUs would also be given a new male. Is that how you remember it, Clement?"

"Yes. I don't think it was ever transcreened – at least, not to us."

"Right. Can I make a suggestion, Sir Clement?" said Marius.

"Please do."

"I propose that you and father approach Sir Bedford Coote to find out exactly how he received the instruction and from whom. Obviously, if he can add any other observations, then that would also be helpful. Meanwhile, I think that Hayden and I should go to Cipherslider. We'll make contact with Stin's old district, and ask them how they were told of the arrangement. We can also take the opportunity to find out if they've ever had anyone return after being sent away."

He paused, and looked at Clement. "I know it's after five, but...well...I'd rather like to get on with it. Do you think it's too late in the day to do it now?"

"Well...first of all...can I assume that everyone is happy with the suggestion?" asked Clement, looking around. Uri and Hayden both nodded.

"Right then. Yes, let's do it. If it's not convenient for Bedford we can arrange another time – and if it's too late for Feardleigh-in-the-Vale, or whatever they're called, well, never mind – we'll get back to them too."

Without another word, Hayden and Marius rose and left.

It was whilst they were walking to the Worthy Hall that the importance of what they were about to do really hit Marius.

"I don't know what the simple explanation is," he said, "but I'm sure there must be one – and hopefully we'll find it. The mind boggles at the thought of having to dream up and consider every possible scenario otherwise."

At that, he stopped talking, because he couldn't bring himself to state the obvious – that many of those scenarios would inevitably have to accept the possibility that Stin was not to be trusted. Although he'd only known Stin for a few weeks, he already considered him to be a close friend.

When they arrived at the Worthy Hall, they went straight to Cipherslider. Marius, now totally comfortable operating the machine for which he held the Distinction of Guardianship, set about calling up Feardleigh-in-the-Vale.

As he finished keying in the name, he said, "Right. Here we go – I'll ask to speak to a Worthy."

The screen went blank for a moment, and then flashed "Please re-key requested District."

Marius did so.

"District not recognised. Is name correct? Is District outside permitted area?" responded Cipherslider.

"Try the new LGU name," suggested Hayden. "Stin said that the Council were refusing to ban reference to the old area entity names. Maybe the authorities have deleted all reference to them in the records."

"Ah…yes. Good thought," said Marius. "What did they call the LGU?"

"Rotherane-in-the-Vale," replied Hayden. "The area entities were Feardleigh-in-the-Vale, Rother-on-Stay and Kilrane."

"OK. Rotherane-in-the-Vale it is."

He keyed in the name, and once again Cipherslider demurred.

"I don't like this," muttered Marius.

"Put the other two area entity names in," said Hayden.

Marius did so – with no more success.

A new message appeared on the screen. "Districts not recognised. Shall I make an observation?"

Marius keyed "Yes," and the reply left them aghast.

"None of four names recognised. Word structure worth consideration. Anagrams. Letters of following names can be reordered to produce phrases on similar theme. Coincidence?

Note:

ROTHER-ON-STAY	=	ANOTHER STORY
KILRANE	=	RANK LIE
ROTHERANE-IN-THE-VALE	=	NEVER OTHER THAN A LIE

Their eyes widened in surprise, but neither spoke. They just stared at the screen – needing time to take in what they were reading. Marius re-read each line slowly, trying to make sense of Cipherslider's observation.

Eventually, Hayden blurted, "Wow! The fact that they aren't recognised as districts *and* produce those phrases surely can't be coincidence, can it?"

Marius creased his brow. Apparently deep in thought, he muttered, "No....but there's one name missing, isn't there...and if it's not coincidence, why would that be?"

"Hmm...I don't know...but you're right...it does seem odd," replied Hayden, "the missing one is Stin's own district too. Why not ask Cipherslider for a comment?"

"Good idea," said Marius, and keyed, "Observation on Feardleigh-in-the-Vale?"

Cipherslider responded immediately.

"Nothing on similar theme, but anagram may be of interest:

FEARDLEIGH-IN-THE VALE	=	REVEALING HEATHFIELD

They stared at the screen in puzzlement for some time.

Eventually, Marius sat bolt upright, took a deep breath and turned to Hayden. In a slow and measured tone, he said, "I think we have to accept that we've probably discovered something of huge importance here. I don't pretend to understand it yet, but I suggest there's more than enough evidence to convince us that something's going on – and that we've only scratched the surface. As much as it pains me to say it, Stin has quite clearly lied to us, and cannot therefore be trusted."

He swallowed and gave a little cough. "We don't know who he is, or why he was moved to Drayling. Clearly the story he gave us about an encryption matrix problem on Cipherslider was simply a lie to explain the lack of any record of his supposed contact with his old home district. None of the places exist."

He stopped speaking, and then, almost inaudibly, added, "Who on earth is he?"

"Let's get back to your house," whispered Hayden, in a rasping, much quieter voice than he'd intended. His mouth was dry, and the words only just escaped.

They had to wait for nearly an hour for Clement and Uri to return.

"Sorry we took a while," explained Clement as they walked in. "Sir Bedford went on a bit. We couldn't just get up and walk out. He was as helpful as he could be, but he really didn't tell us much we didn't know already."

"I think we should start with what Hayden and I have found," said Marius, "…and I think you should sit down first."

Uri and Clement exchanged glances and sat down.

"Feardleigh-in-the-Vale doesn't exist. And neither do Rother-on-Stay, Kilrane or Rotherane-in-the-Vale. They're all the product of an extremely fertile mind."

Uri gasped.

"Are you sure?…" began Clement.

"Absolutely," responded Marius.

"But if that's so, he's lied to us…"

"Oh yes, he's lied all right," continued Marius, "and that's not all. You'll remember I told you that he liked playing with words. Well, Cipherslider's provided us with some observations. The letters of the names of the so-called districts are anagrams of phrases on a similar theme."

He turned to Hayden, who'd copied them onto his IDS.

"Rother-on-Stay makes ANOTHER STORY, Kilrane makes RANK LIE, and Rotherane-in-the-Vale produces NEVER OTHER THAN A LIE."

207

"Good grief...," muttered Clement, momentarily at a loss for anything else to say, "...er...could you read those out again, please?"

Hayden repeated them slowly.

Clement listened intently and, still shaking his head in bewilderment, said, "Er...didn't he say his home district was 'Feardleigh-in-the-Vale'?...Doesn't that make a phrase?"

"Oh, yes – and a very interesting one," replied Hayden. "That makes REVEALING HEATHFIELD."

There were exhalations of breath, followed by a prolonged silence as Clement and Uri struggled to absorb these latest revelations.

Marius looked at his father, who was now staring into space and shaking his head.

"Nothing is as it seems...nothing is as it should be...when will this ever end?" he moaned.

This alarmed Marius, and he walked over to his father and put a hand on his shoulder.

"No...no...don't worry, Marius, I'm all right. I'm just thinking aloud. This is all taking a lot of dealing with – but we're dealing with it...is there any more?"

Clement glanced at Hayden and then Marius. "Look, if you've nothing else to add for the moment, I think we should take a short break, and then go through everything we have together. Hayden, we'll need it hand-recorded again."

"No problem," replied Hayden.

Clement slumped back into his chair and activated the drinksmade.

"No sooner do we get used to the sheer enormity of what's happening to us, then something larger, and even more unexpected, comes along," he observed. "Lesser people than us would find it all very daunting. Don't you agree, Uri?"

"I think Drayling is indeed fortunate to have such a dynamic project team working on its behalf," concurred Uri with a grin.

"What about you two?" said Clement. "What do you think of it all?"

"Well, it's certainly both interesting and testing," replied Marius, "…but, to be honest, it also has a stomach-churning side – and I'm not finding that aspect at all pleasant." He looked at his father and then at the floor. "I'll let you know in due course if I think it was all worth it."

"Yes, and I'll go along with that," echoed Hayden. "I'd be lying if I said I'm finding the emotional side easy, but I'm certain we're doing all the right things, so I'm sure everything'll be fine in the end."

"Good for you," said Clement. "As long as we stick together, I'm sure it will too.

"Right.…let's get down to looking at what we've got in a more structured way. First things first. Now that we know for certain that Stin's been lying to us, let's go through what we know of him, starting with the original announcement. Hayden, you don't need to record this word-for-word, just the key bits as we identify them.

"Bedford said that he received the original "LGU instruction" in the usual way from Regional Administration – via the official encrypted IDS. The additional male bit was included in that. At the time, he had no reason to suspect anything sinister, and was certainly under the impression that the same instruction was going to all Archworthies. In fact, he has a clear memory of the words "to each LGU" in relation to the additional male. Unfortunately, he can't confirm his recollection by looking up the record, because he no longer has the authority – and, of course, I don't have the means to do that yet either.

"I asked if he'd made any other contact with Regional Administration regarding the instruction, and he said that the only subsequent communication related to how the LGU plan affected the existing Worthies.

"The instruction said that the Witan had been concerned for a long time about inbreeding, and that they'd been monitoring it for years. They said that, in addition to the merger of area entities, 'detailed research showed that the addition of a healthy male would have a significant strengthening effect on the gene pool within a few generations'.

"The only other things of note were that he confirmed nothing had ever been transcreened to Worthies about the instruction, and that he didn't envy the new Worthy Council the job it now had to do. He was pleased to be out of it. He added that we have his full confidence – which is nice.

"Hayden, whilst I think of it, would you please make a note that I need to call a closed meeting of the Worthy Council. They need to be told of our discovery."

He looked around. "Does anyone want to make any observations so far?"

Marius spoke up. "Sir Clement, it was you who introduced me to Stin – at the Worthy Hall on the day I was affirmed as a Thinker. At that time, you said that you'd decided that I was the one who should 'make his introduction to our community as smooth as possible' – or something like that."

"Yes, that's right," said Clement. "It was a verbal instruction from Blane. Although I had to accept the responsibility for the decision, it had actually already been taken above me."

"What – that his mentor should be Marius specifically?" queried Hayden.

"Yes. And I have to say it made sense to me too, because Marius was being given the special award, and I thought he was the ideal candidate anyway."

"Since then he's lied to us on a number of occasions," continued Marius. "He told me...us....that he came from Feardleigh-in-the-Vale – 'a district in Mid-BFF,' I think he said. He told me that both his parents were dead, and that he'd taken the opportunity to apply for area-transfer when it arose. He also said that he'd been told he was doing a special service for his country, and that, in return, he would be given preferential treatment by the Local Assessor. He said he was told that the rewards would be tangible."

"I was never given any instruction to give him special treatment," said Clement. "Having said that, though, he *was* accommodated in the living quarters at the Worthy Hall, and he *was* included on the Worthy training list."

"Yes, Marius and I discussed the accommodation question at the time," observed Uri. "Whilst the Archworthy's quarters at the Worthy Hall are obviously very comfortable, they *had* just become vacant, so it seemed to us perfectly sensible, nevertheless, to offer them to a new arrival from outside."

Clement picked up the other point. "...And I can confirm that the decision to include him on the Worthy training list was taken above me. I didn't consider it was necessarily a wrong decision, though. I assumed that appropriate input had been provided by the Local Assessor in his home district, and, as far as I'm concerned, that would've been entirely proper."

He paused for a moment in case anyone wished to comment, and then continued, "What else is there?"

"He told me quite a bit about his interests," said Marius. "He said that one of the jobs he was given involved a lot of sitting around without much to do, and that he used the time to explore national records by IDS. He said he's very interested in history, and certainly seemed genuinely fascinated by the results of our archaeological dig. He said his particular interests are Roman Britain and language... well...words...their derivation, how they're made up, that sort of thing. I remember he said he liked playing with words. I guess that's been well illustrated by the fictional district names. He also told me that the Roman Emperor Constantine had a British mother, and that, if you mix the letters of Constantine, you can get '*Note Stin Can*'."

"The fictional district names are certainly very clever," observed Uri. "Not only do the three area entity names form a phrase, but the LGU name does also – even after taking an element from each of the other three and putting them together – as we did with 'Drayshaw Heath'."

"That suggests that he's telling the truth when he says he's interested in words," said Clement. "In a strange way, though, it also suggests to me that they were designed to be discovered at some point. Otherwise, there wouldn't be any point in the exercise. Does anyone else feel that?"

"Well…yes…I think I see what you mean," volunteered Marius, "…maybe."

"Yes, maybe," said Uri, and stood up. "This is all interesting background, but it doesn't address the two most important, and potentially indicative, aspects of this, does it?"

He didn't wait for an answer. "The sole reason we asked Stin to join our project team was because of his computer knowledge – and, whilst I think of it, you may also remember my fears at the idea of adding someone to our number whose background we didn't know."

"Whoa, steady, Uri," interrupted Clement. "At every stage of this process we've talked out every thought, idea and disagreement, before proceeding. We all understood your legitimate concerns at the time, but we *all* agreed that the computer knowledge we believed Stin possessed was essential to us, and, for that sole reason, as you say, we *all* – including you – agreed that we should go ahead and invite him to join us."

Uri immediately put his hands up.

"You're right, Clement. Sorry. That was unreasonable – and unfair. However, the point about the computer knowledge remains."

Marius stepped in. "Well, I was going on to say that he told me that, whilst his interests in Roman Britain and words were, well, leisure interests, the world of computer technology was his serious study. I remember being hugely impressed with his knowledge of the Ciphersliders."

"Ciphersliders?" queried Uri. "Plural?"

"Yes, he told me about both the Mark One – which is what we've got – and the Mark Two, which he said subsequently became known as 'the first thinking machine'."

Hayden chipped in. "Look, I suppose it's easy to say this with hindsight, but now that we're looking at Stin in a different way, I do find myself wondering how it's possible for someone to reach the level of computer expertise that he clearly has by just 'following an interest'. Some of the stuff he's come up with seems extremely sophisticated for someone – even a highly intelligent and curious individual like Stin – who's simply spent time trawling through IDS records.

"Think of the examples – the use of Cipherslider to contact other districts, encryption, capillimetry, the adaptation of the directional sensor for the multitron scanner, IDS relays…the list goes on and on."

They all nodded and murmured assent. "Yes," said Clement, "his capabilities in that area do seem to be formidable. I wonder where they came from."

He looked at Uri.

Despite the mental gymnastics that they were all going through, Sir Clement remained an accomplished chairman. "And your second important, and potentially indicative point, is…?"

"What does 'Revealing Heathfield' mean?" replied Uri.

They all looked at each other, but no one had an explanation, so no one spoke. Eventually, Marius said, "I think we need to be careful not to make too many assumptions. We know that Stin's lied to us, but we don't actually know much else. And we don't know why. From intuition alone, I feel we should guard against condemning him – or, indeed, fearing him – without good reason. Certainly, let's be cautious, but let's not assume that he's necessarily a threat to us. We don't know that. We need to find out.

"You could say that 'Revealing Heathfield' implies some kind of anti-government stance. If that were so, then he may have a very good reason for keeping his identity secret. It may not be us he's hiding from!

"I know this is only speculation, but I think it does illustrate that we have no reason to be paranoid – at least for the moment."

"We've only known him for a few weeks, but in that time he's been very useful to us," said Clement. "And he's certainly given the impression that he's keen to help."

He made a decision.

"I can see only one way forward. As soon as he's fully recovered, I propose we confront him and ask for an explanation."

No one disagreed, because there seemed to be no other sensible alternative.

"Right," continued Clement, now back to his confident best, "Uri, I'm calling a closed meeting of the Worthy Council for ten o'clock tomorrow morning." He paused, and then observed, "All the other project team business will have to wait until this issue's been resolved – and, for the moment, I think we should keep it to ourselves. Come on, Hayden, let's go home."

With that, they said their goodbyes and left.

20

In closed session the following morning, Clement told the other two Worthies what they'd discovered, and what action was proposed. Whilst obviously surprised, their particular concern was the fact that other districts had apparently not been allocated an additional male also.

They debated the possible reasons for this for some time, but ultimately had to accept that, in the absence of any further information, all they could do was "record their puzzlement and concern."

It was only after they'd arrived at this conclusion that Romford Tester added, "I suppose it's also possible that this may be connected in some way with something we discovered at the medical facility. The colours of Mister Goodman's hair and eyes have been surgically altered. He hasn't always had dark hair and green eyes. In fact, he was originally fair haired and – we think, although we can't be absolutely certain – blue-eyed."

Burcher responded immediately.

"But that's extremely significant...and for at least two reasons! Firstly, it suggests that he may well be hiding from someone who knew him before he came here, and, secondly, I'm not aware that that kind of surgery is available to the average citizen – is it?"

"Well, I don't think I've ever heard of it," said Uri. "I know that many years ago people used to put chemicals on their hair to change its colour, but that was just by dyeing it.

They couldn't change the colour of the growing hair, and when it did grow it reverted to its natural colour. If you're saying it's been surgically changed, Romford, then that's something entirely different.

"So far as eyes are concerned, there was a fashion for a short time in the late 21st Century when some people walked around with each eye a different colour, but I'm almost sure that was achieved by using stick-on lenses. I think some rough-and-ready surgery was probably available around that time too, but it certainly wouldn't have been generally available to the average citizen, and it certainly wasn't sophisticated."

"Obviously, there've been scientific advances since then," said Romford, "and undoubtedly some since Dunstan Heathfield's Revolution of which we're unaware, but I do know that it's not available to us – or to any other normal person. None of us at the medical facility has ever come across it before…but there's certainly no question that it's been done."

Clement was now thinking ahead to the confrontation.

"You said yesterday that he'll be brought out of his coma tomorrow morning. Is that still the case?"

"Yes. There are no complications."

"Good. When's the earliest we can speak to him?"

"There should be no ill-effects, other than some residual bruising," replied Romford, "so tomorrow, mid-afternoon, should be fine."

"Right, thank you, gentlemen," said Clement. "I'll keep you advised of developments."

The following day, just before noon, Della and Urania dropped in on Stin on their way to the food distribution building. Sir Romford had confirmed by IDS that all had gone according to plan, and Della had wanted to see for herself that he was all right. They found him in good spirits, although one side of his face was heavily blackened by bruising. He told them that he had "nothing but praise for the people at the medical facility," and that he felt 'as good as new', despite the fact that it was decidedly strange "to go to sleep on a Thursday, and wake up on Sunday!" They passed on Uri's message that the project team would be meeting in the Heathfield Room, at the Worthy Hall, at three o'clock.

When Stin walked into the room a few hours later, the others were already there.

"Hello, Stin," said Clement. "We were pleased to hear from Sir Romford that you've suffered no serious damage. He said you were very lucky. Do you feel completely recovered now?"

"Yes, I feel fine, thank you, Sir Clement," replied Stin, "although, as I told Marius' mother, it's an odd feeling to lose two days!"

"Yes, it must be," said Clement, in a voice which signalled scant interest. "Right. I'll waste no more time. Sit down, please."

Stin was a little taken aback by the sudden change in tone, and sat down.

"Right. I won't dress this up − I'll come straight to the point. We've made a number of discoveries about you, and we don't like them. Firstly, you've lied to us about your previous home district − we know that Feardleigh-in-the-Vale, and the others, don't exist. That means that you lied to us about contacting them, and, presumably, lied about the computer encryption problem also. In addition to this, none of the other districts we've contacted know anything about the allocation of an additional male to help with an inbreeding problem.

"We also know that you've had the colour of both your hair and your eyes surgically altered.

"Shall I continue, or would you like to explain?"

Stin's jaw dropped. He'd clearly been taken completely by surprise. He looked at Marius, who could only look away.

It was some moments before he was able to regain his composure, and in the meantime nobody spoke. He glanced around at their stony faces.

"You've been busy," he said at last, but didn't immediately continue.

Still no one spoke.

"Well?"

"I guess I've no alternative but to tell you the truth," said Stin.

"That would indeed be a very sensible thing to do," responded Clement.

Stin took a deep breath and swallowed.

"My real name is Turner Zeal. I was assistant to the Archwitan, Spencer Curtis, from January this year until his recent death. I come originally from mid-BFF. When I was a very young child, I was identified as a prodigy by the Local Assessor, and, at the age of fourteen, I was officially selected for potential elevation.

"My duties at Witan Central Office were not onerous. Apart from accompanying the Archwitan on a number of appearances, I simply carried out administrative tasks as and when required.

"My main brief was to 'identify aspects worthy of further personal investigation with a view to gaining as much beneficial knowledge and experience as possible for future governmental responsibility'. That was how I was able to learn about computers. It was also how I became aware of your archaeological excavation, Marius. I actually researched your background in some detail.

"In a few short months, I gained the Premier's confidence – to the extent that his deputy, Kingsley Gryn, warned me that 'jealousies were beginning to manifest themselves in the Witan'. It wasn't long before other rumours – of insurrection and the like – began to circulate.

"I didn't take it too seriously to start with, but then, when Curtis died, I got an IDS message from Gryn that simply said, *'They helped Spencer on his way. They're coming for me, and they'll come for you. Get out now.'*

"I didn't wait for clarification. Whilst Curtis obviously didn't tell me everything, I do know about many of his activities, and of the workings of the Witan. It would appear that I know too much for some peoples' comfort – and it's certainly true that there were factions, including Tujo, whose activities were stamped upon by Spencer Curtis.

"I took the decision to disappear.

"The last instruction that Curtis gave me was to assist the Regional Administrations with their LGU instructions to the Archworthies. I came up with the idea of the additional male, and it was easy for me to alter the message that Drayling received.

"I knew how to get my appearance changed to make identification less likely, and everything else was achievable by the use of computer technology."

He looked around at them one by one.

"I'm sorry I had to lie to you, but I ask you to understand that it isn't you I'm hiding from.

"My situation at this moment is that I have no idea what happened to Kingsley Gryn, but I believe that the warning he gave me referred to Tujo."

He stared at the floor, and shrugged. Then, looking up, he said, "That's it, that's my story. I've told you now, so I'm in your hands. In one way, it's a relief. Although I've only been here a short time, I already consider you to be my friends. I can only hope that you'll still consider me to be yours."

He paused, and looked at Clement.

"I'm happy to answer any questions you'd like to ask me, Sir."

"I think I'd like to ask you to go and sit in the hospitality area, so that we can consider what you've told us," was the reply.

"Comment?" said Clement, as soon as he'd left the room.

"If we believe what he's told us, he's in danger of his life, and, if that's the case, then his desire to fabricate a story would be entirely understandable," observed Uri.

"The trouble is, just how much is fabrication?" said Marius. "We don't know how much of it is true."

"But why would he want to fabricate still further?" asked Hayden. "We know who he is now, so what would he have to gain?"

"I'd like to ask him why we should believe his story..." said Marius, "...and ask him to prove it in some way."

"OK," said Clement, "...we can do that."

Uri made a cautious observation. "Let's be careful not to over-react. We know we've been lied to, and we don't like it. It's natural that we're angry and feel let down...and I think, if I were Marius, I'd feel especially hurt. He's spent more time than any of us with Stin – or whatever his name is – and that means he's probably been lied to more than the rest of us too. That must be painful.

"Having said that, I agree we should ask the question."

Marius looked at his father and gave an appreciative half-smile. "We could also ask him to tell us the real name of the area entity in which he was brought up," he added.

"Agreed," responded Sir Clement. "Hayden, would you note these please? Any other questions?"

"Yes, I have one," said Hayden. "He said that he made significant use of computer technology to help him hide. How?"

His father nodded. "Right, I think that's enough for the moment. I'm sure his answers will prompt us to ask others anyway, but if at any point we need to adjourn again, there's no reason why we shouldn't.

Let's call him back in."

Uri, who was nearest to the door, did so.

"We have some questions for you," said Clement, "...and the first is – why should we now believe what you're telling us? Can you prove your story?"

"I can't prove it one hundred per cent conclusively, Sir Clement, but I believe you already have enough hard evidence to show that I worked at Witan Central Office.

"The extent of my computer knowledge – from which you've already benefited – and the fact that I had access to appearance-altering surgery are strong indicators, but the fact that I was in a position to change the LGU instruction to Drayling to say something different from what the other districts received – and you've already verified that – is, I submit, heavily suggestive of the truth of my story."

"How do we know you're not some kind of 'plant'?" asked Clement.

"As far as I understand it, you'd done nothing to concern the authorities at the time I amended the LGU instruction. There would've been no reason, at that time, for such a plant."

"What is the name of the real district in which you were brought up?" said Marius.

Stin blew out his cheeks and exhaled. "Look, if you really want me to answer that, I will. But please don't try to contact them, because it would create a trail back to me here. I think Tujo will already have thought of that."

Clement intervened. "If your story's true, you'd have good reason to keep it a secret – and we wouldn't need to know. If your story's not true, then not telling us really doesn't change much either, so we'll leave that one for the moment. Hayden, what's the next question?"

"Thank you, Sir Clement," said a grateful Stin.

"You said you used computer technology to help you hide...how?"

"I laid false trails which end in elaborate 'loops'. I think I know how Tujo would use technology to look for me, so I created a means by which a new trail is generated every time it's used. Theoretically, it will go on doing that – and failing to find me – forever. I arranged for an encrypted message to be automatically generated two weeks later – to be sent to the Archworthy of Drayling (or whatever designation had by then been given to the newly-established LGU) to 'confirm' my grading from my previous district, and recommending that I be 'considered for high office when appropriate'. Obviously, with a new identity, I have a new IDS, and the record of the LGU instruction at Southern Regional Administration is identical to the one received by all the other Archworthies – it says nothing about an additional male. Their system contains no record of the automatic message either, because I programmed it to be sent, in its entirety and without trail, to my new IDS. I have it here, but I appeal to you not to ask me to call it up, because to do so would significantly increase the likelihood of monitoring."

"Hmm. The automatic message will have gone to Grindon Blane," observed Clement.

"So that would be why you were given the Archworthy's living quarters and a place on the Worthy training list," said Uri.

"I wasn't expecting the luxury accommodation," replied Stin. "I think that was simply a case of it being available at the right time – but it was very welcome nonetheless."

Hayden was thoughtful.

"There must have been a risk that our Archworthy would mention you in one of his communications to Regional Administration," he observed.

"Yes, that's true, and it's been one of my biggest worries," replied Stin. "The best I could come up with was to arrange for all communications that included any of the words 'Stin, Goodman, additional, male, newcomer or inbreeding' to be re-routed to my new IDS here. It was no problem setting it up so that there'd be no record of the diversion. My intention was that I'd then edit them, as appropriate, and send them on their way. In fact, I haven't received any, so I don't actually have proof that the system works. However, I have no evidence that it doesn't either."

Marius decided to change the subject. "You told me your parents were dead…"

"That's right," replied Stin. "They died when I was very young. I was brought up by my grandparents – but they're gone now too. I was telling you the truth when I said I have no family ties."

"What lies *have* you told me?" asked Marius, laying bare his acute feeling of betrayal.

"I knew that the power-route wasn't an old internet conduit, so I'm afraid the attempt to use it to contact Frawton was a bit of a charade. I was confident that it must be important though, because I knew that the Regional Historian had lied to you, Sir Uri. Er…I made sure we weren't in any real danger when we were digging. I faked the 'imminent danger' message to avoid us getting too close."

"Hmm…then what's the purpose of the power-route?" queried Clement.

"I don't know the answer to that," replied Stin, "but I'd like to. The sheer magnitude of flow is so huge, that it has to be of monumental importance. I'd like to think that we're still going to find the answer."

"Did you know about the armed guards?" asked Uri.

"Yes…or, at least, I knew there were men who could be sent anywhere in an emergency. Gryn told me that someone called Tujo was the National Commander – but that was off the record, and it was all I was ever told."

"Do you think Spencer Curtis was murdered?" said Hayden.

"Well, that's what Kingsley Gryn said – or at least implied – in his IDS message. Somebody said he'd been ill for some time, and had been keeping it a secret, but I wasn't aware of that."

"You told me you were interested in the structure of words," said Marius, "and we discovered that the names of your fictional home district could be reshuffled to form phrases such as *Another Story, Never Other Than A Lie,* and so on. Very clever. But what do they mean? And what is the significance of the Feardleigh-in-the-Vale one – *Revealing Heathfield*? I assume there is one."

"From all the recent events, and from what I've told you, I think you'll agree that there are things going on of which the people of BFF are unaware, and which would not sit comfortably with the average citizen's understanding of the spirit of Dunstan Heathfield's Revolution. I had the idea that, at some point in the future, I would seek to reveal these things. I thought the fictional names might help me to explain my situation at that time. Failing that, in the event of my death, their discovery might help someone along the road to the truth…I'm surprised you've remembered my interest in words, Marius."

"Yes, you also told me that the Roman Emperor Constantine makes *Note Stin Can*," smiled Marius, relaxing slightly now for the first time since the interrogation began.

"And he can also make *Neat Stin Con*," responded Stin, "…but let's not dwell on that one."

"Hmm. Has anyone else got anything to say?" asked Clement.

He looked at each of them in turn, but no one said anything.

As soon as it was apparent that there were no more questions, Stin said, "Could I say something more, please, Sir Clement?"

"Of course."

"As I've already said, I've come to regard you as friends.

"I was delighted when you asked me to join your team, because, as I'm sure you can now see, your objectives fit very well with my own. I'd genuinely like to help.

"I suggest that what you're trying to do is far more important than your relationship with me – or any of our personal feelings, for that matter. To achieve the objective must transcend everything.

"And you need me.

"I ask you to retain your trust in me, and to continue to call me Stin."

He stopped speaking and smiled.

"It's an amazing story," observed Marius.

"It is indeed," concurred Sir Clement. "Stin, I think it's only right that I give everyone the opportunity to reflect on all that's been said. For myself, I'm glad that you seem to have fully recovered from your cricket accident. Perhaps you shouldn't play such dangerous games."

Everyone laughed, and the tension was broken.

"We'll meet at our house tomorrow morning at ten," said Clement. "Now…I'm going home."

They dispersed without further ado.

As he left, Marius turned to Stin and said simply, "See you tomorrow."

About an hour later, Clement called up Uri on his IDS. "Uri, we need to talk. Sara's gone out with Della this evening, so there's no one here. Could you come over at, say, seven?"

Uri agreed immediately, and as soon as he'd arrived and selected a drink, Clement said, "What do you think?"

Uri took his time to answer.

"Well, it's a amazing story…and whether it's true or not, he's certainly a remarkable young man. We know he's a convincing liar, and we therefore can't be a hundred per cent certain one way or the other.

"I don't think he's some kind of plant – for the reasons we said before – but, even if he were, I think we're damned already, so there's not much point in worrying about that side of it.

"To me, his story rings true. Incredible – yes – but, on balance, I'd say it's probably true."

"So you say we pick up where we left off, and go ahead with our plan?"

"Yes. Frankly, I don't think we have a choice anyway. I mean, the expedition was always going to be dangerous, so that hasn't changed. Marius and Hayden's feelings on the subject are important, of course, because they'll need to trust him, so we should talk to them. As Marius' father, I was already concerned about the trip, and I still am, but the need for it to go ahead hasn't altered. I think we should have another meeting, though, to ask Stin if there's anything he hasn't told us that might cause us to change our plan – anything about district boundaries, for example."

Clement considered Uri's words for a while, and then said, "Right. We'll ask Hayden and Marius for their views in the morning. If they say we go ahead, we'll have the project meeting. I'll update the other Worthies, as appropriate, after that."

"There's one other aspect," said Uri. "Despite our undertaking to our wives, I suggest we *don't* tell them about Stin – at least, not for the time being. If the expedition goes ahead, they'll be worried enough. There's no point adding to it."

"And, in any event, if his story's true, it *must* remain a secret," pointed out Clement.

Marius had also felt the need to share his thoughts, and had invited Hayden over for a drink.

"It's very quiet here today," said Hayden as they sat down.

"Everyone's out," replied Marius. "My mother's with your mother, my father's with your father, and Urania's out with a friend, so we can talk freely. What's your reaction to Stin's revelations?"

"I think it's such an incredible story that it must be, at least substantially, true...and if it's substantially true, then I can't see any reason why he'd need to embroider it around the edges. So I guess it's probably all true.

"There are some aspects which seem to me to go a long way to verifying it. He had access to both sophisticated surgery and Regional Administration's systems. That says to me that he must have been involved, in some way at least, at a high level of government.

"Also, as someone else said, the decision to change his appearance could only have been to try to hide from someone who knew what he looked like before he came to Drayling.

"What are your feelings on it?"

"I think I agree," said Marius. "To be honest, I'm having more difficulty dealing with the fact that we've been deceived than with the story itself. I'm finding it all very unsettling. It's quite upset me actually. I mean, if we can't trust each other, we've got nothing. The breakdown of trust is the very thing we've been spending all our time grappling with these last few weeks.

"Having said that, I can understand Stin's need for the elaborate deception. After all, he's only known us for a very short time, so he has no more of a guarantee of our good faith than we have of his.

"Hopefully, having gone through this process, our mutual respect will've been strengthened, not weakened. The fact of the matter is he's in our hands now. Whether he likes it or not, he's going to have to trust us – with his life."

The atmosphere at the meeting the following morning was altogether different from the previous one – lighter, more relaxed, and not without humour.

The subject matter remained deadly serious, however.

For his part, Stin seemed genuinely relieved to have unburdened himself of his secret, and was readily answering the many questions they were still firing at him – some of which were follow-ups to questions he'd answered already.

After about an hour and a half, Clement called a halt and said, "Right. Let's pull all this together. Because of the nature of your situation, Stin, we're not going to make a record. I'm going to summarise the position, and if anyone disagrees with anything I say, speak up."

He looked around. "OK?"

They all nodded.

"We've all been surprised by Stin's revelations and, in truth, made to feel a little uncomfortable. However, we all

227

now accept the position as he's explained it to us. We realise the responsibility we now have to protect his secret, and he can rest assured that we'll do so.

"Stin has never actually met Archwitan Tujo, but knows various things about him. He knows there was no love lost between Tujo and Spencer Curtis, and was told that Tujo was the National Commander of what I'll call the Emergency Guard. He believes his life would be in danger if Tujo knew his whereabouts. Our ultimate objective remains the removal of Tujo.

"We've agreed that the power-route expedition should go ahead, and Stin has confirmed that he's not aware of anything further that would help us in that regard. Indeed, he's as interested as we are to find out more about both the power-route and the district barriers.

"One personal observation I would make, Stin, is that, if I were in your position, I'm sure I'd think twice about embarking on a mission that carries a real risk of drawing the very kind of attention you're seeking to avoid."

"Whilst Tujo's around, I can never be completely comfortable, Sir Clement," explained Stin. "Your declared aim is to get rid of him. That's why I'm here – because it has to be mine also. The power-route expedition is part of the plan to reach that objective, and I can help with it…so when do we start?"

Clement nodded his understanding. "That's what I was coming to. I've received a message from Sir Romford Tester proposing that the tree-planting ceremony in Stowly Heath take place this coming Saturday – the sixteenth. Whilst that's nearly a week away, I do feel we should allow it to pass before embarking on the expedition."

He looked around. "Does anyone disagree?"

It was apparent from the immediate reaction around the room that there would be no dissent.

Marius caught the mood. "I think we would all wish to be there, Sir Clement. Delaying our mission for a few days isn't a problem."

As a consequence, and after a brief further discussion, they agreed that Marius, Hayden and Stin would commence their journey on the evening of Sunday, 17th October.

21

Clement called a Worthy Council meeting for the following afternoon. It was effectively the first full working meeting since the formation of the new Council, and as soon as it was over, the following report was transcreened to every resident in Drayshaw Heath:

Matters agreed at meeting of Worthy Council –
Tuesday 12th October 2466

1.   The tree-planting ceremony in memory of the sixteen citizens who died on 27th September will take place outside the Worthy Hall in Stowly Heath on Saturday 16th October at 2pm. All residents of Drayshaw Heath are invited to attend.

2.   Starting in November, a monthly access opportunity, or 'surgery', will be held in each of our three districts by the appropriate Worthy Council representative (see below). This will create a convenient, additional means by which residents can make known any concerns that they have. Citizens are still welcome to contact councillors at other times if they wish to do so. Times of surgeries will be notified in daily IDS information.

3.   The six citizens recently designated as Worthy Trainees will be seconded to councillors as follows, with immediate effect:

Gordy Wester will assist the Local Provider to identify what benefits, if any, might be achieved by centralising food and non-food storage, processing and distribution. They will also review livestock procedures and arrangements for the provision and treatment of water.

Glebba Day will assist the Local Genworthy to identify what benefits, if any, might be achieved by centralising the medical facilities. They will also set up a transport facility to enable citizens to travel between our districts more easily.

Zeke Darwin will assist the Local Genworthy to identify what benefits, if any, might be achieved by centralising the machine maintenance facilities. They will also review building erection and maintenance procedures.

As previously announced, a new Local Culturist will be appointed in due course. In the meantime, the other members of the Worthy Council have taken on temporary additional responsibilities, and are assisting each other as required. The duties of the other trainees – Hayden Burcher, Stin Goodman and Marius Graves (Th.) – are therefore less specific at this stage, and will be clarified later.

SIR CLEMENT BURCHER (Archworthy and Acting Local Assessor/Culturist)
SIR URI GRAVES (Local Historian and representative for Drayling)
SIR ROMFORD TESTER (Local Genworthy and representative for Stowly Heath)
SIR GARTH WELDON (Local Provider and representative for Burshaw).

The next few days gave everyone the opportunity to relax a little.

Uri caught up on some of his more mundane Worthy duties, and Clement stayed in touch with Romford over the arrangements for Saturday's ceremony. Both made the effort to spend some time with their wives, Uri making a special point of discussing the forthcoming power-route expedition with Della.

No one relished the idea of their son disappearing through a hole in a district barrier, but all knew it had to be done.

Marius, Hayden and Stin spent most of the week together, although Stin took a couple of hours out to visit – and provide welcome reassurance to – the Stowly Heath resident whose cricket bat had almost killed him.

It took a while for Marius, in particular, to re-establish his relationship with Stin. Intellectually, he understood the reasons for the deception, but it didn't alter the fact that he'd been prepared to lie to him. Emotionally, that part wasn't so easy to come to terms with.

By the time Friday came, however, that difficulty had – at least partially – been put to one side, and the three of them carried out a full and careful check of the equipment that they were going to take with them. Everything was now ready, and it was just a case of waiting until Sunday evening.

The following afternoon, every able-bodied resident of the LGU – and most of the others – massed outside the Worthy Hall in Stowly Heath. At 2pm precisely, Sir Romford Tester began to speak.

"Ladies and gentlemen, today is the sixteenth, and we are here to pay tribute to sixteen of our citizens who lost their lives in the recent tragedy.

"The Local Provider has selected a British oak, to be planted here – on the very spot at which they fell.

"The Archworthy will hold the young tree in place, and I shall call out the names of the young men – one by one. As each name is called, a member of his family will come forward to empty a quantity of soil onto the roots. The planting will then be completed by a Local Worthy Trainee."

It was an emotional occasion. Each family representative came forward at the appropriate time, some formal and serious, some tearful, and some requiring physical support. When the names had all been called, Zeke Darwin packed earth around the sapling to ensure that it was firmly established. Sir Clement Burcher then stepped forward.

"This tree shall be called 'The Sixteen Tree'…"

He paused. "…May it stand strong and proud, and act as a living memorial to those who fell. May it also be a symbol of a new and better future for their families, their friends, and for all of the residents of Drayshaw Heath."

He then stopped speaking, and stood in silence, facing the tree.

After a respectful time had elapsed, conversation began to break out in the crowd, and one of the family representatives walked over and said, "Thank you, Sir Clement, that was a fine tribute. Kirk would've been proud."

Clement couldn't suppress a tear as they shook hands warmly.

Some twenty yards away, Marius muttered, "That was a very moving ceremony."

"It was indeed," agreed Hayden. "...And not a single mention of Grindon Blane."

22

When the following morning dawned warm, sunny and bright, it did so in stark contrast to the mood in the Graves' residence at breakfast. Perhaps unsurprisingly, there was virtually no conversation, although Della took the opportunity to say that she and Urania would not be coming to Burshaw later, as they preferred to "say their goodbyes" at home.

Marius realised that there was no point in telling his mother not to worry, so he gave her a huge hug and promised solemnly that he'd do his very best to look after himself.

The day seemed interminable to Marius but, eventually, Clement, Hayden and Stin arrived in late afternoon for a final run through of the plans.

Clement wasted no more time.

"Right," he began, "Hayden, Stin, you've left your own identiscreens at home, haven't you?"

They nodded their confirmation.

"Good…Marius, you must also. An attributed IDS out of area would almost certainly be detected. You'll need to use one of the unattributed ones to send back your reports. Either Sir Uri or I will be beside Cipherslider at all times. Have you decided who's carrying what?"

"Well, we've divided it all up so that each load is equally unwieldy and troublesome, so there's no problem there," grinned Hayden.

He turned to Stin and Marius. "I think that's everything, don't you?"

"I think we're as prepared as we're ever going to be," agreed Stin.

"Yes…come on…let's go," urged Marius.

He sought out Della and Urania in the kitchen and kissed them both, and then, without further ceremony, the five men left the house. Uri went straight to the Worthy Hall – to Cipherslider – and the others headed towards Burshaw. They took the precaution of going the least populated route, although it wasn't really very likely that a party including the Archworthy would attract unwanted questions anyway.

"I can carry some of the equipment if you wish," offered Clement.

"No, we must carry it, Sir Clement, thanks all the same," said Stin. "If there's any problem with the transport of the stuff, it's better that we find out now, and not after we leave the district."

They walked for some time in silence, each with his own thoughts.

When they finally arrived at Burshaw's Southern Agricultural Area, they stopped. Stin put down his load and said, "Right, this is it. Who wants to bury the first screen?"

"This is it?" exclaimed Clement incredulously, "I know you told me the barrier goes across the middle of a field, but how on earth can it be here?"

"I assure you it is, father. Just one of the many things we don't yet know the answer to," said Hayden. "I'll bury the screen if you like, Stin."

Clement and Marius watched as he and Stin walked slowly forward – the latter holding the multitron scanner in front of him.

"Right, stop here," said Stin in a whisper that was probably unnecessary, but somehow seemed appropriate. "See where the spoor passes that small grey stone?…"

He pointed. Hayden nodded. "That's the entrance…it's the same size and shape as last time…roughly semi-circular…about three feet wide. It's only about two feet high, though. The tunnel it forms is approximately six feet long."

He put his hand out and touched Hayden's arm. "Remember, we don't know precisely what happens if we touch the barrier, but we do know that now's not a good time to find out."

Hayden gave him a meaningful look and a half-nod. "Does the spoor go precisely down the middle of the tunnel?"

Stin nodded in turn.

"Clever things, animals, aren't they?" said Hayden as he slithered towards the barrier on his stomach.

When he reached the grey stone he pointed to the ground and looked questioningly back over his shoulder.

"I reckon the optimum place is probably three feet in," said Stin. "But remember the shape of the tunnel. Can you do it?"

"It can obviously be done, but it isn't going to be easy. There's very little room for manoeuvre, and that's not helpful when you're lying flat on your stomach. It's going to take time, and it also depends on the condition of the soil. Another thing occurs to me now – if we bury the screen before we've all gone through, we'll disturb it as we pass over it. So the last person through will need to bury it from the other side."

Hayden hadn't yet entered the tunnel, and slid backwards carefully. As he did so, he muttered, barely audibly, "We should've practised this."

Stin heard him. "We still can," he said. "There's no reason why we have to go through tonight. Getting through the barriers safely and undetected is, after all, key to the success of the whole enterprise."

"It is," agreed Hayden, still on his knees. "However, having said what I said, I don't actually think that practise is likely to tell us anything particularly meaningful that we don't know already."

He turned and looked up at the others. "All we've got to do is get the equipment and ourselves through without touching the barrier. I think we're ready to go now. I say we go for it."

Marius was thoughtful as ever. "I think we're all mentally prepared now. Unless it's really necessary, I don't think we should wait – I too would just like to get on with it."

"Then we're agreed," said Stin. "Let's go."

"Good luck," said Clement, and tapped Hayden on the shoulder. "We'll be looking out for your reports."

He watched as first Stin, and then Marius, pushed small piles of equipment through the barrier, and he walked slowly backwards as Hayden, too, disappeared.

It was only then that he realised, with some alarm, what he'd just witnessed – *they'd disappeared.*

He looked at the field in front of him. Although it was late afternoon, it was still daylight and he could see perfectly clearly. He could see also the spoor running through the point at which they'd left, and continuing on the other side. Yet Marius, Hayden and Stin were nowhere to be seen.

For a time he gaped, unmoving and in disbelief, at the spot at which his son, and the others, had vanished in front of his eyes. He then turned and hurried to the Worthy Hall.

He found Uri beside Cipherslider, and told him what had happened.

His friend, whilst amazed, was philosophical.

"Well, Clement, the sole objective of this expedition is discovery – and, unfathomable as it seems, I suppose this is just something else to add to the list of things we don't understand…and, frankly, I've a feeling it won't be the last."

Stin, Marius and Hayden had taken their time getting through the barrier. They'd agreed that their safety in that situation took precedence – even over their desire not to be seen.

Once they were through, Hayden buried a screen with a quickly-perfected turf-lifting technique, and they then hurriedly made their way to the comparative safety of a clump of bushes.

Having looked around to satisfy himself that they weren't being observed, Stin announced, "I've some news for you. And it means that we're going to have to be even more careful than we've already realised."

Hayden and Marius looked at him.

"Marius, whilst you were coming through the barrier, I could see the field on the Burshaw side perfectly clearly – but there was no sign of either Hayden or Sir Clement."

"But I was standing there talking to him," said Hayden.

"Indeed," replied Stin. "Yet you weren't visible from this side. So, assuming the same applies in both directions, your father will have seen each of us disappear – one by one."

"But we can plainly see the spoor on the other side of the barrier…and when we were testing the scanner we stood and watched the swallows swoop down, go right through, and then – quite clearly – fly away on the other side," exclaimed Marius.

"I know – and I can't explain it either," replied Stin, "but it's a fact, nonetheless. Maybe it's to do with being in contact with the ground, or maybe it only applies to humans – I don't know. But as we've already said, there are many things we simply don't understand.

"For the moment, however, the important point is that we can't confirm that the coast is clear on the other side of a barrier simply by looking from the side we're leaving. The first one through the tunnel is going to have to check visually – on arrival, so to speak.

"It's just another risk, I guess."

As they waited for nightfall, they decided to use the remaining daylight to send a test message back to base. Marius watched Stin carefully pull an IDS from his pack, and shuddered as he realised that he and Hayden were now totally at his mercy – if he should prove, after all, to intend them harm.

"Would either of you two like to send this?" asked Stin.

238

Marius and Hayden looked at each other.

"No, you go ahead," said Hayden. "It doesn't matter who sends it."

"OK," replied Stin, and keyed: "All through OK. Nobody else around. Waiting for dark. Assume you noticed strange invisibility phenomenon. IDS indicates the name of this LGU is Gillersbush. Will be in touch. MHS."

As soon as he hit the 'send' button, he received automatic confirmation of successful transmission.

"Good. That's working," he said, and returned the screen to his pack.

As he did so, he became aware that both Marius and Hayden were staring at him.

Neither spoke, but their demeanour was sufficient to prompt him to say, "Look, I know what you're thinking, and I know I lied to you. I had to. I'm really sorry...but I hadn't known you for very long.

"But you know my story now, and you know why I lied to you. I promise you – I'm on your side. You don't have anything to fear from me. If this project is to succeed, we have to work together – as a team – and that means trusting each other. I want to find out what the power-route's for just as much as you do."

Hayden was the first to reply.

"Well, we don't have much choice, given the circumstances," he said, "and yes, of course we understand your reasons. But you must appreciate that, being human, it isn't easy for us to accept being deceived to such a degree. The fact that we now have an intellectual understanding of your situation doesn't actually make things much easier for us in that respect.

"However, having said that, it's true that we have to pull together, and I think Marius will agree unreservedly that that is what we're going to do."

"Absolutely," confirmed Marius immediately.

Clement and Uri were elated when the message came through.

"They're OK," said Uri, "...so the barrier-crossing process works."

"And the reporting system," added Clement, "...and they seem to have realised that the 'strange invisibility phenomenon', as they call it, means that they need to double-check for people each time they go through."

"I hope they're going to be all right with Stin," said Uri. "There are enough risks involved in this expedition without any new ones from that quarter."

Clement replied with more confidence than he actually felt. "Well, we talked it out as best we could – and Stin did explain his reasons. We couldn't have done any more than that...and they all understood the position, so I'm sure they'll be fine.

"Now, they're unlikely to report again for some hours, and we undertook to man Cipherslider at all times, so how do you want to do it?"

After a brief discussion, they decided to take alternate nights, but – as a general rule – both be present during the day. They agreed that Uri would take the first night shift, so Clement wished him goodnight and went home to tell Sara that they were fine, and that everything was going according to plan. Uri sent a brief IDS message to Della saying much the same.

A while later, Marius, Hayden and Stin decided it was time to move. They picked up their packs with great care.

"It looks like we're in for some moonlight," observed Marius. "Which is good – it'll be useful."

"It'll certainly be safer if we can avoid using the hand-illuminators," agreed Stin.

He activated the multitron scanner and said, "This way."

They walked slowly, keeping their ears and eyes open, and making as little noise as possible. Even so, every little sound they made as they stumbled across the uneven ground seemed to resonate in the still of the night, threatening imminent discovery. In fact, as they'd surmised, the route crossed open agricultural land, so the risk of being seen or heard, whilst ever present, was as small as they could reasonably have hoped for.

They made steady and unimpeded progress.

As the hours passed, they crept on in silence – communicating in hushed tones only as necessary when traversing a gully or circumventing some other natural obstacle.

Eventually, Stin whispered, "We're approaching the next barrier, and it'll be dawn soon. As there's plenty of woodland here, I suggest we hole up until night comes round again – we don't know what we're going to find on the other side. What do you think?"

Marius and Hayden agreed that the proposal made sense, so they found some thick bushes and crawled into them. Making themselves as comfortable as they could, they settled down to see out the coming hours of daylight.

"We're going to need to eat and sleep," said Hayden, "but I suggest that at least one of us should be awake at all times. I'm happy to take first watch."

"I'm not sure how much sleep we're going to get in here, but I'll certainly give it a try," declared Marius. "Didn't we ought to send a report back first, though?"

"Yes, I agree," said Stin. "Do you want to send this one?"

"No, you go ahead, you're more practised," replied Marius, "but please tell them I hope the rest of the journey'll be as uneventful as last night's."

The message Stin sent was: "Have crossed Gillersbush. Uneventful. Illuminators unnecessary most of the time due to moonlight. As expected, the route stuck to the agricultural area. Now camped in bushes. Will cross the barrier this evening. MHS."

As dawn approached, Clement found Uri dozing next to Cipherslider.

"Uh? Oh…hello Clement…what time is it?"

"About five o'clock I think. I couldn't sleep, so I thought I'd join you. You don't appear to have had the same problem."

"I tried to stay awake all night," said Uri, "but it would seem I succumbed eventually."

As they were speaking, the expedition party's second message came through. Clement read it aloud.

"Excellent. No problems. It's all going according to plan. Look – why don't you go and get your head down for a few hours? I'll call you if anything comes through."

Uri was happy to agree, and went home.

Clement settled down next to Cipherslider and, within minutes, was asleep himself.

Back in Gillersbush, the day started fine, if a little cold. After a while, Marius, Hayden and Stin were able to make themselves surprisingly comfortable and, in an uneventful day, snatched a little sleep, consumed some rations and crawled away from time to time to attend to the necessary calls of nature. At one point, they heard a couple of agricultural workers chatting some distance away, but that was as close as they came to meeting anyone.

"It's just the same as in Drayling," observed Stin. "No one goes anywhere near the barriers."

Eventually, after a long day, evening approached and the light began to fade. Marius shivered involuntarily as he emerged, sluggishly, from his sleep-roll.

"It's a bit colder than it was last night," he muttered. "I don't think it's going to be quite as pleasant this time around."

"I agree. I reckon we'll have to put our overjackets on," concurred Hayden.

"Yes…you're probably right," said Stin, "…but I suggest we don't put them on until after we're through the

242

barrier. They'll tend to make us bulkier and less agile – and neither of those things are going to be helpful in terms of getting through safely. We can put them on when we get to the other side."

The others readily accepted the common sense of this, and, after double-checking that no one was around, they approached the barrier.

In the half-light, they could see some trees a couple of hundred yards away on the other side, but there was little cover prior to that.

"We'll need to make for those trees," said Stin, "but remember to check that there's no one around when you first get through."

They didn't hurry, and went through – taking great care – in the same order as previously. Again, Hayden buried a screen, and soon they were standing together in the relative safety of the trees they'd identified from the other side.

They donned their overjackets quickly and Stin activated the multitron scanner. After moving it from side to side a couple of times, he pointed and whispered, "This way…"

The cold, clear sky once again gave them moonlight and, for a couple of hours at least, they made good progress in much the same way as they had the previous night. Once again they were crossing agricultural land, and there was nothing to slow them down.

They walked on in silence.

Suddenly – and without warning – Stin stopped abruptly and Marius bundled into the back of him.

"What th…"

"Sssh," cautioned Stin, "I think we may have a problem…look up ahead."

"What is it?" asked Hayden.

"Lights…," whispered Stin, "look – can you see? …There…" He pointed. "…Straight in front of us."

Hayden and Marius peered forward and, after allowing their eyes to adjust to the murky distance, could just pick them out.

"We must be getting close to people," said Hayden.

"Sssh...listen," hissed Marius.

They stopped talking and, through the silence, they could just hear the sound of music being played.

"They must have built right on top of the power-route," observed Stin.

"I knew our luck was too good to last," sighed Hayden, "what do we do now?"

"It seems to me we've got two choices," replied Stin. "Either we follow the route and risk where it takes us, or we branch out right or left and try to pick up the route again on the far side. Either way, we don't know what we're going to find."

There was a pause whilst they considered their situation. Then, as Marius opened his mouth to speak, fate resolved the issue for them. There was a sudden flash of light about twenty yards to their right, and a voice bellowed, "Hey, you there...it's a bit cold to be stuck out here isn't it? We wondered if we might find you here."

Marius, Hayden and Stin froze.

The shaft of light, seemingly from a hand-illuminator, passed over the three of them, checking each in turn. "So...there are three of you, are there?...There's only two of us....we only ever have two...I'm Jerome by the way, and this is Fin – he shone the beam onto himself and his companion. It doesn't seem very fair does it? Why should everyone from Drowlsden be allowed to attend the celebration, whilst the likes of us from Gimpston and Wignorth have to go out on patrol? Actually, we weren't sure if you folks operated in the same way as us, but we thought it was quite likely."

Stin was the first of the three to react.

"Well, pleased to meet you, Jerome and Fin. You gave us quite a start there for a second – I certainly didn't hear you coming – so I suppose I must commend your patrol technique. I'm Stin, by the way, and these two gentlemen are Hayden and Marius."

Marius gulped as Stin announced their real names. Why on earth did he do that? Surely he realises it can only make the situation even more dangerous for them? He glanced at Hayden, but his face was in deep shadow, so he was unable to read his expression.

"Yes, we obviously operate as you do…," continued Stin in a confident voice, "…presumably Drowlsden don't."

"No they don't," replied Jerome, "but surely the amalgamation of our districts is reason enough to allow all of us to attend the official celebration – just for this once. It's not as if we're going to catch anyone trying to get out or in – everyone knows it's only a symbolic exercise anyway."

At that point, Fin chipped in. "Our Archworthy's a stickler for tradition, you see. He says that the patrol's been carried out daily since the time of Dunstan Heathfield – and he's not prepared to be the one who breaks that kind of continuity."

"Well, I suppose when you put it like that, it does sound sort of reasonable," replied Stin, "but as you say, Jerome, it is only symbolic – unless you count us as aliens, that is!"

Everyone, including Marius and Hayden, laughed – and Stin continued, "Look, we've still got a patrol to finish, whether we like it or not. I don't want the Local Assessor on my back again – I've had enough of that. Why don't we all meet up again in a day or two and have a proper chat? After all, the Council's encouraging us to get to know each other, and it'll be more comfortable then. I could contact you by IDS in a few days, Jerome." He turned to Hayden and Marius, "I assume you two are happy with that?"

Marius and Hayden nodded, and the latter added, "Sure, that'll be fine."

Jerome looked at Fin, who also nodded. "OK, we'll look forward to it. Just one thing before you go though. What's that?" He pointed at the multitron scanner that Stin was holding.

Without hesitation, and in the same fluent and assured voice that he'd used earlier, Stin replied, "It's a people detector. Our Local Culturist invented it, and he's asked us to test it. Actually, he hasn't quite got it right yet though, because it didn't detect you two! I don't think it'll take him long to sort it out, though."

"That's interesting," said Jerome, "we'll look forward to hearing more of it. Come on, Fin."

They said their goodbyes, and Jerome and Fin walked off, directly away from the buildings, whilst Stin, Marius and Hayden continued slowly towards them.

Keeping careful watch over their shoulders, they were able to make out the retreating forms of their two new acquaintances for a surprisingly long time in the moonlight.

Eventually, when they judged they were far enough away, they stopped.

"Phew, that was lucky," breathed Stin, "for a moment there I thought we were in trouble."

"Why did you tell them our real names?" blurted Marius. "Isn't our situation dangerous enough?"

"I thought, on balance, it was the safer option," replied Stin smoothly. "They're highly unlikely to question our names, but if we invent false ones for ourselves, we immediately put pressure on ourselves to remember them – and also run the risk of perhaps not reacting normally if, say, someone suddenly shouts our name, or something like that. I had no way of knowing how long we were going to have to keep up a pretext."

Even in the half-light, he could see the expressions of his two companions – and he immediately sensed their incredulity. Realising the heavy irony of what he'd said, he just shrugged.

But it was all too much for Marius.

"What?...look...you've already told us that Stin isn't your real name!...You've told us that you're on our side...that we have nothing to worry about. You've told us that you've lied to us. You've told us an incredible story by way of explanation. We've just witnessed you fabricate yet another story for Jerome and Fin. The ease with which you come out with these lies is, quite simply, frightening. You had almost no time to think, yet it all came spewing out – all perfectly plausible. Why shouldn't I be concerned that you decide to tell them our real names? Why should I accept whatever explanation you choose to give us? You clearly don't need any time to prepare your stories – so how can I accept anything that you say?"

Hayden decided to step in. He put his hand on his friend's shoulder.

"Come on, this isn't the time for this conversation. Our priority at the moment has to be to get to somewhere safer. We're too exposed here. My suggestion is that we strike out to the left and try to get around the built-up area and pick up the power-route on the other side. I think it's better to stay as far away from the buildings as possible."

Marius nodded his acceptance, and Stin, apparently affected by the outburst, added somewhat meekly, "Sorry, Marius…"

Turning left did indeed take them to an agricultural area, and very soon they were making good progress once more. As soon as they sensed they'd gone far enough, they veered back towards the right to pick up the power-route again. At one point, they spent an annoying amount of time negotiating a deep, wooded gully, but, other than that, it was a relatively straightforward exercise and they were soon making themselves comfortable, as best they could, in some heavy brush, in preparation for the approaching day.

As it was still very early, and not yet fully light, Stin announced that he was going to take a closer look at the barrier. "It looks a bit more overgrown this time – I won't be long."

As soon as he'd gone, Hayden took the opportunity to whisper to Marius.

"Marius…are you all right?"

"Yes, I'm OK, Hayden," responded Marius in a rather braver voice than he actually felt. "Obviously, I'm frightened

247

sick about this whole journey – I'd be lying if I said anything else – but we're all in it together, and we all knew from the start what a risk we were taking. We all know there'll be huge trouble if we get caught…"

"…And Stin…" continued Hayden, "…what about Stin? You told him a few things back there."

"Yes, I'm sorry about that – I probably haven't helped things much. It's all the conflicting emotions, I suppose. I thought he was my friend, although I know I haven't known him for very long. His ability to lie to order scares me greatly, and we still don't really know if he's a danger to us or not. He certainly could be. On the other hand, we went ahead because we seemed to share a common purpose…and I can't see any reason why he'd want to harm us…but I still don't know…"

"Take it easy," said Hayden, in as reassuring a voice as he could muster. "As you say, we're all in this together. Stay calm, and remember we've undertaken – both to our fathers and to Stin – to work as a team…to find out the reason for the power-route. That has to be our number one priority."

At that point, Stin returned. As he crawled in beside them, he looked at their faces – the light had by now improved considerably – and realised immediately that they'd been talking about him.

He opened his mouth, as if to speak, and then closed it again. He looked from one to the other, and then, apparently having changed his mind, said, "It's very overgrown at the point where the power-route crosses the barrier. However, once again, there's an animal spoor going through the gap, and the space available to us is the same as before. The ground's pretty worn, but I reckon there'll be lots of roots this time. I hope it won't be too much of a problem burying the IDS. Having said that, there's no sign that people come here much anyway."

Neither Marius nor Hayden said anything.

"Right, I'll get some sleep then," said Stin and, after a short pause, he lay down, wrapped himself in his sleep-roll and turned his back on them.

Hayden and Marius exchanged glances and did similarly.

When Uri had returned to the Worthy Hall the previous evening, he'd found Clement still fast asleep beside Cipherslider.

He roused him gently.

"Uh? Oh, hello Uri…er…what time is it?"

"About five o'clock in the afternoon," smiled Uri. "I assume you've been asleep all day?"

"Oh…yes…I think I must have been," admitted Clement, sheepishly.

"Well, you obviously needed it," observed Uri.

He looked at Cipherslider.

"They don't appear to have sent any more messages yet. I hope everything's going OK."

"There's no reason to think otherwise," said Clement, as he stretched his aching limbs. "They're probably preparing to cross another district at this moment. I expect they'll report back tomorrow morning when they've done that."

He paused and considered. "However, as I don't now need to sleep, I think I'd prefer to stay here if you don't mind, despite what we agreed."

Uri understood at once his friend's desire to be on hand. "Of course I don't mind – that's fine," he replied.

They chatted for a while, and then Clement said, "Look, if we're going to be here for some time, I think I'll take the opportunity to practise my new computer skills. If I don't use them, there's no doubt I'll forget them!" He moved over and positioned himself in front of Cipherslider.

"I'll go and get us a drink," said Uri, and walked through to the hospitality area.

After thinking for a moment, Clement recalled what Marius had said about the Emperor Constantine, and keyed "Comment on Constantine."

Instantaneously, Cipherslider responded with "Facts relating, word structure or both?"

Clement keyed "Word Structure."

"There are many combinations of letters. Best phrases are: NINE NOT CAST, NOTE ANTICS, ANTS NOT NICE. Do you require more?"

Clement keyed "Phrases to include the word STIN."

"NOTE STIN CAN, NEAT STIN CON."

Clement was pleased with himself, because he recalled that these were the two phrases that Marius had mentioned.

Cipherslider continued, "Observation on word STIN?"

"Yes."

"STIN = TUJO."

Clement didn't react immediately. Then, as the words in front of him registered, he gasped. For a moment, he froze, and then, gathering himself, he keyed "Explain."

"Simple Cipher slide. Move each letter of STIN to next letter alphabetically. Result...TUJO."

Clement stared at the screen.

He re-read it again, and again.

He shook his head, as though to deny what he was seeing. Could it be coincidence? No, of course it couldn't. Could it be a young man's joke?...What *was* this?

"Uri! Get in here – now!" he yelled.

Uri was already on his way back with their drinks, and spilled most of the contents as he dashed to join Clement.

"What's the matter?...Whatever's happened?"

Clement, in a state now approaching distress, pointed at the screen with a shaking finger.

Uri read the words. "What does it mean?" he asked.

Clement took him through the last few screens.

"Oh, my life..." began Uri, "but surely it can't mean...surely Stin's not...no, no, he couldn't be...it's not possible..."

"We…must try…to be calm," said Clement with a huge effort. "We wouldn't have believed Stin was anything other than our additional healthy male a few days ago. Then we discovered he'd lied to us. Then he told us he was an assistant at Witan Central Office. His story's fantastic. Why shouldn't it be even more fantastic still? Why shouldn't he be Tujo himself?"

"Well…it's stupid," responded Uri. "Why would Tujo want to come here? Why would he want to be here when all those strange orders were received from Regional Administration? And why would he want to go off on an expedition with Marius and Hayden? It doesn't make any sense at all."

"No it doesn't, but, having said that, we're not in the best position to know what makes sense and what doesn't are we? I agree it's unlikely. He has to be too young for a start. I can't see how someone of his age could get into that position. The whole idea is too ridiculous for words. I reckon what we have here is another of Stin's games with words. I certainly hope so. If I truly believed he was Tujo, I wouldn't know what to do with myself whilst he was off on this expedition with our sons. It's bad enough knowing he isn't even Stin."

"So what do we do?" asked Uri. "Should we contact them? Is there any way we *can* contact them?"

"To tell them what?" snorted Clement, "…that we have this incredible notion that Stin's Tujo? What good would that do?"

The sun was high in the sky when Marius opened his eyes. He blinked and looked around him. Hayden was snoring gently a couple of yards away, and Stin was sitting up, reading an IDS.

He looked up.

"Morning Marius. Sleep well?"

"Um…yes, I think so," answered Marius. "What time is it?"

"About midday," replied Stin. "We're going to need to stay here for a while yet. Er...we didn't send a report back to base before we all went to sleep, so I took the decision to send one about an hour ago...I thought we ought to...I hope you agree...it went through OK."

He handed Marius the screen.

The message read: "Have crossed Drowlsden/ Gimpston/Wignorth (LGU name not known). Now camped in bushes again. Will cross next barrier this evening. MHS."

"Seems all right," shrugged Marius. "Short and to the point. I agree we should have sent one."

"I was just reading about this district," continued Stin, apparently wanting to make conversation. "They don't appear to have given their LGU a name yet...I think we're in Wignorth at the moment."

At that point, Hayden grunted and turned over. "Uh? Oh, hello...have you two been awake long?"

"Well, I haven't," replied Marius, "but I don't think Stin was asleep for as long as we were. He's sent another report."

"Oh?...oh...yes...we should have done that when we first got here, shouldn't we...what did you say, Stin?"

Stin read out the message.

"Well, it tells them where we are, and the fact that the expedition's still ongoing, I suppose," commented Hayden, "I guess that's all they need to know for the moment."

"...and I've also had a look around," said Stin. "I don't think anyone ever comes here – I can't see any evidence of recent human activity in the immediate vicinity at all."

"In that case, I have a very human need, and I shall go and attend to it," announced Hayden, and crawled off.

23

The hours of daylight seemed to Marius to drag on forever. He didn't feel like saying much, and, as a result, it was simply a case of waiting for the end of the day.

Eventually, when the time did finally arrive to resume their journey, they remained cautious and took no chances – despite Stin's assertion that they were unlikely to meet anyone – at least prior to going through the barrier.

Once again they didn't hurry.

They went through in the now-established order – with Hayden bringing up the rear and burying a screen. Each checked for himself that no one was around before emerging from the tunnel into the new district.

"Right," whispered Marius. "Which way now, Stin?"

Stin didn't answer. He was peering at the scanner closely and moving it from side to side.

"That's odd."

"What's the problem?" asked Hayden.

"The scanner's saying that the next barrier is only about twenty yards in front of us, but the power-route seems to be turning to the right."

"But couldn't that be because we just happen to have crossed at a corner of the district, or something like that?" queried Marius.

"Well, yes...I wondered that," replied Stin, "but a full right-to-left sweep is showing a consistent reading – which sort of suggests that we're in some kind of corridor between barriers...or the scanner could be malfunctioning, I suppose."

He pondered for a moment, and then appeared to come to a decision.

"Right. I can't think of any reason why the scanner would suddenly cease to function properly.

"...And I therefore think that we must assume it's working OK, and must therefore trust what it's telling us, despite our expectations to the contrary. Do you both agree?"

"I can't see that we have much choice," said Marius, "...but what about an IDS? Couldn't that tell us something?"

"Yes – good thought," agreed Stin, and took a screen from his pack.

He activated it and gasped. "Whoa...good thought indeed! It says the name of this place is 'BFF Parkerspont'."

"BFF?" said Hayden, "What does that mean?"

Stin didn't answer immediately. He looked around in the fading light. There was no sound, and he couldn't see much.

"Hmm...I'm not sure...," he whispered. "Come on....and stay behind me."

He began to edge forward slowly holding the scanner in front of him, with Marius and Hayden following him closely.

After only about ten yards, he stopped abruptly and Marius almost bumped into him.

"What...are we at the other barrier already?"

"No, no...but I'm getting some rather strange readings. This barrier's definitely not the same as the others...in fact...actually, I'm not sure we're quite as close to it as I thought."

He adjusted the controls on the scanner.

"Ah...yes...I see now. This barrier is indeed very different from the others. I made an assumption that it would give similar readings to the others, so I set the levels accordingly. But it doesn't. This barrier isn't far away, but it's a bit further than I thought. The difference is that it's much, much bigger and much, much more powerful than the others."

He turned and looked at Marius and Hayden. "I think we've found the reason for our power-route."

"What – a huge barrier?" said Marius.

"Yes," replied Stin, "and I suggest we should find somewhere to hide as quickly as we can, because if my assumptions are correct, we could be in imminent danger of discovery."

Marius looked at Hayden, then back at Stin.

"Look, we'll have time to talk later, but I think 'BFF' could mean we're on government property," said Stin, "…and that means danger. Come on – let's move."

There was a well-worn path, running parallel to the barrier they'd just come through.

"Look at this track. It's certainly not an animal's spoor," said Stin with certainty, "…it's far too well-used for that. We need to keep our eyes and ears open. If I'm right, and this is indeed government property, then there could be regular patrols along it, even at night."

"Then why don't we get off the path?" said Hayden.

"Well, we could," replied Stin, "but we don't know what the security measures are. My feeling is that we're less likely to trip alarms and sensors if we stick to areas where people are normally expected to be. What do you think, Marius?"

Before he could answer, Hayden said, "Yes, OK. I think you're probably right. Come on, let's move."

They turned right along the path – Stin still leading the way, holding the multitron scanner in front of him.

After about half an hour of silent walking, he stopped suddenly and raised his hand. "Listen!" he hissed, "can you hear something?"

They all froze. As they stood motionless, holding their breath, they could just sense that the silence of the night had indeed been replaced by a barely audible low hum.

"What do you think it is?" asked Marius softly.

"I don't know, but I think I can make out some kind of structure up ahead. Look…there…can you see it?"

He pointed, and they all crept slowly forward, peering into the darkness.

Soon a small building became clearly discernable in the gloom.

"The power-route seems to be going straight towards it!" whispered Stin.

They made no sound as they approached, but a sensor detected their presence and a door opened. Lights came on both inside and out.

"We may or may not have been spotted already," breathed Stin hardly audibly, "but, either way, we're committed now – and there'll almost certainly be someone not far away."

They walked forward cautiously and, as soon as they'd entered the building, were confronted by a large screen displaying the words, "New personnel – identify yourself within 20 seconds."

"Oh no," gasped Marius in alarm, "what do we do now?"

"Enter a security code I guess," replied Stin, and tapped something into the keypad.

Despite all that had happened to them in recent days, Marius and Hayden were simply not prepared for what happened next.

The words on the screen changed to "Code TUJO/WHD/CM1 accepted. Welcome, Archwitan Tujo."

Neither was able to suppress a gasp, and, as they struggled to comprehend what they'd seen, a man wearing a BFF uniform appeared from the next room. Hayden recognised the uniform immediately. It was identical to those worn by the guards at Stowly Heath.

The newcomer looked at the three men, and apparently unsure which of them to address specifically, came to attention, saluted, and – looking straight ahead – said, "BFF Officer Steadlaw, Sir! Welcome to Parkerspont Four, Sir!"

Stin stepped forward.

"Relax, officer, this is an informal visit. I just wanted to see things for myself. These two gentlemen..." he indicated

Hayden and Marius… "are my assistants. Is everything in order here, as far as you're concerned?"

"Er…yes, Sir," replied Steadlaw.

"Good, good. Is anyone else here?"

"No Sir. I'm due to be relieved in about three quarters of an hour, Sir."

"What do your duties entail? What would you normally do for the next three quarters of an hour?"

"Monitor the Force Field, Sir. I maintain a constant check on the operational data for this sector – and all the security detectors, of course."

"Ah, yes. The security detectors. When did you first notice our presence?"

"When you were on the patrol path, Sir."

"Good…very good. Well done, Steadlaw. Excellent job. Now…is there somewhere I can sit down with my assistants and talk in private?"

"Er…yes, Sir, you can use the ops room." He gestured towards the door through which he'd appeared. "I can stay in here and use this screen."

"Thank you, Steadlaw…that'll be fine…and don't worry, we won't inconvenience you for long."

"It's no problem, Sir…er…thank you, Sir," responded the still-bewildered officer.

During the exchange, Marius and Hayden had said nothing. Their natural instinct for survival had enabled them, with some difficulty, to contain their inner turmoil and appear confident and detached, despite what had played out in front of them. Stin motioned to them to join him in the next room. As soon as they were out of sight of the officer, he put his finger to his lips. He turned back to the door and said, "Oh, Steadlaw, do you think you could de-activate the roomscriber please?"

"Oh, yes Sir – sorry Sir."

As soon as Stin was satisfied that they weren't being monitored, he selected a drink from the single drinksmade console, and settled himself into the only chair – still warm

257

from having been occupied only a short while ago. Marius and Hayden exchanged glances, and the latter walked wordlessly to the roompad and keyed 'Seats/2'. Two occasional chairs slid out of the wall.

"I thought that code might come in handy at some point!" grinned Stin. "I stumbled on it when I was re-programming aspects of the Regional Administrations' system. I must admit my heart was in my mouth for a moment there, though."

He looked at his two colleagues. Neither said a word, but their haunted demeanour was sufficient to prompt him to add, "Look, I know this must all seem a bit strange, but please don't worry. I don't think we're in any immediate danger. I suggest we should send a report to your fathers telling them what we've discovered. We can also tell them we're on our way home. Would either of you two like to send this one?"

Still neither Marius nor Hayden spoke.

"OK," shrugged Stin. "I guess I can do it."

He took an IDS from his pack and despatched: "Have discovered the reason for the power-route. A huge barrier. Far bigger than local border-barriers. All is well. Details when we see you. Now on our way home. MHS"

"Right. Happy with that?…OK. I'll just go through to the other room and ask Steadlaw to make our journey home a little easier." He got up and left them alone.

Hayden opened his mouth to speak, but initially nothing came out. With a major effort, he rasped, "We're in big trouble. Did you see that code?"

Marius nodded. "Well…yes, we were very lucky there."

"No, no…you don't understand," persisted Hayden, his voice now close to panic, "…it's much, much worse than that. The code Stin input was 'TUJO/WHD/CM1'! Don't you see? It has to stand for 'TUJO… *Worthy…Hall…Drayling…Cipherslider…Mark One*'! It simply has to be far too much of a coincidence to stand for anything else…! The computer not only recognised him as Tujo, but part of the code was Drayling Worthy Hall! …And

258

that can only mean..." he stopped speaking to take in a gulp of air, "...it can only mean that Stin *is* Tujo! It can't mean anything else!"

"But he said he remembered it from the RA's system..." began Marius, "surely that's feasible isn't it?...if we accept he had access to it, then it makes sense that he should make a mental note of it."

"No – Marius – you're not thinking!" hissed Hayden, whose mind was functioning with remarkable clarity despite his highly emotional state. "That code couldn't have been conceived until after Stin moved to Drayling! Can't you see?..." He was becoming frantic now. "...And not only that – the kind of technology used in a government installation like this simply wouldn't permit a misuse such as Stin's suggesting. It can't be as simple as that! Look, we've come through barriers which somehow prevent humans from being seen through them, and we've discovered a massive forcefield of some kind here. The level of technology involved is way, way beyond our comprehension! Yet he's suggesting that all he had to do to satisfy the security system was to enter someone else's code? That has to be rubbish! For goodness' sake, Marius, even identiscreens can sense a particular individual's 'innate ambium' – or whatever it's called – so it's simply not conceivable that the security here could be fooled in such a way..."

His voice tailed off, and he said nothing more. He just slumped.

Marius gaped.

His mind was still racing when Stin returned a little while later.

"Steadlaw's given me three personal field-negaters. We'll be able to walk straight through the local barriers... and the Archworthies of both LGUs are being informed, so there'll be no problem there either."

"Stin..." began Marius, "look...please...this is all too much for us...are you going to tell us what's going on?"

Stin looked from one to the other, and appeared to come to a decision.

"All right…yes…I'll explain everything…

"You're right, of course – there *is* something strange going on, and now that we've confirmed the existence of this huge force-field, I'm in a position to tell you it all.

"However, I think it's only right that I tell both you and your fathers at the same time – so I ask you to be patient for just a little while longer – until we get back to Drayling."

He paused and smiled. "Look, I know this is hard for you, but I promise you you're perfectly safe. In fact, I believe you've done your country a great service."

Marius looked at Hayden, and then at Stin, and then back at Hayden. He had nothing to add. There was so much information to absorb, much of it ambiguous and none of it making any sense. He knew they were totally exposed, totally vulnerable and totally helpless. Neither he nor Hayden knew how much of what they were being told was true, or indeed whether they were still in great danger or not.

Eventually Hayden shrugged and said, "You know we're totally in your hands, Stin – or whoever you are – we've no choice but to go along with what you say."

24

The walk home took a little under five hours, and during that time virtually nothing was said. Eventually, after crossing into Burshaw, Marius sent an IDS message to Uri saying simply "Meet us at Drayling Worthy Hall in one hour – just the five of us. We're fine. M."

Despite Marius' reassurance, Clement and Uri couldn't disguise their huge relief when the three finally arrived. Uri wept as he hugged his son.

"We were so worried…I'm so glad you're safe…"

He turned to Stin, and with obvious fear in his voice, said, "What…do you intend to do now?"

Stin looked straight into his eyes. "Sir Uri, I intend to tell you everything."

Then, turning to Clement, he said, "Sir Clement, do you think we could use a roomscriber? I believe it's important that you have a record of what I'm going to say."

"All right. Let's go through to the Heathfield Room," replied Clement.

As soon as they were seated, and the roomscriber activated, Stin began to speak – slowly and deliberately.

He looked at each of his listeners in turn.

"Sir Clement…Sir Uri…Hayden…Marius. This is an historic moment. It's the moment at which you'll hear the whole truth, and you'll know that it's true."

He paused for a moment and gathered himself.

"During my time at Witan Central Office, I was privileged to learn many things – and much of what I learned troubled me."

Again he paused.

"Gentlemen, Dunstan Heathfield's Revolution is a complete sham. It is a fabrication from beginning to end, and the deception has been perpetuated by every Archwitan since the formation of the Government of National Unity in 2320. For over one hundred and forty years now, the people of this country have been fed lie upon lie. It is, without question, the most cynical and sustained example of social engineering in the history of the world."

Again he stopped speaking for a few moments to give his audience time to absorb his words.

"Dunstan Heathfield took advantage of new technology to build a force-field of massive proportions around the whole of mainland Britain. It was so powerful that nothing, absolutely nothing, could breach it – not even from above. It was effectively a huge bubble, in which he then set about creating a Britain in line with his vision of how he thought British life should be. All that stuff about "showing the world how, by non-violent, yet determined, political means, global peace could be won" is a load of rubbish. Heathfield never travelled the world – never mind convincing it politically to stop fighting.

"The force-field has been in place ever since.

"The list of subsequent lies is almost infinite. International trade has never been abolished. Even the BFF has continued to trade – without the knowledge of its inhabitants. The claim that "moral leadership had solved the old problems of starvation, deprivation and envy" was, sadly, a fantasy, and the assertion that "world peace and harmony" had been achieved would be a joke if it weren't so tragic.

"At no point since Heathfield's time has there been a single year in which there has not been serious fighting – and much devastation – somewhere. And the BFF itself has been directly involved in at least two international conflicts during the intervening years, despite the fact that almost all of its citizens remained blissfully unaware."

Clement, Uri, Marius and Hayden were awe-struck. Every word Stin uttered dismantled their world still further, yet it was already apparent to them that what he was telling them was the truth.

In the absence of interruption, he continued.

"Inside the country, Heathfield abolished travel, non-administrative communication, religion, currency and many other things, and the people went along with it all because they believed that he'd brought about world peace and prosperity. His monumental achievements made such sacrifices seem trivial by comparison.

"In subsequent years, a new reality evolved inside the bubble, and successive Witans have lied and cheated, as appropriate, to perpetuate the myth and protect the way of life."

Once again, Stin paused – expecting someone to say something – but still no one did.

"When Spencer Curtis died, I found myself in a unique position. I knew that, in accordance with tradition, he'd decided who his successor as Archwitan was going to be, and that it was my responsibility to send out the announcement that he'd prepared prior to his death."

He looked at his audience's faces. "Er…I think I ought to tell you at this point that he didn't actually have a deputy as such. There never was a Kingsley Gryn. I invented him for the purpose of my deception…sorry."

He continued, "However, when I accessed the relevant record, I discovered that he hadn't yet made any approach to his selected successor.

"It was at that point that I realised that fate had dealt me a rare opportunity. I formulated a plan to expose Heathfield's Revolution. Using the computer knowledge I'd acquired, I changed the message to say that the next Archwitan was to be one 'Tujo', who wished his identity to be kept secret, at least for the time being, to enable him to "get a better understanding of the true state of affairs in every aspect of government." I implied that he'd been an active member of Curtis' Witan, and included strict instructions that the fact that the new Archwitan wished to be called 'Tujo' was all that anyone needed to know. Actually, the name 'Tujo' comes from the first two letters of each of my first two names – Turner Josef.

"In the guise of Tujo, I sent messages to the six Regional Administrations telling them that they would receive their future instructions by IDS, and I assured the existing Witanates that their position was safe – at least for the moment. I told them that my future communications with them might be direct, by IDS, or via the Regional Administrations.

"At that point, I'd effectively become the new Archwitan.

"You may wonder why I didn't just come out and shout the whole sordid story. The reason is simply that I didn't think I'd be believed. By its very nature, the 'world' created by Dunstan Heathfield's Revolution was based on an exceptionally deep trust, and I felt that a simple statement 'out of the blue' would be summarily dismissed. And then I'd be silenced – quite possibly forever.

"So I determined to provoke a group of people into seeking the truth for themselves, so that, when they found it, they'd know it was the truth.

"I needed a sufficient, and increasing, number of people to discover the truth – before the Witan became aware of it and moved to 'disprove' it. I had to force the people into a position in which they had no alternative but to believe."

He looked rather sheepishly at Clement. "Er... those people are you...Sir."

He looked at the floor. "I could go on and on, but maybe it would be better if you asked me any questions you may wish to. Er...once again, I apologise for all my deceptions...although I feel sure you'll understand now why I felt they were necessary."

Whilst he was waiting for someone to speak, he selected a cool drink from his drinksmade. Clement was the first to find his voice. He spoke in a slow, measured, almost bewildered whisper.

"You must appreciate…that what you're telling us is that the whole of our lives…that is…everything that has ever happened to us up to now…both to us and to our families…has taken place in a kind of 'protected environment' which was the brainchild of an unscrupulous, albeit possibly idealistic, man.

"And…further…that it's been perpetuated by every government since that time. That we've been duped – I can't think of a more suitable word – into believing that we were living in a far better world than in fact we were. You must appreciate…that it isn't an easy thing for us to come to terms with…"

Uri interrupted – also in a low, rather unsteady, voice. "…And I can only echo that. This is…very… very…hard. Nonetheless, it is true that what you say does indeed seem to fit the facts as we know them.

"It seems, therefore, that I must accept that I've lived in a bubble for all of my 55 years, and that my environment – my life – has, in fact, all been an illusion.

"Added to that, as Drayling's Local Historian, I've been an unwitting agent of the government, and have helped to reinforce the lies to hundreds of men, women and children for many years. Is that about the size of it?"

Stin looked at Marius, and then back at Uri.

"I'm afraid that's essentially true, Sir Uri," conceded Stin, "although I wouldn't say anyone's life has been an illusion. It's the environment that's been manufactured, not the people."

"Hmm…maybe," responded Uri, clearly far from convinced. "…Maybe…"

He paused briefly as though in thought, and then carried on in something more akin to his normal voice. "Er…it seems to me that, in order to maintain such a deception, an

Archwitan would have to have a very loyal and well-organised team behind him. Are you able to tell us how, precisely, our Government of National Unity is made up – who's responsible for what, and so on? The information has never been available, although I've often wondered."

Stin swallowed some drink and replied, "Heathfield had five Witanates in his team, and it's probable, although not totally verifiable, that every Archwitan since then has stuck to precisely the same formula.

"I can certainly confirm that that is the case today. Would you like to know their titles and responsibilities?"

"Yes, please," cut in Clement.

"Right. Well, the 'Archwitan', as you know, was...is...the head of state and head of the Witan. Ever since Heathfield's time, the Archwitan's been portrayed as all-powerful, and – incidently – has always been male. It isn't a coincidence that most positions of authority are still held by men, although there's never actually been any regulation preventing the advancement of women. Heathfield believed that there were jobs that each of the sexes were best-suited to, and set about creating his vision accordingly. The BFF culture as we know it today has simply developed from there.

"The 'Head of Defence' is responsible for anything relating to national defence, whether inside or outside the country. He's also responsible for the coastal force-field and the Channel Dredging Project.

"The 'Global Informer' is responsible for keeping the Archwitan informed of events outside the BFF, whilst the 'National Informer' keeps him informed of events *inside* the BFF. The latter also has responsibility for the monitoring of IDS traffic, and works closely with another Witanate – the 'Guardian of Truth'.

"The key function of the 'Guardian of Truth' is the management of all information given to the people. He controls and ensures the consistency, appropriateness, creation and credibility of 'truth'. He's in charge of propaganda, which of course includes the image of the

Archwitan, and the government in general. In addition, he also has overall responsibility for the issue of identiscreens and the provision of daily IDS information to all citizens – via Regional Administrations and Local Worthies as appropriate.

"That leaves the 'Quality Controller', whose responsibility is, generally, anything relating to the quality of life of the people. Food and drink, leisure activities, alleviation of worry, health, happiness – that sort of thing. He's also responsible for the suppression of travel and inter-regional communication. In this latter respect he, like the National Informer, works closely with the Guardian of Truth."

"It would seem that propaganda is extremely high on the agenda," observed Marius. "And that consistency is more important than truth."

Stin half-smiled. "Absolutely. When the whole thing's based on a lie, there's little point in worrying about the truth. It's become more important to ensure that all information fits into the official picture."

"…And we've had recent evidence of that," interposed Uri, "when I was instructed by Grindon Blane to delete all reference to the old area entity names from IDS records."

Clement nodded and, adopting a formal tone, said, "OK, does anyone else have a question?"

"Yes," said Hayden. "What can you tell us about the huge force-field?"

"It runs right around the coast of mainland BFF – generally about two or three miles inland. Its purpose is to protect the country and, as far as I know, nothing has breached it yet. Of course, we now also know that it's the reason for the power-route. It requires quite phenomenal power, and the sole reason that we were able to get so close to the conduit was that the flow was controlled by the direction-specific Cumber Pulse technology. If that were not so, Marius, Hayden and I wouldn't be here now."

Uri suppressed a shudder.

"How on earth was Heathfield able to build it without anyone knowing?" asked Marius.

"He abolished inter-district travel and communication first. That involved the establishment of the local barriers – which, incidently, is a subject we should discuss later. It would have been easy to explain away the network of power-routes in inland districts as supplying the needs of other area entities.

"He used the inhabitants of the coastal districts to do all the necessary construction work, and then simply cut them off from the rest of the country. That meant that the only citizens who may have any knowledge of the force-field were outside it. Those communities became an entirely separate social group, and have remained so. That's where the members of our armed forces, and everyone involved in major undertakings such as the Channel Dredging Project, now live. As you've already realised, no one who leaves a district inside the force-field ever goes home."

"What exactly do you mean by 'major undertakings such as the Channel Dredging Project'?" asked Clement.

"There've been many ventures over the years which have utilised manpower drawn from the coastal communities – support for our forces in times of conflict, major repairs to the force-field, that sort of thing…and it's true that there's long been a dredging programme in the Channel to combat rising sea-levels. However, what 'the Channel Dredging Project' generally refers to is a huge undertaking ordered by Dunstan Heathfield in the south-east of the country. At the same time as constructing the force-field, he took the view that mainland Europe was a little too close. He therefore ordered that about half of Eastern Kentover, as that corner used to be called, should be returned to the sea. That's meant that, ever since he made the decision, there's been an ongoing, and highly labour-intensive, process of redistributing millions upon millions of tons of earth to all the various coastal communities around the country. As a result, there's now an almost continuous range of hills –

much of it frankly unstable – running parallel to the coast, just outside the force-field."

"Are you saying that many of the districts to the east of us are simply no longer there?" said Uri incredulously.

"Yes, Sir, I am. If you travelled due east from Burshaw, you'd reach the force-field, and then the sea, after about thirty miles. It's a continuing project, so it's likely that you'd also see a great deal of activity. There have, of course, been many accidents – and many deaths. Working conditions are pretty primitive, despite the modern technology available. Many of the stories that you uncovered will have been true, although dredging accidents have undoubtedly been used as a convenient explanation for many other disappearances over the years."

"And all the citizens that have been sent away from area entities all over the country for all the various reasons have ended up in the coastal community," mused Clement. "A sort of permanent exile...or life sentence."

He sighed. "Has anyone else got a question?"

"Yes," said Marius. "In all of this, you constantly refer to technology. There must have been a wealth of progress made over the years since Heathfield – all of which has, presumably, been deliberately kept from us. Are you able to tell us anything about that?"

"I can tell you what I know. Yes, there've obviously been advances, and I can show you how to gain access to the records available about all of it. You've already come across Cumber Pulse, force-fields, local barriers, capillimetry, hand weapons, innate ambium, proximetry and some of the advances in the medical world. There are many, many more – including some frightening innovations in the field of international warfare – but I suggest that that's a subject for later."

"We'll certainly be interested to find out about it all," commented Clement. "Now, I have a rather simpler question – why did you choose us?"

Stin smiled and looked a shade embarrassed. "Well, actually, the original target was Marius. You'll recall I told you I used to spend a lot of time investigating stuff by IDS. In this instance, one of the Witanates suggested that I take a look at an archaeological excavation being carried out in a South Country area entity called Drayling. I discovered that the instigator was a sixteen-year-old youth named Marius Graves, who was the son of the Local Historian. I investigated his IDS activity over the preceding two years, and also noticed that the searches carried out on his father's screen in the few months leading up to his fourteenth birthday weren't in any way consistent with Sir Uri's previous access patterns, so it was reasonable to assume that they too had been made by his son.

"The nature of the searches, and his depth of inquiry, confirmed to me that here was someone who could think for himself, and think logically.

"Wider, subsequent investigation also showed me that Drayling had an efficient and progressive Worthy Council – er, actually the exact opposite of what you were told by Grindon Blane, Sir Clement. Sorry about that.

"Drayling also had another advantage – it was only a short distance from Witan Central Office, so it would be relatively easy to get here."

Clement nodded slowly. "Hmm. You were quite right about Marius, of course, although the intrusive nature of your monitoring makes me shudder. And, on the subject of the Worthy Council, I suggest it's Sir Bedford Coote you should apologise to, not me."

Stin took a deep breath, sighed and replied, "I knew, of course, that the actions I'd decided to take were always going to create problems – not to say anguish – for someone. I told myself that, whether or not I achieved my aim of revealing the truth, people were going to suffer in one way or another in any event. I clung to the premise that this thing was too big to worry about individuals in that way, and that, for the greater good, I had to at least try to do it.

"Rationalising it in that way didn't make it any easier though. The deaths at Stowly Heath, and similar tragedies elsewhere in the country, were so needless...so unnecessary...and so sad. Once again, those events made me question myself, but by that time I was already committed, so I simply had to suppress the feelings of guilt and carry on."

At that point, Clement came to a decision. "I think it would benefit all of us if we take a break for a while to gather our thoughts. Stin, would you be kind enough to go to the hospitality area to allow us to discuss what you've told us? You will, I know, appreciate the momentous nature of the information you're giving us, both to the nation and to us as individuals. Whilst it's true to say that, in recent times, we've almost become accustomed to being bombarded with far-reaching revelations, the enormity – and importance – of what you're telling us now is such that I think it would be wise to give ourselves time to consider it, and try to come to terms with it, properly."

Stin accepted the wisdom of his words readily, and withdrew to the hospitality area.

After de-activating the roomscriber, Clement said, "Gentlemen, I called the break because I want to know whether we all believe his story or not before we go any further. Uri, what do you think?"

Uri took his time. "What I think is that we're probably in shock at this moment – at least to some extent – because his story impacts on our lives, both past and potentially future, to such a degree. For that reason, we should treat our initial thoughts with caution. Having said that, his story is so incredible that I can't see any purpose to it unless it's essentially true. Many aspects of what he's said fit very well with facts that we're already aware of. If it's true, this thing changes our lives, Clement."

"Indeed, old friend," replied Clement. "Hayden?"

"Marius and I have seen the evidence for the force-field, and we've also seen Stin dealing with the engineer – BFF

Officer Steadlaw. I think it must be true – it explains all his earlier deceptions as well, of course."

"Marius?"

"I agree with what father says about the need for caution, but I feel that the case for accepting Stin's story is so overwhelming that I'll be amazed if I think differently in the morning. Also, Hayden and I saw evidence on screen that Stin is indeed Tujo."

Clement interrupted. "Actually, your father and I also have evidence of that. We haven't been able to tell you. Whilst you were away, I asked Cipherslider for observations on 'Stin'. It responded that Stin equalled Tujo. Nothing else. Just "STIN = TUJO."

"To say we were extremely alarmed would be something of an understatement. As you can imagine, it made us even more worried for your safety. When I asked the computer for an explanation, it said 'Simple Cipherslide code – move each letter to the next alphabetically'. The word 'Stin' becomes 'Tujo' – or vice-versa. That's where he got the name Stin from. I can't tell you how relieved we were when you both returned safely."

"Hmm. So he's been playing word games again," mused Marius. "He likes those, doesn't he?"

Clement smiled. "I interrupted you, Marius, did you want to say anything else?"

"Yes, Sir…as you know, I was more than surprised when we discovered that Stin had lied to us. It just didn't seem in character – even though I hadn't known him for long. What he's now told us seems to me to fit much better. It justifies all the deceptions, and what he's done is frankly nothing short of heroic – and much more in character as far as I can see. I think he's an amazing man, and, yes, I believe his story."

"Right, then it would seem we all accept that what Stin's told us is the truth. On that basis, I think we ought also to realise that what's happened here today is a momentous event in the history of our country. Let's ask Stin to come back in."

Marius walked out to the hospitality area and found Stin fast asleep in a reclined chair. Just as he was on the point of waking him, he hesitated. He turned and went back into the Heathfield Room.

"He's asleep," he told Clement, "…and with all the pressure he's been under in recent weeks, I reckon it's pretty likely he hasn't been sleeping particularly well. It may well be that the relief of finally telling us his full story has enabled him to relax a little. I'd like to suggest that we leave him to get some rest.

"We could come back at, say, ten o'clock – or whatever time you think would be best."

"I think ten o'clock will be fine," concurred Clement. "We can leave him an IDS message.

"One final thought for today though. Difficult as it may be, all of this must be kept strictly between ourselves for the time being. The way that this information is to be released will need to be given very careful consideration indeed."

Despite the enormity of the issues facing them, the mood was altogether different when they met again a few hours later. Stin had had his first proper sleep for ages, and the undercurrent of distrust of the last few days had completely disappeared. By three o'clock that afternoon, the historic meeting was over and all four members of the Graves family were sitting in their favourite chairs.

"…And that's why he couldn't simply come out and say that Dunstan Heathfield's Revolution was a sham," said Uri, as he came to the end of the story. "He's a remarkable, and exceptionally brave, young man. He created a situation in which we became so angry that we went and discovered the truth for ourselves."

He paused briefly.

"He was absolutely insistent that we tell our families everything. Obviously, we're all sworn to the strictest secrecy until the news is made known to the country as a whole, but he was adamant that all those who've been so directly affected by the discovery process should know the truth. He said he felt it would be an intolerable burden otherwise."

"He must know all there is to know about intolerable pressure," said Della. "The whole thing is quite incredible. What's he going to do now?"

"Wife, you're a source of never-ending, wonderful surprises," rejoiced Uri. "I've just told you that the whole of our lives to date have been lived in a fantasy land, and your first reaction is concern for Stin's future."

"But I can't do anything about the past," replied Della, "...and anyway, we've been perfectly happy, so it wasn't a problem. It's the future we have to worry about, isn't it?"

Uri affected a bewildered expression and threw his hands in the air. "Well, the answer to your question is that he wants to stay in Drayling and be known as Stin. He was telling the truth when he said he has no family, and he had some rather nice things to say about the new friends he's made here. He said he doesn't want to be anything other than a normal young man of his age, and that he hoped he could still take part in the Worthy Training programme if it goes ahead. Obviously, that'll have to be one of the many decisions to be made in the coming weeks and months.

"He was particularly concerned about the effect of his revelations on Marius personally. You see, he came up with the idea of making him a 'Thinker' so that the subsequent award of the Distinction of Guardianship of Cipherslider wouldn't be questioned – you see, he needed the computer to be installed here in Drayling to enable him to carry on his activities as Tujo."

"Well, he needn't worry," explained Marius. "As you know, I was quite uncomfortable about that whole thing when it first happened. Now that I know there was a rational reason behind it, and that I've been, albeit unknowingly, a key figure in the process, well…it all makes more sense to me now."

"What effect is all this going to have on the BFF?" asked Urania, who'd been listening quietly up to that point.

"The Archworthies are going to get together and work out what needs to be done," said Uri. "It'll almost certainly be a long process of change, involving the whole country, but I'm confident that they'll make every effort to retain all the things that we believe are good about our way of life.

"Actually, Stin told us something interesting about the name 'BFF'. He said that Spencer Curtis told him that Heathfield never specifically planned to change the country's name to the British Friendly Federation. Apparently, during the long period that the huge construction project was going on, he got into the habit of calling it 'that bloody force-field' – which he subsequently shortened to BFF. The story goes that an unauthorised person overheard him say it one day, and asked him what it meant.

"Being the politician he was, he thought quickly on his feet, and lied.

"It stands for British Friendly Federation," he said, "I'm considering changing the name of our great country – what do you think of it?"

"It's said that the reaction he got was so positive that one thing led to another, and now we're all proud citizens of the BFF."

"Is that really true?" asked Urania, wide-eyed.

"I don't know," smiled Uri, "but it makes a good story, doesn't it?"

It was a welcome opportunity for them all to laugh.

Later, when Della and Urania had gone to bed, Uri and Marius stayed up to talk. Standing side by side with drink in hand, they gazed at the night sky through the open window as colleagues who had been through much together.

275

"You know, he's a great man," mused Uri. "Despite his relative youth, he'll go down in history as one of our country's heroes."

"Actually, he's almost too decent," replied Marius. "His insistence that, in due course, he should be tried in an appropriate court of law, because his actions may be said to have led to the deaths at Stowly Heath, Choperton and various other places, seems, on the face of it, completely unnecessary."

"I think it'll be a long time before we get to that point," said Uri, "and I doubt very much if he'll be held responsible.

"Actually, I'm more concerned about him in the short term. For the moment, at least, he must stay in contact with the Witanates and Regional Administrations via Cipherslider to maintain the illusion of normality for their benefit. Meanwhile, Clement'll push to get things moving as quickly as possible.

"In the interim, there's a real risk that your visit to BFF Parkerspont and the return hike through Gillersbush and the other district will give an astute hawk enough information to work out where he is, or at least set alarm bells ringing. We don't want anyone, Witanate or otherwise, to take any kind of precipitate action at this stage.

"However, I'm sure it won't take long for the friendly Archworthies to get together and formulate an initial plan, despite the size of the task ahead. I think they'll seek to expand their numbers as quickly as they can. Obviously, their priority will be to deal with the existing Witanates and Regional Administrations – and to release the news in an appropriate way to every resident of the BFF.

"After that, a stable – albeit probably temporary – administration will be in a position to take a more measured approach to dealing with the multitude of other issues – such as the coastal force-field, all the people living on both sides of it, the BFF guards, the travel restriction laws...and of course every other law. They'll also have to consider our relationship with the rest of the world. Actually, the list is almost literally endless.

However, as I said earlier, I'm sure they'll seek to retain everything that's good about our existing culture – I certainly hope so."

They looked at each other, and, with tears in their eyes, hugged.

After a short pause, Uri added, "You know, we've all lived happily for so long. It isn't going to be easy dealing with the changes that are going to have to happen."

Marius nodded.

"But it must be better to live in the real world…

…mustn't it?"

The author lives with his wife in Sussex. He is a member of English Heritage, the National Trust, Brighton & Hove Albion Supporters' Club and Mensa.